EXPERIENCE THE ULTIMATE IN FIREARMS TRAINING!™

Welcome to Gander Mtn. Academy™, the most advanced, professional firearms training academy in America. With its unique combination of highly trained instructors, live fire range, and exclusive, state-of-the-art simulation technology, no other firearms training facility compares with Gander Mtn. Academy. In fact, nothing even comes close! Gander Mtn. Academy offers a wide variety of classes designed to address many firearms issues, for beginners to advanced enthusiasts. Taught by highly trained instructors, our classes are the foundation of our proprietary and proven FRS Learning System™ techniques.

Gander Mtn. Academy is your starting point for gaining the knowledge, practical experience, and Reality Based Training (RBT) necessary to fully develop a personal protection plan – a plan designed to not only *avoid* violent encounters whenever possible, but also a plan to *survive* a violent encounter if you have *no other choice* but to defend your life or the lives of loved ones.

OUR FRS LEARNING SYSTEM™

At Gander Mtn. Academy, we believe that Fundamentals, Repetition, and Simulation are the cornerstones of firearms safety, proficiency, and preparedness. In the classroom, our expert instructors will provide you with the best possible instruction on the *fundamentals* of firearms safety, gun handling, and marksmanship. Next, we believe that *repetition* is the key to perfection, and Gander Mtn. Academy offers two complementary ranges that combine for perfect practice: Our V-Range™ for virtual training, and our L-Range™ for live fire, both designed and developed for exclusive use within our Academies by industry leaders in firearms training and technology. Finally, we'll place you in stunningly real, high-definition video *simulations* to prepare you for real-life situations using technology previously available only to elite military agencies and law enforcement. Read on for the details!

Fundamentals. **R**epetition. **S**imulation.™

The cornerstone of firearms safety, proficiency and preparedness.

Experience perfect practice in Gander Mtn. Academy's exclusive V-Range, our state-of-the-art simulated training range using actual firearms modified for laser technology and full-felt recoil.

BEST IN CLASS, FROM PROFESSIONAL INSTRUCTION TO HIGH-TECH SIMULATION

As a firearms owner, you have an obligation to be safe and responsible. When it comes to purchasing and handling firearms, the questions are endless. As the major retailer of firearms in America, Gander Mtn. has the answers. In our classroom, we'll begin to answer those questions with the wealth of information in this course book and more. As a next step, we'll provide you with practical experience on the safe handling of personal protection handguns and the proper use of self-defense shooting fundamentals on our exclusive V-Range – the world's most accurate simulated firing range. On the V-Range, you'll wear eye and ear protection, and use an actual handgun modified for laser fire and full-felt recoil. You'll experience the stunning clarity of over two million pixels per lane as you practice on a wide variety of targets, qualifications, exercises, and marksmanship drills. Each simulated bullet leaves a hole punch in a simulated paper target, and you'll be able to "zoom-in" to examine your results, and even send a picture of your target to your email! Once you've mastered the V-Range, you'll continue to build your practical experience and hone your fundamentals through live fire on our L-Range, under the guidance of your instructor or a trained range master. Real bullets. Real shooting. One safe environment.

Collectively, the knowledge you'll gain in our classrooms, on our V-Range, and on our live-fire L-Range will exceed the type of training you'd receive at even the most elite training schools. But at Gander Mtn. Academy, you're just getting started!

THE FUTURE IN REALITY BASED TRAINING, HERE AND NOW

As you'll read in Chapter Five, the body and mind undergo dramatic, automated responses when we're faced with extreme stress (the "fight or flight" responses). Every person will react differently to varying levels of stress in different situations, and accurately predicting your reaction in a given situation would be impossible. What Gander Mtn. Academy *can* do, however, is to provide you with the unique opportunity to participate in stunningly realistic, multi-screen, HD video simulations that will enable you to experience *first-hand* the effects of adrenaline, tunnel vision, auditory exclusion, and the other automated responses discussed in Chapter Five, all while dealing with realistic life-or-death scenarios. During your training, we'll take you through multiple scenarios under the guidance of a skilled instructor, which will enable you to recognize the automated responses when they occur, and learn to compensate for their effects. You'll understand how these physiological responses affect your performance and judgment, and you'll build the skills to deal with real-world violent threats, rather than merely building the skills to punch holes in paper.

180°

180 degrees of realism. The Pro V SIM 180™ features three borderless 8' x 10' screens for enhanced Reality Based Training. The action extends to the extreme limit of your peripheral vision.

300°

300 degrees of the unexpected. The Pro V SIM 300™ is the ultimate in full-immersion virtual reality training. The action surrounds you with five 8' x 10' screens, and threats can approach you from behind!

THE PERFECT FUSION OF TRAINING AND TECHNOLOGY

Our fully immersive, interactive, multi-screen HD video virtual simulators are so cutting edge and lifelike that until now, they have been available only to elite military and law enforcement agencies. Our Pro V SIM 180™ features three borderless 8' x 10' screens that surround you to the extreme limits of your peripheral vision. Our Pro V SIM 300™ is the ultimate in full-immersion reality based training (RBT) where the action surrounds you with five borderless 8' x 10' screens, and threats can approach you from the rear! You'll use the same actual firearms modified for laser fire and full-felt recoil that you use in our V-Range. Our simulator scenarios replicate and prepare you for self-defense situations you may face in real life. While some facets of our Academy primarily train your *body* by focusing on mechanics to improve your gun handling techniques and marksmanship, our Pro V SIM 180 and Pro V SIM 300 specifically challenge your *mind*. Multiple decision points exist within each scenario, allowing a variety of outcomes based on your decisions. Test your judgment. Learn how you perform under stress. Train yourself for the unexpected.

After your simulator experience, you and your instructor will replay and critique your actions and decisions in debriefing rooms using our sophisticated Trainee Monitor and Recording (TMaR™) performance auditing software. We can also upload a short video clip of your simulation training to YouTube® so you can share your Gander Mtn. Academy experience with friends!

OUR MISSION. OUR GUARANTEE.

As the major retailer of firearms in America, Gander Mtn. believes it's our responsibility to offer the highest level of professional firearms training available. That's not just our mission. It's our guarantee. And we're confident Gander Mtn. Academy delivers on that guarantee.

Exclusive technology. Professional training. Unparalleled safety. Welcome to Gander Mtn. Academy and Experience the Ultimate in Firearms Training.

Be Safe. Be Prepared.

Basic Handgun & Concealed Carry
FUNDAMENTALS

MICHAEL MARTIN

FIRST EDITION – JANUARY 2011

©COPYRIGHT 2011, MICHAEL MARTIN

LICENSED EXCLUSIVELY TO GANDER MTN.

PUBLISHED BY KEY HOUSE PRESS

Published by Key House Press
Woodbury, MN 55125

Printed in the United States

Library of Congress Control Number: 2008933390

ISBN 978-1-4507-3724-1

Basic Handgun and Concealed Carry Fundamentals. First Edition.

Written by Michael Martin.

Design by Ken Wangler,
RedShed Design, Saint Paul, MN

Cover design by Concept Group, Saint Paul, MN

Experience the ultimate in firearms training., Fundamentals. Repetition. Simulation., FRS Learning System, the FRS logo design, Gander Mtn. Academy, the Gander Mtn. Academy logo design, L-Range, V-Range, Pro V SIM 180 and Pro V SIM 300 are trademarks of Gander Mountain Company. The Flying Goose Medallion, Gander Mtn. and WE LIVE OUTDOORS are registered trademarks of Gander Mountain Company.

Photos on pages X, 38, and 103 by Oleg Volk, used by permission. All other photos and illustrations are licensed for use; used by permission of the manufacturer; or are copyright© Michael Martin. NRA and Eddie Eagle logos are trademarks of the National Rifle association. Nighthawk and Talon are trademarks of Nighthawk Custom. TMaR is a trademark of VirTra Systems, Inc. YouTube is a registered trademark of Google, Inc.

Key House Press is a registered trademark of Key House Press LLC. To contact the author or publisher, or to see other books by Michael Martin or Key House Press, visit us at www.keyhousepress.com.

To contact Gander Mtn., visit www.GanderMtn.com.

ACKNOWLEDGEMENTS

This book would not have been possible without the overwhelming number of instructors, authors, and advocates who were so generous with their time and knowledge during the past several years. Whether that knowledge was passed to me in the classroom, on the range, over a cup of coffee, or over e-mail, I'll be forever grateful. To quote one of my own instructors, I like to think of myself as a good instructor, but a great student, and I've had the pleasure of being a student of some of the best and brightest. Specifically, I'd like to thank Ben Stairs, Director of Training at Gander Mtn. Academy. Ben's advice on shooting fundamentals helped to improve my own shooting to the best it's ever been, and I'm happy to share that advice in Chapter Three. I'd also like to thank Rob Pincus, owner and director of the I.C.E. training company and author of the book "Combat Focus Shooting: Evolution 2010." Rob's research and writing on the automated responses experienced during violent encounters had a major influence on my own interest in the topic, and you'll see that reflected in Chapter Five. Rob and his staff were also responsible for developing several of the exercises that you'll see in Chapter Seven, and Rob was a major help in making sure those exercises were fully explained. I'd also like to thank Dr. Alexis Artwohl, author of the book "Deadly Force Encounters." Dr. Artwohl offered wonderful support as I was writing the section on human physiology in Chapter Five, including providing me with access to a number of her research papers, which we've listed in the "Suggested Reading" section at the end of the book. I'd also like to thank Marc Berris of Segal, Roston and Berris. Marc is one of the most respected firearms attorneys in my home state of Minnesota, and Marc provided countless hours of assistance to ensure that our chapter on the legal use of force was accurate and complete. I'd also like to thank my friend Oleg Volk (www.a-human-right.com). Oleg's photographs of my family used in this book tell a story that I could never have told in words alone. I'd also like to thank a number of other individuals who provided invaluable advice, ideas, and corrections, including: Paul Blincow, Len Breure, Rick Bruels, John Caile, Jeff Cater, Paul Horvick, Don Larson, Bob Leeper, Mary Lou Martin, Roger Martin, Loren Moriearty, Sam Netherly, Joe Penaz, Patrick Sacco, Andrew Shapiro, David Slomkowski, Tom Tousignant, and Jason Walberg.

Finally, I'd like to thank my wife Sara for her patience with this and other projects, especially her patience as she sat through "just one more photo shoot" (you'll see Sara in Chapter One and Chapter Five.) Without Sara and my little boys, life would have much less importance and would seem far less worth protecting.

This book is dedicated to my wonderful wife, Sara, and
my two wonderful little boys, Jack Ryan and Samuel August.

INTRODUCTION

In the late 1980s, fewer than ten states provided law abiding citizens with the right to carry firearms for self-defense, and fewer than one million citizens were granted that right. Fast forward to 2011, when the number of right-to-carry states stands at 39 (with more on the way), and the number of concealed carry permit holders increased to more than six million nationwide. At the same time, the FBI's uniform crime report showed an overall drop in violent crime, and a dramatic decrease in the number of deaths attributed to firearms. That is, unless you live in one of the jurisdictions with the strictest gun-control laws, such as Washington D.C., where the gun homicide rate is more than *five times* the national average. Today, only two states, Illinois and Wisconsin, provide no ability for law abiding citizens to receive a permit, even if they can demonstrate a need. While the laws vary from state to state, right-to-carry states *require* the controlling authority to issue a permit if the applicant has met specific criteria such as passing a detailed background check, and completing a training course conducted by a certified individual or organization.

The decision to apply for a permit and to ultimately carry a handgun for personal protection is a big one, but no different than other decisions you've already made for the protection of yourself and your family, such as a decision to maintain smoke alarms and a fire extinguisher in your home, or a decision to learn CPR. Each of these decisions is nothing more than the recognition that your city's police, fire, and EMT services are not omnipresent and will not suddenly materialize when you and your family are confronted by a fire, a heart attack, or a violent crime. When it comes to fires and heart attacks, we know that prevention matters, and the same is true for violent crime. To that end, Chapter One will kick the book off with a variety of topics focused *entirely* on prevention, avoidance, and awareness. Chapter Two will then introduce you to a wealth of information on different types of handguns and ammunition, and we'll provide easy to understand explanations of the common terms used so frequently. The goal of this chapter is to de-mystify what can sometimes feel like a topic reserved for experts. Chapter Three will continue with the basics, including a very visual overview of what we call the "building blocks" or the fundamentals for accurate and safe shooting. Chapter Four covers important legal topics, including the laws governing the legal use of force. Chapter Five covers violent encounters and their aftermath, including a detailed section on the physiological reactions that you should expect to experience if you're ever involved in a "critical incident." This section will take you on an amazing tour of the inner workings of the brain, which should convince you why we take the "simple versus complex" approach in our shooting fundamentals section in Chapter Three. This chapter goes on to explain what our options might be during a critical incident and what we should know when dealing with the police after an incident has ended. Chapter Six will introduce you to the variety of gear and gadgets available, including holster options and other gear such as lights and lasers. Chapter Seven summarizes the book with a number of basic and advanced drills designed to take your skill level beyond the building blocks introduced in Chapter Three, and dramatically elevate your speed, accuracy, and enjoyment at the range.

Before we kick off the book, we thought we'd help answer a question that you might be asked some day – "Why do you carry a firearm?" Until recently, we'd answer that question by using the analogies mentioned on the previous page, and we'd compare carrying a firearm to taking the time to learn CPR or taking the responsibility to keep fire extinguishers in our home. We'd also have thrown out a variety of statistics to prove our point (which are included in this book), or we'd have discussed the meaning of the Second Amendment. But our answer to that question got a whole lot easier after a long day shooting photos with Oleg Volk (www.a-human-right.com). At the end of the day, we were heading back home with Oleg trailing behind us, snapping a few last minute pictures. When we sat down to look at the results of the day, the photo on page X caught our eye. Sam (three years old) was about ready to fall asleep, and Jack (six years old) was dragging his feet after the long day. A casual observer of this photo would tend to see nothing more than a protective father walking home with his kids, and it might take a closer look to realize that there's a firearm on the author's hip. That photo, above all others, reminded us why we carry. Carrying a firearm isn't about statistics or constitutional arguments, it's not about analogies or comparisons, it's not about the gear, and to be honest, it's not even about the gun. It's about taking a *small measure* of personal responsibility for our safety and the safety of our families. It's about making it home safe at night and being safe while in our homes. It's about recognizing that we *are* our families' first responder and we'd better start taking that responsibility seriously.

TABLE OF CONTENTS

CHAPTER 1:
DEVELOPING A PERSONAL PROTECTION PLAN 2

CHAPTER 2:
HANDGUN AND AMMUNITION BASICS 38

CHAPTER 3:
SHOOTING FUNDAMENTALS FOR
DEFENSIVE ACCURACY 82

CHAPTER 4:
THE LEGAL USE OF FORCE 104

CHAPTER 5:
VIOLENT ENCOUNTERS AND THEIR AFTERMATH 122

CHAPTER 6:
GEAR AND GADGETS FOR THE PERMIT HOLDER 164

CHAPTER 7:
BASIC AND ADVANCED SKILLS & SELF-LED AND
INSTRUCTOR-LED RANGE DRILLS 186

DEVELOPING A PERSONAL PROTECTION PLAN

In this Chapter we'll be discussing a number of topics associated with developing a personal protection plan, including situational awareness, conflict avoidance, and how to prepare for a potential violent encounter through planning and mental preparation.

— How Common is Violent Crime in the United States? —

— Why is Conflict Avoidance So Important? —

— Situational Awareness —

— The Color Codes of Awareness —

— Observing Our Environment —

— More on Conflict Avoidance —

— Planning for Home Defense —

— Mental Exercises —

— Other Use of Force Options —

Chapter 1

Developing a personal protection plan is a key component of not only preparing for how we should (or might) react if confronted by a violent crime, but also how we might avoid violent crime in the first place. The first topic we'll cover in this chapter will take a look at violent crime itself in the United States. We'll help you understand just how common it is compared to other risks we've already prepared for in our lives, such as the risk of a heart attack or the risk of a home fire. Within this chapter, you'll also discover that developing a personal protection plan is about much more than becoming proficient with a firearm or writing up a home invasion plan. It's a plan that must encompass awareness, avoidance, and preparation, so that we're *less* likely to find ourselves in a situation where we have no other option than to use our firearm, rather than *more* likely.

Think about it this way – if we *only* focused on becoming proficient with our firearm, but spent no time considering ways of avoiding violent crime, we'd be no different than individuals who expend enormous amounts of effort to become experts at putting out a variety of fires and using a variety of fire extinguishers, yet fail to take even an ounce of preventative action and continue with risky behavior such as smoking in bed and leaving flammable materials next to their furnaces. Those individuals virtually guarantee that someday they'll have a chance to put their firefighting skills to the test. We need to be better than that.

Topics in this chapter also include an overview of situational awareness and how we might take the idea of the President's protective bubble and apply it to our own lives. We'll expand on that topic by walking through the color codes of awareness, developed by a gentleman named Jeff Cooper, whom we've profiled in this chapter. These color codes are designed to make us more aware of our surroundings and to avoid what Cooper describes as the "Oh my God, I can't believe this is happening to me!" situation.

We'll continue with a topic on "observing our environments," which explains not only how to watch for and avoid areas that might be attractive to criminals, but to also look for objects in our environment that can work to our advantage. We'll also look at a number of additional ideas on conflict avoidance, planning for home defense, and a discussion of how mental exercises can take us beyond the drills that we can run at the range. We'll wrap up the chapter with an overview of a couple less-than-lethal options that we might consider, including explanations of how pepper spray and tasers work.

> 66 *"(The Constitution preserves) the advantage of being armed which Americans possess over the people of almost every other nation... (where) the governments are afraid to trust the people with arms."* 99
>
> *Thomas Jefferson*
> *3rd President of the United States*

HOW DOES THE RISK OF VIOLENT CRIME COMPARE TO OTHER RISKS?

When contemplating whether or not to get a Concealed Carry Permit, many people ask the question, "Just how likely is it that I'll be a victim of violent crime?" While violent crime has been decreasing over the last three decades, it can occur anywhere, at any time.

In the United States there were more than 1.4 million violent crimes in 2008, including 16 thousand murders, 89 thousand rapes, 442 thousand robberies, and 835 thousand assaults. That means that you are 508 times more likely to be a victim of violent crime in the U.S. than you are to die in a house fire, and 15 times more likely to

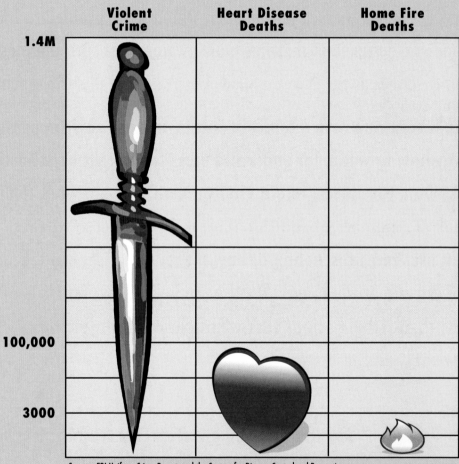

Violent Crime   Heart Disease Deaths   Home Fire Deaths

1.4M

100,000

3000

Sources: FBI Uniform Crime Report; and the Centers for Disease Control and Prevention.

be a victim of violent crime than you are to die of a heart attack for those 60 or under, and twice as likely for all age groups. Getting a Concealed Carry Permit is just one step in developing a Personal Protection Plan. Situational awareness, mental preparation, planning, conflict avoidance, and ongoing training are all components of this lifestyle to ensure that we use force as a last resort; but if required, we're prepared to defend ourselves and our families.

DEVELOPING A PERSONAL PROTECTION PLAN

What exactly is the goal of a personal protection plan? At its most basic level, a personal protection plan is designed to help keep us physically, legally, financially, and morally safe. While our personal protection plans should include becoming proficient with a firearm or other defensive tool, our ultimate goal should be to avoid violent encounters in the first place by developing an acute awareness of our surroundings and by making intelligent decisions about our actions, behavior, and precautions. Three options typically exist when it comes to a violent encounter: avoid the situation entirely; escape from a situation that is already in progress; or defend ourselves from a situation that we weren't able to avoid and are unable to escape from. While the choice isn't always left up to us, the topics in this chapter help to increase the likelihood that we'll have an opportunity to avoid or escape from dangerous situations *before* a use of force is required.

CONFLICT AVOIDANCE

So why is avoidance or escape so important, if legally, we have the right to defend ourselves from a violent attack? The answer is more than just the fact that the only guaranteed method of surviving a violent encounter is to avoid it in the first place. It's also because as a permit holder, the law will place a special emphasis on our decisions and actions leading up to any incident, and we'll be expected to have "known better" if we could have avoided a situation that turned violent. Prosecutors will want to know more than just "Who was the assailant?" and "Who was the victim?" They'll want to know *what did we do* to avoid or instigate the fight? In part, prosecutors will use what's known as a "reasonable person test." That means they'll weigh whether or not they believe a "reasonable person" would have believed the same things we believed to be true and would have reacted the same way we did. Here's the catch: "reasonable person" doesn't mean our friends, our family, the gang at the local shooting club, or other permit holders. It means 12 likely jurors, many of whom may hate guns. Because of that test, a use of force on our part must carry such seriousness attached to it that it's a fair question to ask: "Is this situation worth going to jail over?" or, "Is this situation worth dying over?" If the answer is "Yes," then we'll need to be prepared to live with the results. If the answer is "No," then we'll need to work hard to remove ourselves from the situation (quickly!) before the only option remaining is a use of force.

Said another way, a use of force on our part should only be done as a last resort, when we have no other choice, and when the risk of death or jail time is secondary in our minds compared to the necessity of defending ourselves from an unavoidable situation that we didn't start, and we couldn't escape from. On the next page, we've borrowed a few thoughts from one of our favorite classes, the NRA's Personal Protection Outside the Home, which asks some very serious questions we'll need to consider.

National Rifle Association

founded 1871

Since its founding, the NRA continues to be the leader in firearms education. Over 50,000 Certified Instructors now train about 750,000 gun owners a year. Since the establishment of the lifesaving Eddie Eagle® Gun Safety Program in 1988, more than 21 million pre-kindergarten to sixth grade children have learned that if they see a firearm in an unsupervised situation, they should "STOP. DON'T TOUCH. LEAVE THE AREA. TELL AN ADULT."

With 4 million members and another 40 million U.S. Citizens who identify themselves as "NRA Members" (yet who fail to pay the dues), the NRA is the largest organization in the U.S. dedicated to continued support of our 2nd Amendment rights. To join, visit: **www.NRA.org**

Am I prepared to take the life of another human being to save my own or someone else's life? The taking of another person's life, even to save our own, would be the second worst thing that could possibly happen in our lives. The worst, of course, would be losing our own life or the life of a loved one to violent crime. But many individuals who *did* successfully defend themselves or their loved ones from violent attack discovered that the result wasn't euphoria at having survived. Instead, it was the guilt of knowing they took the life of another person.

Am I prepared to risk my own life or the life of a loved one? While the vast majority of violent encounters are ended when permit holders simply expose their firearm (without firing any shots), there are no guarantees that you'll be that lucky. Think about it this way – if your behavior and actions can either put you in close proximity to a bad guy's knife, gun, or fists, or leave you hundreds or thousands of feet away, which behavior and actions are the prudent ones?

Am I prepared to tolerate the judgment of my friends, family, neighbors, and the media if I must defend myself with force? If you are involved in a shooting, however justified it may be, you should expect to be the lead story on all local TV stations and make the front page of your local papers. And that's not because you'll be getting an award. Be prepared for your attacker to be called the "victim" and for the press to use phrases like "the prosecuting attorney has not yet decided whether charges will be filed against the permit holder." Your case will be debated over water coolers and on pro- and anti- Second Amendment message boards, and you may discover that people you *thought* would be on your side are not on your side after all.

Am I prepared to go to jail over my decision? Even if a shooting is found to be justified, you should expect to spend tens of thousands of dollars defending yourself with the help of a quality lawyer who understands and has experience with self-defense cases. You should be prepared to lose your concealed carry permit, your right to own firearms, your savings, and quite possibly your freedom.

SECONDS COUNT

After asking ourselves the difficult questions on the previous page, we'll need to remember that a use of force is *not* the only possible outcome when it comes to a violent encounter. The *three* possible outcomes of avoidance, escape, or defense, share a key element: "Seconds count." If we go through life with a complete lack of awareness of our surroundings, the first two options are typically off the table and our ability to defend ourselves is seriously limited. Think about the warning time that each of the outcomes might require. For us to *avoid* a dangerous situation in the first place, we might need anywhere from 60 seconds to five minutes to be somewhere else. For us to *escape* from a dangerous situation that's already in motion, we might require at least 30 seconds of prior warning. For us to *defend* ourselves from a dangerous situation when it's too late for avoidance or escape, we'll still require at least several seconds of warning to find cover and/or draw our firearm. You can see pretty quickly that being unaware of our surroundings doesn't leave us with too many options.

OUTCOME	WARNING TIME	POSSIBLE RESULTS
Avoid	1 – 5+ Minutes	• You'll never know for the rest of your life whether or not you just avoided a violent crime or whether you overreacted. Personally, we can live with that. • If you were right about the situation, you've just gotten a "Get out of jail for free" card and possibly a "Get out of the hospital for free" card. • Your blood remains in your body where it belongs; your money remains in your bank where it belongs; and you'll remain at home with your family, where you belong.
Escape	30+ Seconds	• You've identified a dangerous situation in time to "exit stage left" before your options are limited to defend, but you're still in the middle of a bad situation.
Defend	3 – 5+ Seconds	• While you still have plenty of options other than "shoot the bad guy," you've now crossed a *significant* line where every action you are about to take will be second-guessed by the police, the media, the prosecuting attorney, and quite possibly a grand jury and jury. On the other hand, if it was your *only* choice, you do have a good chance of surviving. • Think about it this way – if you *knew* that the use of your firearm in self-defense would result in your incarceration (that's not a true legal test, but it is a good litmus test) and would cost you tens of thousands of dollars in legal expenses, how would that knowledge affect your decisions leading up to your use of force?

SITUATIONAL AWARENESS

So how do we gain those crucial seconds necessary to avoid or escape, or the few extra seconds that we'll need to find cover or draw our firearm if "defend" is the only option left to us? A good start is to develop a keen sense of situational awareness. Like it sounds, situational awareness is an awareness of our immediate vicinity and of the people and objects within that environment. Being aware of our surroundings doesn't mean that we need to hire a reconnaissance team to scout out our shopping area in advance, but it *does* mean that we need to lift our heads up and observe more than just the cell phone in our hands while we text a message, or the few feet of sidewalk immediately in front of us.

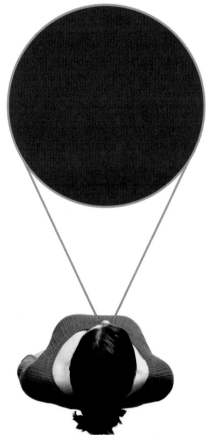

"Smart" phones and MP3 players can cause us to focus our entire attention on a three-inch circle in front of us, making us oblivious to the rest of our environment.

Even without the distraction of an electronic device, too many people focus no farther than a circle of a few feet in front of them when they're in public.

AWARENESS MEANS 360°

When thinking about an awareness of our environment, we need to think about the 360 degree circle surrounding us, not just the individuals or objects to our front. When we move through public areas, we should think of a "bubble" surrounding us and our loved ones and we need to be aware of everything and everyone inside of that bubble. Think of the way the secret service keeps a mobile bubble around the President of the United States. The secret service observes and categorizes everything within that bubble to identify any possible threat before it strikes. While we operate our own lives on a different scale, we can be no less vigilant – we are, in effect, our own bodyguards and first responders. Since we're lacking dozens of agents and overhead imagery, how do we go about monitoring that bubble around us? First off, it means that we need to lift our heads up from the sidewalk or our cell phones, and we need to watch where we're going. To get a 360 degree look at our surroundings, we'll need to use not only our peripheral vision (which provides about 180 – 200 degrees of visibility), but we'll also need to actually swivel our head to scan the area to our front, sides, and rear.

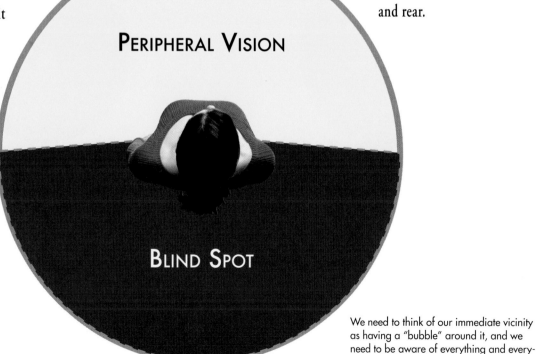

PERIPHERAL VISION

BLIND SPOT

We need to think of our immediate vicinity as having a "bubble" around it, and we need to be aware of everything and everyone in that bubble.

OUR PROTECTIVE "BUBBLE"

If you have a firearm and your attacker has a knife, you survive every time, right? Not necessarily. Lieutenant Dennis Tueller of the Salt Lake City Police Department demonstrated that simply having a firearm doesn't necessarily mean you could bring it into action in time to protect yourself, unless you closely observed threats (think situational awareness) within your protective bubble. Lieutenant Tueller observed that with practice, the average shooter could place two shots on target at a distance of 21 feet in about a second and a half. Tueller then ran another set of tests to determine exactly how quickly an "attacker" could cover that same distance and discovered that it could be done in that same 1.5 seconds. Based on Tueller's experiment, most police departments in the U.S. now consider anything within 32 feet to be within the "danger zone," where an officer should be prepared to issue commands, increase distance, or gain access to a firearm.

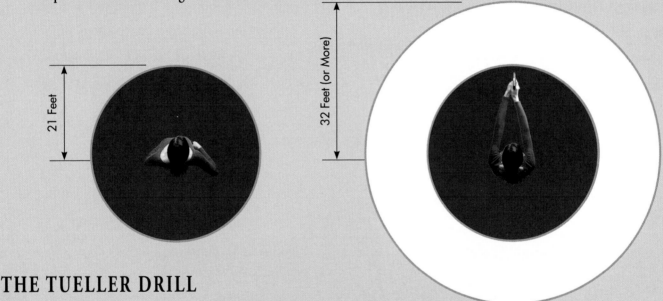

THE TUELLER DRILL

1 Version One. With the defender armed with a blue or red replica gun and the "attacker" armed with a blue or red replica knife, this drill begins with the defender's replica gun holstered and the attacker 21 feet away. Without warning, the attacker charges the defender. The defender is successful if she can clear her replica gun from the holster and get it on "target" prior to the attacker touching her with the replica knife. Most individuals CANNOT bring their firearm on target in time.

2 Version Two. With instructor supervision, an outdoor range version of the drill can be run with the "attacker" and shooter positioned back-to-back. At the signal, the "attacker" runs away from the firing line and the shooter unholsters her gun and fires down range at a target 21 feet in front of her. The "attacker" stops as soon as the shot is fired. This exercise can help each individual calculate his or her own danger zone.

3 Version Three. Visit a Gander Mtn. Academy for an opportunity to do the Tueller Drill in a 300-degree, real-world simulation.

We also need to actually *look* at the individuals in our immediate vicinity (including those behind us) to do two things. First, we want to make a quick assessment of the threat level of the individual; and second, we want to send the simple message "I see you." That doesn't mean that we need to "eyeball" potential threats, and our look shouldn't signal "I'm tougher than you" or "I'm carrying a firearm." It simply needs to imply "I see you."

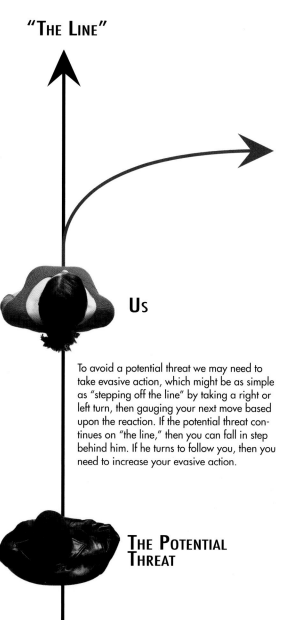

"THE LINE"

This individual turns her head to observe anyone in her immediate area, and quickly makes eye contact to inform the individual "I see you."

Us

To avoid a potential threat we may need to take evasive action, which might be as simple as "stepping off the line" by taking a right or left turn, then gauging your next move based upon the reaction. If the potential threat continues on "the line," then you can fall in step behind him. If he turns to follow you, then you need to increase your evasive action.

THE POTENTIAL THREAT

If we see something or someone who sets off our warning bells, we need to move away from the potential threat by slowing down, speeding up, changing direction, or turning around. If someone is approaching us from the rear, the "polite" reaction is to not turn around. We're not worried with polite. If we *do* hear (or otherwise sense) an individual behind us, we should turn to observe and if the individual causes us concern, we should take evasive action by changing direction and observing his reaction, if any.

NOT LOOKING LIKE A VICTIM

When we observe our surroundings in this manner, it will be obvious to anyone watching us that we're being observant, and that fact alone will make us less attractive to potential assailants. We can increase that "unattractiveness" by walking with "purpose" – that is, we need to walk with our bodies erect and our heads up, and we should walk faster than the crowd, not slower.

Imagine two individuals walking down the street – the first individual is walking with purpose, moving at a quick enough pace that she looks like she's going somewhere. That individual swivels her head to scan the area and she makes quick eye contact with any individual in her immediate area. The second individual is shuffling along at a slow pace, focused on a three-inch circle in front of him while he sends a text message on his cell phone. Which person do you think a criminal will want to target? When sizing up the first individual, the criminal will realize "She's moving too fast and she saw me. She won't be easy to approach." On the other hand, he'll look at the second individual and think "I can get right up on him, and he'll never see me coming." Notice that we said nothing about the size or other characteristics of the potential "victims." The truth is, an observant 110 pound woman is a *less* attractive victim than a 200 pound man who is *entirely* absorbed in his cell phone and who is *completely unaware* of the attacker approaching from behind.

MAKING A GAME OF IT

We don't need to think of situational awareness as something that we have to turn on, or as a chore. We personally make a game of it – when we're in public, we like to be people watchers, looking for a few different things. First, we like to challenge ourselves by trying to identify anyone else who might be carrying a firearm. It might be a slight bulge on the hip of another permit holder, or it might be the outline of a pistol grip under the shirt of a gang member, but that simple exercise ensures that we at least look at everyone around us. We watch hands, we watch eyes, and we pay extra close attention to people approaching or within our "danger zone." We also like to make a game of looking for individuals in condition white (more on that on pages 16 and 17); that is, we like to look at things from the criminal's perspective. Next time you're in public, give it a try – look for individuals who are talking on their cell phones or texting and are completely absorbed by that task (and *completely unaware* of their surroundings). Watch for people who shuffle along slower than the crowd around them, looking as if they're going nowhere. One of our favorites (or biggest pet peeves) is observing people who walk down the middle of the driving lanes in parking lots or parking garages, and are completely unaware that a vehicle weighing several thousand pounds is bearing down on them. If they're not aware that a 5,000 pound truck is behind them, do you think they'll notice if a 150 pound rapist is sneaking up behind them? Finally, take the time to monitor yourself – how often do you find yourself out in public, immersed in a cell phone call and oblivious to your surroundings? How often do you discover that you're tailgating the only other vehicle on the freeway, when two or three other lanes are clear?

To hone our situational awareness skills, we like to use the color codes of awareness developed by the late Jeff Cooper.

THE "COLOR CODES OF AWARENESS"

These were originally developed by the U.S. Marines in the Pacific during World War II to help mentally condition Marines to prepare for an attack. They were later modified by Colonel Jeff Cooper for use in educating civilians to help us to become more aware of our surroundings, and to not only prepare for violent encounters, but if possible, to avoid them in the first place.

The "Color Codes" developed by Cooper include:

Condition White: Unaware
Condition Yellow: Aware
Condition Orange: Heightened Awareness
Condition Red: Action

On the following pages, we've detailed what type of mental awareness we should have at each level, and what our actions might be. We've also included a quote from Jeff Cooper with his thoughts on each level of awareness.

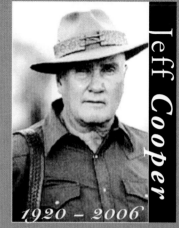

Jeff Cooper
1920 - 2006

Father of the "Modern Technique" of Pistolcraft

Jeff Cooper's accomplishments include author, columnist, professor, and WWII and Korean War veteran. Cooper is also widely recognized as the Father of the "Modern Technique" of Pistolcraft, including the development of the four universal safety rules; updates and refinements to Jack Weaver's classic "Weaver Stance;" and development of the four "color codes" of awareness. In 1976, Cooper founded what is widely recognized as one of the premier firearm training organizations in the world, the Gunsite Academy in Paulden Arizona. Cooper died in September, 2006, and will be sorely missed by thousands of students and fans.

UNAWARE

In Condition White, you are unaware of what's going on around you:

- You don't think anything bad will happen and may believe that violent crime happens to "other people."

- Modern technologies such as cell phones, smart phones, and MP3 players create a perfect environment to lull individuals into condition white, allowing criminals to approach within inches of their potential victim, making avoidance or escape nearly impossible.

- Individuals in condition white often fail to recognize emotions or aggressiveness in others and they might enter into arguments without realizing that they've moved beyond what's safe, or they might believe that they can talk their way out of trouble. They will also be unaware when they've strayed into unsafe areas such as poorly lit areas, areas with blind spots, or areas away from the crowds; or they might put themselves into unsafe situations by allowing their gas tank to go to "E" or forgetting where they parked their car.

- It's the condition of most victims, and it's the condition that criminals look for.

- You should never allow yourself to be in condition white when armed, because your ability to avoid or escape a dangerous situation is compromised – that means that a defensive shooting might occur when it could have been avoided!

> **"If attacked in this state the only thing that may save you is the inadequacy and ineptitude of your attacker. When confronted by something nasty your reaction will probably be, 'Oh my God! This can't be happening to me'."**
>
> *Colonel*
> *Jeff Cooper*

Unaware
This individual is preoccupied with her MP3 player, and is *completely unaware* of her surroundings.

AWARE

In Condition Yellow, you are aware of your surroundings:

- This is the condition you should be in any time you're in public.

- You are aware of what's happening in the immediate vicinity, and you proceed with caution.

- You are not paranoid or overreactive, but you keep an eye out for potential threats and their sources.

- Your posture, eyes, and demeanor say "I am alert" and you walk faster than the crowd.

- You should become comfortable with simple habits such as scanning an area (rooms, street corners, etc.) before entering; and identifying exits and cover wherever you are.

- You make brief eye contact with individuals in your immediate area, letting them know "I see you."

- Individuals in condition yellow have developed safe habits such as avoiding arguments, identifying everyone and everything within their protective "bubble" (including objects that can work to their benefit such as cover, barriers, and exits), and following the conflict avoidance ideas outlined in this chapter.

- If you are armed, you must be in yellow.

> *"Relaxed alert. No specific threat situation. Your mindset is that 'today could be the day I may have to defend myself.' You are simply aware that the world is an unfriendly place and that you are prepared to do something if necessary. You use your eyes and ears. You don't have to be armed in this state but if you are armed you should be in Condition Yellow. You should always be in Yellow whenever you are in unfamiliar surroundings or among people you don't know."*
>
> *Colonel*
> *Jeff Cooper*

Aware

This individual is aware of her surroundings and is not distracting herself with any electronic device. She not only observes the area to her front, she also swivels her head to look to her sides and directly behind her. She makes momentary eye contact with anyone within her protective "bubble."

HEIGHTENED AWARENESS

In Condition Orange, you have identified a possible threat or threats.
This is a heightened state of awareness:

- You realize that something *may* be wrong.

- There *may* be a danger to yourself or others.

- You make a plan on how to react, including identifying cover, barriers, or an exit strategy.

- You may begin to take preemptive action such as turning around, stepping off "the line," increasing your distance, or making simple, direct verbal commands such as "Stay back!" or "Don't come any closer!"

- You decide on a mental "trigger" that will move you to take action, such as an individual refusing your verbal commands and moving closer into your "bubble."

- You mentally prepare yourself for a confrontation or a rapid escape.

- You may begin to feel the effects of adrenaline or other automated responses described in our physiological section in Chapter Five.

- Your pistol may remain holstered, but you should prepare to access it, such as brushing aside outer clothing; putting your hand in the pocket where you have your firearm in a pocket holster; or reaching into your purse and getting a tight grip on the pistol.

> **"Specific alert. Something is not quite right and has gotten your attention. Your radar has picked up a specific alert. You shift your primary focus to determine if there is a threat. In Condition Orange, you set a mental trigger. If the threat proves to be nothing, you shift back to Condition Yellow."**
>
> *Colonel*
> *Jeff Cooper*

Heightened Awareness
This individual has sensed or observed something or someone that causes her concern and takes preemptive action by taking cover. She closely observes the situation to determine if there is a threat, and makes a plan on how to react. Even if she can't definitively categorize the situation as an actual threat, she may decide to avoid the situation entirely and take evasive action by walking, running, or driving away.

ACTION

In Condition Red, action is immediate:

- Your mental trigger has been tripped and you execute your plan, either to escape, take cover, or engage the threat.

- Trust your instincts – it's better to run away from a situation that turned out *not* to be a threat than it is to get stuck in a mental block of "this can't be what I think it is" and guessing wrong.

- Instinct and adrenaline will cause involuntary reactions and *must* be calculated into your training program (See the section on the physiological reaction to stress in Chapter Five.) You should expect your hands to tremble and your fine motor skills to degrade.

- If engaging the threat, operate within the rules governing the use of force, including the obligation to retreat if possible, and the obligation to use something less than deadly force if it will suffice. See Chapter Four for a full definition of your obligations and rights when it comes to a use of force to defend yourself.

- A use of force is *not* the required outcome. If you've closely observed the immediate area and have identified an escape route, retreat may be the most logical and prudent course of action.

" *"Condition Red is (action). Your mental trigger has been tripped (established back in Condition Orange). The mental trigger will differ depending upon the circumstances. Whatever trigger is selected, it is a button that once pushed, results in immediate action on your part."* **"**

Colonel
Jeff Cooper

Action: Verbal Commands
In this example, the individual forcefully barks out verbal commands while raising her hands in a "stop" gesture.

Action: Escape
In this example, the individual has identified a threat early enough to make a rapid escape or to head toward cover.

Action: Draw Firearm and Issue Commands
In this example, the individual forcefully issues commands with her firearm at a low ready position (and the finger outside the trigger guard).

Action: Engage the Threat
In this example, the individual points her firearm at the attacker and is ready to take whatever action is required to stop the threat.

OBSERVING YOUR ENVIRONMENT

Observing your environment is as important as observing the people within it. Look for (and avoid) areas that might be attractive to criminals looking for easy victims; but also look for things in your environment that can work to your advantage, such as barriers, cover, concealment, and escape routes.

BLIND SPOTS

Criminals count on surprise when targeting prospective victims, and they'd be more than happy to have their victims approach them, rather than the other way around. When approaching blind spots at the corners of buildings, or when approaching trees, tall bushes, concrete pillars, or vehicles, give them a wide berth, and turn to observe the hidden area as you approach.

AWAY FROM THE CROWDS

Just as criminals count on surprise, they also count on an easy escape with no witnesses. Regardless of how convenient a shortcut might seem or however safe you might feel heading to your car late at night all alone, that's the kind of behavior that criminals count on to find easy victims.

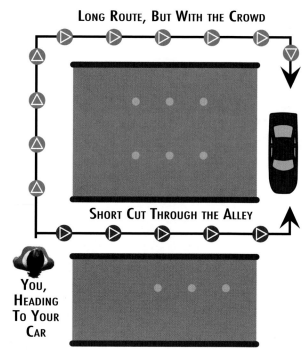

LONG ROUTE, BUT WITH THE CROWD

SHORT CUT THROUGH THE ALLEY

YOU, HEADING TO YOUR CAR

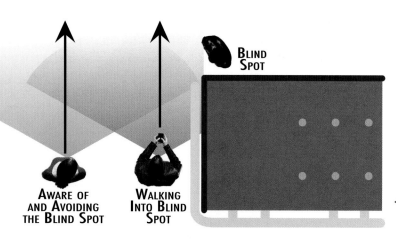

BLIND SPOT

AWARE OF AND AVOIDING THE BLIND SPOT

WALKING INTO BLIND SPOT

◀ Be especially observant when approaching blind spots such as corners of buildings, tall vehicles, pillars, dumpsters, bushes, etc. Make a wide berth around these areas, and turn your head to look as you approach. Get ready to run.

Although you may be perfectly within your rights to walk down a dark alley all alone, you've already made two mistakes. The individual above might be looking for a handout, or he might be looking for your money or your life. Fix your mistakes before it's too late by turning around and returning as quickly as possible to a crowded area.

LOW LIGHT AREAS

Back entrances of homes or businesses, dark alleys, parking areas with burned out lights; these are all areas where criminals may hover when looking for easy victims. Especially dangerous are areas with a rapid transition from bright lights to low light or darkness. It takes our eyes as long as 20 minutes to adapt to low light, and criminals who are stalking victims in these areas will be well adapted to the low light while our eyes are still adjusting. In the example on the opposite page, you should plan a route through the well-lit area of the parking garage rather than the route with the burned-out lights. If a criminal is in the area looking for a victim, he's much more likely to hover behind a vehicle or pillar in the dark area rather than in the brightly-lit areas.

BARRIERS, COVER, AND CONCEAL-MENT

When under threat, any barrier between you and the threat increases your ability to escape. Vehicles, tables, chairs, even a display case at a convenience store is better than nothing. Concealment is anything that hides you from the threat (a closed door, a wall, or anything you can duck behind) while cover (things like concrete pillars, or the front of vehicles where the engine block is) protects you from incoming bullets.

As part of your situational awareness when in public, you'll need to be aware of how different objects within your environment can help serve as barriers, concealment, or cover. Whether you are under attack yourself, or you find yourself in the vicinity of an attack on someone else, you should place as many of these objects as possible between the attacker and you.

ESCAPE ROUTES

Identify routes and opportunities to increase distance between you and a threat (walking, running, or driving away) or to reach cover or concealment. You'll foil an attacker with a knife if you can remain at least arm's distance away (and if you can keep barriers between you and the attacker), and if he has a gun, you'll need to spoil his aim by getting "off the line" and increasing your distance as quickly as possible. Picture how the difficulty increases at your local range when you increase the distance between you and the target from 7 feet to 14 feet to 21 feet. How about pushing it out to 100, 200, or 300 feet? The attacker will find it just as aggravating.

Cover
Behind engine blocks and concrete pillars.

Exit Strategy
Out of garage or back to mall.

Area to Avoid
Where lights are burned out.

MORE ON CONFLICT AVOIDANCE

As mentioned earlier, avoiding conflict requires more than simply observing our surroundings, it's also dependent upon our actions, behavior, and precautions. The following list is not all-inclusive, but it does contain some good ideas to keep ourselves and our families safe.

1 PERSONAL SECURITY

- There is safety in numbers. When in public, travel with a companion.
- Move faster than the crowd and be a people watcher. Always be in condition yellow.
- Never go to a stranger's house alone and never allow a stranger into your house when you're alone. That includes when buying/renting/selling a home or when buying or selling from one of the popular auction websites.
- As silly as it sounds, when dining out, don't take a seat with your back to the door and know where the exits are. At the first sign of trouble, leave the area.

2 AUTOMOBILE SECURITY

- Keep valuables out of sight and do *not* leave paperwork in your car with your home address.
- Note where you parked your vehicle and be observant of the immediate area when entering or exiting your vehicle.
- Be especially observant when loading the car or buckling in children. If in doubt about a potential threat, you may need to literally toss the kids into the car and drive away immediately. Stop when you can and double-check seat belts and child seats.
- Lock your vehicle immediately upon entering.
- Leave room to maneuver when you come to a stop.
- Be a courteous driver – allow other drivers to merge, don't tailgate, keep off the horn, and keep that middle finger to yourself.

- If you are involved in a fender bender, call the police and stay in your vehicle until you can evaluate the situation. If in doubt, remain in your vehicle until the police arrive, even if (or especially if) the other driver has exited his vehicle.

3 HOME SECURITY

- Keep doors locked and the garage door closed, even when at home.
- Have ample exterior lighting – don't be the only house on the block with the lights out.
- Leave an interior light on a timer.
- Use good quality door locks and add a deadbolt and/or a hotel type "throw over" lock to both front and back doors. When installing deadbolts, use 3-inch or longer screws when mounting the "strike plate," which will be deep enough to anchor in the wall stud, rather than just the door frame.
- Get an alarm system and set it religiously, especially when at home. You can afford to lose property; you can't afford to lose your life or the lives of your loved ones during a home invasion.
- Keep driveway clear of snow and front steps clear of newspapers, especially when home.
- Consider getting a dog. Not an attack dog, just a dog that will bark at the first sign of an intruder.

4 PHONE SECURITY

- Use caller ID and don't answer calls from unknown numbers.
- DO NOT give out personal information, such as whether you live alone, whether you have a security system, etc.
- Keep a cell phone in your bedroom so that you can call 911, even if your home phone becomes disabled.

Chain locks run the risk of being cut by an intruder and don't perform to the level of deadbolts or throw-over locks. Regardless of your lock choice, mounting them with extra deep screws will dramatically increase the force required to breach the door.

PLANNING FOR HOME DEFENSE

We plan for what to do if a fire occurs in our homes and we need to do the same type of planning for what to do if a home invasion occurs. Although the rules governing the use of deadly force inside the home are typically less stringent than those for outside the home, our advice is to focus on remaining safe and *not* on keeping your property safe. When discussing a home invasion plan with the family, review the checklist items below and ensure that all family members are aware of how to dial 911 and all age-appropriate family members are aware of the location of the home defense firearm and how to use it. Plan a route for all family members to head to the most secure areas of the home and include in the plan who will get the phone (and dial 911), who will access the defensive firearm and tactical flashlight, and who will assist loved ones. While you don't necessarily need to draw a floor layout of your home with your plan, you should at least *have* a plan and discuss it with everyone in your household, including your children. Think of this as no different than discussing a plan in case of fire. Finally, it's important to discuss what *not* to do in the event of a home invasion. For example, if everyone in the family is in the same part of the house, then it is not necessary, prudent, or smart to "clear rooms" looking for the intruder. In addition, it's extremely important to discuss what to do if a family member is coming home late or unexpectedly and how to communicate it if a guest will be in the home. The use of a family "code word" or "challenge and reply" can avoid tragedy if your teenage son or daughter has decided to sneak a significant other into the house for a late night rendezvous, or if your spouse has gotten up for a late night snack.

THE "HOME DEFENSE" CHECKLIST

- Are the front and back lights on?

- Is the alarm on?

- Are all doors locked (including deadbolt and/or throw-over lock)?

- Is the home defense firearm in its proper location and is it loaded? (Keep in mind that you'll need to follow federal and state safe storage laws.)

- Where is the phone and how do I dial 911 (in the dark, with a head full of cobwebs)?

- If the home is invaded, what room do we move to?

- What commands do we give?

- How do I identify a friend from a foe?

- What's a family code word to identify whom and where you are?

- How do we inform our family that we'll be coming home late, or that a guest will be in the home?

- Does each family member know how to dial 911?

- Does each age-appropriate family member know how to use the home defense firearm?

- What do we do when the police arrive?

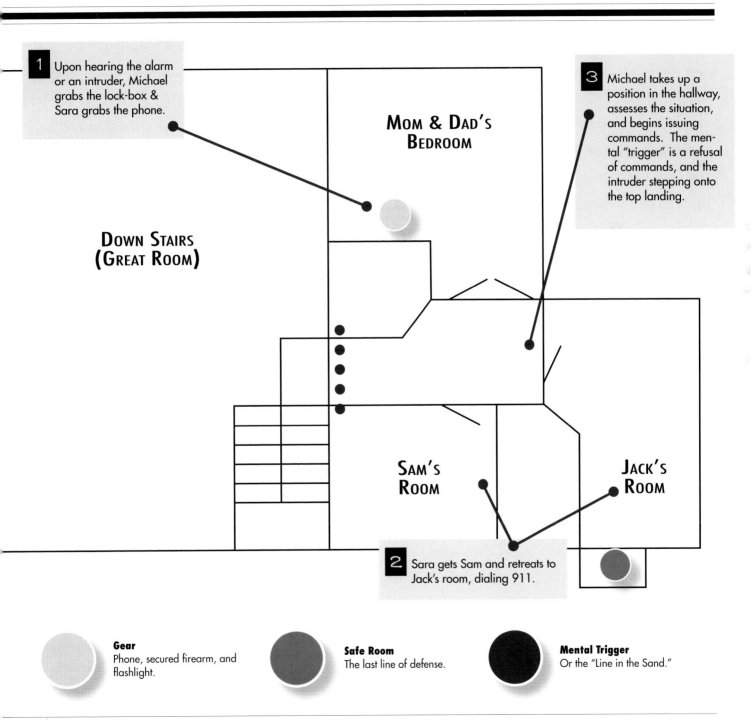

1 Upon hearing the alarm or an intruder, Michael grabs the lock-box & Sara grabs the phone.

MOM & DAD'S BEDROOM

3 Michael takes up a position in the hallway, assesses the situation, and begins issuing commands. The mental "trigger" is a refusal of commands, and the intruder stepping onto the top landing.

DOWN STAIRS (GREAT ROOM)

SAM'S ROOM

JACK'S ROOM

2 Sara gets Sam and retreats to Jack's room, dialing 911.

Gear
Phone, secured firearm, and flashlight.

Safe Room
The last line of defense.

Mental Trigger
Or the "Line in the Sand."

With enough time and money, dozens of advanced shooting schools are available to the average citizen, including advanced topics such as force-on-force, low light shooting, shoot/no-shoot scenarios, etc. In fact, we're sure that a school exists that would teach us to use infrared gear, rappel from a helicopter, breach doors, and rescue hostages, but let's face it – the average permit holder is lucky to get to the range once a month. So how do we bridge the gap between the training that we *do* perform, versus the type of scenario we might find ourselves in if a critical incident does occur? One simple alternative we can do while sitting in our armchair at home is to run through a series of mental exercises.

Mental exercises shouldn't be confused with paranoia, or with a law abiding citizen fantasizing about getting in a shootout with a bad guy. It's simply a process to have a mental checklist of items that wouldn't normally be part of our time on the range. For example, when walking through a parking garage, picture what you would do if someone stepped out from behind a car with a knife. What commands would you give? Where would you find cover? What would be your mental trigger? At home, mentally walk through the step-by-step process that you would go through if you heard the front door being kicked down. These simple mental exercises can help to avoid the "Oh my God" reaction described by Cooper.

Mental exercises can extend to our time on the range as well. One goal of mental exercises on the range may seem counterintuitive, which is to elevate our stress level to the point that our body will generate higher levels of adrenaline. This might be done by converting a relaxed round of shooting at 21 feet to an exercise where we imagine the target is an attacker, charging us with a knife. The goal should be to place several rounds into critical areas within one to two seconds (the time it would take for the attacker to reach us). The results might be lower accuracy compared to a more relaxed practice round, but it will force us to learn to shoot safely and accurately, while having a pounding heart and shaking hands. When running mental exercises at home or at the range, you'll need to create hypothetical problems (such as the examples on the opposite page) that require a solution. Your solution will need to be a *complete* solution; that is, it should include the checklist items on the opposite page, including evaluating your options and preparing for the aftermath.

AT HOME:

- What if I hear the front door being kicked down, or a window shattered?
- What if my burglar alarm goes off in the middle of the night?
- What if a stranger at the door suddenly produces a weapon?
- What if I find the door to my house open upon arriving home? (This is an easy one – stay outside, call 911, and let the police do their job.)
- What if I hear someone in the house at night? How do I distinguish a family member from an intruder?

IN PUBLIC:

- What if I'm approached by one or more individuals who cause me concern?
- What if I "step off the line" and they follow me?
- What do I do if they produce a weapon? What if it's a knife? What if it's a gun?
- What if a threat materializes between a loved one and me?
- What if I see an attack in progress on someone else?

MENTAL EXERCISE CHECKLIST

- What are my options?
- What cover or barriers are available?
- How do I move "off the line?"
- How do I draw from the holster?
- What commands do I give?
- What are the requirements for speed versus accuracy?
- How do I work the physiological reactions into my response?
- How do I disengage/re-engage any safety devices including holster retention, manual safeties, or decockers?
- How do I clear a malfunction?
- How do I perform a reload?
- What do I do in the aftermath?
- Whom do I call and what do I say?
- What do I say to the police?
- What will I do when I'm arrested?
- Where is my lawyer's contact information?

HOW DOES A CONCEALED CARRY PERMIT FIT?

When it comes to our personal protection plans, a "Concealed Carry Permit" simply provides us with one more tool that might be used if we find ourselves unable to avoid or escape from a dangerous situation. But, as discussed on the opposite page, possessing a firearm actually *elevates* our legal and moral need to find ways to avoid or escape. A concealed carry permit should *not* be confused with any additional authority under the law, beyond the right to carry an object that would otherwise be illegal. In most of our experiences, the only individuals that we've known who have carried firearms on a daily basis have been law enforcement (who *do* have additional authority), so it's understandable that confusion can occur about what exactly our permit authorizes us to do. Let's look at some things that our permit is NOT.

WHAT A PERMIT IS NOT

An Invincibility Shield

We cannot look at our concealed carry permit as a permit to go to places, do things, or say things that we shouldn't otherwise. If we ignore the guidelines on conflict avoidance and allow ourselves to be placed in a dangerous situation that we could have avoided, we'll quickly discover that our permit does not stop incoming bullets and it will *not* shield us from an aggressive prosecutor who believes that we were spoiling for a fight.

A Shield of ANY Kind

Never confuse a concealed carry permit with a "Junior Police Officer" badge. Police have specific responsibilities (such as chasing down bad guys) that would put us in legal peril if we tried to imitate them. For example, if we tried to prevent a property crime (such as attempting to stop someone from breaking into a car or chasing down a purse thief), or if we followed an individual whom we suspected was up to no good and the situation escalated to the point where we used force to protect ourselves, we could be charged with a felony since we've broken nearly every one of the rules governing the use of force or deadly force outlined in Chapter Four. On the same topic, we'll occasionally hear of an enterprising organization selling "Concealed Carry Permit" badges, modeled after police badges. These are *really* bad ideas, not only because they could be confused with actual police badges (possibly resulting in a charge of impersonating a police officer) but they may also give the "holder" of the badge the incorrect impression that they have some special powers or authority. Save your money.

A "Fix" For Bad Attitudes

If you pull out your handgun and wave it at someone in an attempt to adjust his behavior (such as the guy who just cut you off in traffic), you'll quickly find yourself on your way to jail, charged with assault or worse.

SO WHAT'S IT GOOD FOR?

A concealed carry permit is just that – it's a permit to carry an object in public that would otherwise be illegal. EVERY other law that applies to non-permit holders also applies to us, including the rules governing the use of force and deadly force. In fact, our permit may put us in *greater* legal jeopardy compared to non-permit holders, since many state and federal statutes provide additional penalties when a firearm falls into the mix. For example, if a non-permit holder verbally threatens someone with death or great bodily harm for cutting him off in traffic, he might be charged with misdemeanor assault. Insert a permit holder and a firearm into the same situation, and he should expect to be charged with felony assault, and anything else the prosecutor can come up with.

If you're unlucky enough to see this charming fellow in the lane next to you, keep calm, don't react, and keep that middle finger to yourself. ▶

OTHER USE OF FORCE OPTIONS

As part of our personal protection plan, we may want to consider other "use of force" options, in addition to a firearm. Legally and morally, we may want to consider the ability to use some other method of force that has a lesser chance of killing an attacker, and a lesser chance of putting us in legal peril. However, other use of force options including tasers, pepper spray, knives, etc., almost always require the defender to be within 10 to 12 feet of the attacker (for tasers and pepper spray) or within arm's reach (for a knife) and they rarely have the same deterrent effect as exposing a firearm.

In addition, both tasers and pepper spray can sometimes have no effect on an attacker, particularly when he may be high on drugs. In this section, we've profiled both tasers and pepper spray, as well as another use of force option that's really kind of silly.

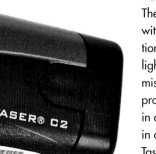

Taser C2

The C2 comes in a small package with replaceable cartridges. Options include a built-in laser and LED light to assist in aiming. If the user misses an attacker with the ejected probes, the device can also be used in a direct contact mode, using built-in contacts on the face of the device. Taser has a lifetime guarantee and will replace the device for free if it is used in a defensive situation.

HOW DO TASERS WORK?

More properly called an Electronic Control Device (Taser is a brand name), these devices are designed to send a high-voltage, low-amperage electrical charge through the body of an attacker. The charge confuses the body's own natural electrical signals, incapacitating the attacker.

Consumer models, such as the Taser C2, utilize cartridges that when fired release compressed air to shoot two probes connected to wires in the direction of the attacker (up to 15 feet), which then embed themselves in the attacker's clothes or skin. The device is designed to deliver a 30 second shock, allowing the victim to drop the Taser, and retreat to cover.

Detractors have claimed that criminals will use Tasers to incapacitate their victims, however, Taser has developed an innovative device within the C2, which showers the ground with 20 to 30 "confetti like" tags, containing an identification number that can be traced by police. Taser also requires that purchasers pass a background check prior to device activation.

A SELF-DEFENSE SUGGESTION, THAT'S, WELL, SORT OF DUMB

In the summer of 2006, a Minneapolis Police spokesperson suggested that a ring of keys laced between your fingers would make a "great defensive tool." We think that that advice is, in a word, dumb. First of all, using anything contained in your fist as a defensive tool requires that the attacker be within arm's reach, and a fist full of keys is more likely to enrage an attacker. Most people would consider a firearm to be a *bit* more of a deterrent to the prospective criminal. Most criminals think so too.

SABRE Pepper Spray
SABRE combines both CS military tear gas and oleoresin capsicum in this small canister, capable of delivering up to 25 shots. SABRE Red contains 10% oleoresin capsicum measuring 2,000,000 Scoville Heat Units, which SABRE says is the hottest on the market.

Kimber PepperBlaster
Kimber sells the PepperBlaster (shown above) and the JPX Jet Protector (fashioned to operate like a traditional pistol, sights and all). Both models store OC and benzyl alcohol in separate tubes, which are mixed when the trigger is depressed. The PepperBlaster delivers its spray at 90 miles an hour, while the JPX is capable of delivering its spray at 270 miles per hour.

HOW DOES PEPPER SPRAY (OC) WORK?

The active ingredient in pepper spray is oleoresin capsicum (OC), a chemical found in cayenne peppers (hence the name "pepper" spray). OC affects mucous membranes like the eyes, nose, throat, and lungs and causes instant capillary dilation, causing the eyelids to shut. The bronchial tubes may also swell tightly, making it hard for the attacker to breathe. Sprayed into an attacker's face, pepper spray may incapacitate an attacker for as long as 45 minutes.

With all chemical sprays, there exists the possibility that an assailant will not be affected by the spray, or that the wind can deliver the chemical spray back into the face of the victim.

HANDGUN AND AMMUNITION BASICS

This chapter reviews the fundamentals of handguns,
the universal firearm safety rules, ammunition basics, and
ammunition & semi-automatic malfunctions and their clearance.

— Four Universal Safety Rules —

— Properly Clearing Semi-Automatics and Revolvers —

— Additional Safety Considerations —

— Double Action vs. Single Action —

— Detailed Revolver and Semi-Automatic Explanations —

— Handgun Sizes and Weights —

— Pros and Cons of Different Handgun Options —

— Ammunition —

— Ballistic Basics —

— Ammunition & Semi-Automatic Malfunctions and their Clearance —

— Handgun or Shotgun for Home Defense? —

Chapter 2

Handgun and ammunition basics should be an enjoyable topic for new and experienced shooters alike. In this chapter we'll start by reviewing what are called the "Universal Safety Rules" that are non-negotiable when it comes to safe firearm ownership, handling, and use. We'd love to say that the universal rules were our idea, but that's not the case. Like the color codes of awareness, the Universal Safety Rules were developed by Colonel Jeff Cooper and have been adopted by nearly every firearms training organization in the world. We'll also cover a number of other safety considerations that are part of safe firearm ownership including topics associated with firearm maintenance, safety on the range, and safety considerations when selecting a holster. We'll also cover the proper clearance (unloading) procedures for both semi-automatics and revolvers, including lots of good pictures to help you through the process.

In this chapter, we'll also explain the difference between double action and single action. This might sound like kind of a technical topic, but it's an important one to understand because it not only affects the operation of your firearm, it's an important safety consideration when selecting a firearm. In our example, we'll be using a pistol called a SIG SAUER P229 (for you Cliff Clavins, that's the same pistol used by U.S. Air Marshals), but the theory is the same for both semi-autos and revolvers. Once we're through that topic, we'll be reviewing several different types of revolvers and semi-autos.

Revolvers have been a mainstay of repeating handguns since Sam Colt developed the first modern design in 1836 with his Colt Patterson model. More than 170 years later, Colt would still recognize today's modern revolvers as having many of the same functional components as his designs, although he'd probably find them a bit less attractive than his beauties. As you'll see in our examples, revolvers have a revolving cylinder, which typically has between five and eight chambers, each capable of holding a cartridge.

Semi-automatics have been on the market since the late 1890s, but it took another famous inventor, John Moses Browning, to perfect the design with his Model 1911 (which was adopted by the U.S. Army as its standard sidearm). Fast approaching its 100th birthday, the 1911 is now produced by more than 15 manufacturers and remains one of the most popular handguns made. We've included a walkthrough of the 1911, as well as three other semi-autos, including the Glock, the Springfield XD, and the SIG SAUER P250. We'll even help explain how these gadgets work with a step-by-step cutaway of what happens when you press the trigger.

In the remainder of the chapter, we'll help you understand the pros and cons of selecting a revolver versus a semi-automatic; and we'll talk about other important factors to consider when selecting a handgun such as size and weight (where we've included a side-by-side comparison of several different models). We'll also explain ammunition types and care, ammunition and semi-automatic malfunctions, and how to safely clear malfunctions. We'll wrap up this chapter with a discussion on what you should know when considering a shotgun for home defense.

THE UNIVERSAL SAFETY RULES

By itself, a firearm is an inert object. By itself, it doesn't just "go off." Insert a human being and a negligent discharge can occur when the proper safety rules aren't followed. The following safety rules were developed by Jeff Cooper and must be followed whether at home, on the range, or carrying in public. All firearm "accidents" can be eliminated by following these easy to remember rules.

1 **Treat all guns as though they are always loaded and always perform a clearance check every time you pick one up!**
Most firearm "accidents" occur with firearms that the users had sworn were unloaded. Never, never, never grow careless with a firearm. Every single time you pick it up, perform the proper clearance procedure and educate those in your household how to do the same. Treat a firearm that you've just unloaded with the *exact* same respect as one that you've just loaded.

2 **Never point your gun at anything that you are not willing to destroy!**
While your firearm has to point somewhere, you should always ensure that it's pointed in a direction that can serve as a backstop if the firearm were to discharge. A good method to practice this rule is to pretend that a laser extends out from the end of the barrel. You should NEVER let that imaginary beam touch anything that won't stop a bullet (that includes any wall, ceiling, or floor that could

not stop a bullet) or ANYONE (that includes your own hands, legs, or body) unless you are in a defensive situation and all criteria is present for the use of deadly force.

3 **Keep your finger OFF the trigger and outside the trigger guard until you are on target and have made the decision to shoot!**
Until these criteria are met, your trigger finger should be straight and placed firmly on the slide of a semi-automatic or the side of a revolver's cylinder. In a defensive situation, do NOT put your finger in the trigger guard unless all requirements have been met for the use of deadly force. Training consistently with this method will avoid a negligent discharge in a stress situation, when your body's natural adrenaline dump will cause the strength of your grip to increase.

4 **Always be sure of your target and beyond!**
Said another way, you must POSITIVELY identify your target before you shoot and you MUST be convinced that anything that you shoot at (a target on the range, or an attacker in a parking garage) must have an effective backstop to stop your bullet, otherwise you MUST NOT SHOOT!

THE TALE OF THE TAPE

As simple as the four universal rules sound, unless they've been ingrained into our lives, they're sometimes easy to ignore (or forget) and tragedy can result. Even experts occasionally blow the rules – in the two examples below, two law enforcement officers are caught on tape with one or more safety violations. In both cases, the officers were only faced with embarrassment rather than tragedy, but you may not be so lucky. Never, never, never forget the Universal Safety Rules.

| An unnamed Las Vegas police officer points her firearm at a suspect while her partner handcuffs him. Her finger is in the trigger guard. | She lowers her firearm slightly. | Her firearm discharges inches from the suspect and her partner. A cloud of debris is clearly seen in the video. | She puts her hand to her mouth in shock and surprise. | She holsters her firearm. |

| An unnamed DEA agent discusses the dangers of firearms in front of a classroom full of students and their parents. | Using his Glock pistol as a prop, he declares it unloaded, and steps off camera to have his assistant confirm that it's unloaded. | He holds the pistol over his head with the slide locked back. | He releases the slide. | And shoots himself in the leg. |

As mentioned in Universal Safety Rule #1, we *always* do a clearance procedure *anytime* we pick up a firearm (other than the exceptions noted below). This might seem a bit ridiculous (as in "I *just* cleared the pistol, why would I clear it again?") but this habit will ensure that you avoid the "I thought it was unloaded" type of accident described on the next page. During the clearance procedures that follow, always remember all four Universal Safety Rules, including maintaining muzzle control and keeping your finger OUTSIDE of the trigger guard.

The *only* exceptions to this rule are: when operating on a "hot" range and picking up a previously loaded firearm from the benchrest in preparation to fire; when retrieving a loaded handgun from a gun vault to holster it for the day; or, when placing a loaded handgun in a gun vault at the end of the day.

Properly clearing a semi-automatic takes four steps. Clearing a revolver? Just two steps.

1 Drop the magazine.

2 Lock the slide back.

3 Look through the top of the slide, through the entire magazine well. All you should see is the floor or your other hand waving underneath. You should NOT see a magazine or bright, shiny rounds staring back at you. Notice the finger OUTSIDE the trigger guard.

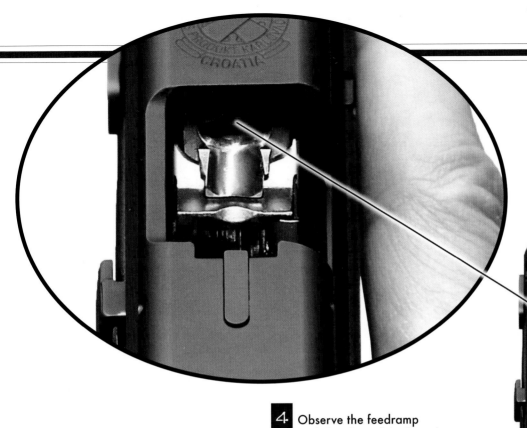

"I THOUGHT IT WAS UNLOADED!"

In March of 2006, L. Pan of Saint Paul left a loaded 9MM handgun under a sofa cushion in his home. His two-year-old son found the gun but his mother took the gun away. She removed the magazine, and believing it was unloaded, left the gun within reach of her child. The child picked up the gun and fired the chambered round into his mother's knee.

4 Observe the feedramp and chamber of the barrel to ensure that no round is chambered, and double-check by sticking your pinky into the chamber. We know this sounds like we're getting a bit anal, but this is the best method to ensure that your firearm has been properly cleared.

One additional piece of advice – make sure that your fingers are nowhere near the slide release when your pinky is inserted into the chamber, otherwise you'll get a painful lesson on how quickly (and forcefully) the slide will slam closed.

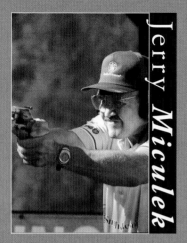

Jerry Miculek

Fourteen Time International Revolver Champion

What do you think can be fired faster: a semi-automatic or a revolver? Which one do you think can be reloaded faster? If you guessed a semi-automatic, don't be so sure. Jerry Miculek is a speed shooter and firearms instructor, experienced in nearly every type of firearm made, but revolvers are his first love. He is recognized as the world's fastest revolver shooter, with four world records held, including firing six shots, reloading, and firing six more shots from a revolver in 2.99 seconds. To see this incredible feat, search for Jerry Miculek on YouTube. You won't believe your eyes.

CLEARING REVOLVERS

1 Open the Cylinder.

2 Look through each chamber, and confirm that they are completely clear.

ADDITIONAL SAFETY CONSIDERATIONS

In addition to the four Universal Safety Rules, we've added a few additional topics here:

SAFETY

1. Educate others on the four Universal Safety Rules, and do *not* feel bad asking someone to "watch your muzzle" or to take his finger out of the trigger guard.

2. Prior to handling any firearm, know how to operate it safely. If you're not sure, ask someone who does, but don't assume the guy behind the gun counter is an expert on each and every firearm. Most owner's manuals can also be downloaded from the manufacturer's website.

3. Never depend on safeties, de-cocking levers, or magazine disconnects in place of the four Universal Safety Rules. Mechanical devices can and do fail! The ultimate "safeties" are your brain and trigger finger.

4. Know how to clear (unload) both revolvers and semi-automatics and always perform a clearance check when picking up a firearm, handing it to someone else, or accepting a firearm yourself. Always maintain muzzle control!

5. When handing a firearm to someone else, the action should be open – either the cylinder opened on a revolver or the slide locked back on a semi-automatic.

6. Use only the correct ammunition for your gun, matching up the caliber on the barrel, the ammunition box, and the stamp on the bottom of the cartridge. In addition, prior to using any ammunition with a higher than normal pressure rating (indicated by a +P or +P+ designation) ensure that your firearm is rated for these pressures. The most common risk is in using .38 Special ammunition with a +P rating in an older .38 Special revolver, not rated for that pressure.

7. Never use drugs (including prescription or over-the-counter drugs) or alcohol prior to or while handling firearms. That's common sense, but doing so may also put you in direct violation of federal and state law.

8. Removing the magazine from a semi-automatic will not remove the round that has been chambered, and most semi-autos will still fire without the magazine in place. Those that can't fire with the magazine removed have what are called magazine disconnects. We don't like them, since they can lead to a malfunctioning firearm if the magazine isn't tightly seated.

9. Be sure the barrel and action are clear of obstructions including dirt, mud, snow, squib loads, etc. If in doubt, perform the proper clearance procedure, then disassemble your firearm, removing the barrel so that you can perform a visual check.

10. Never shoot at a hard, flat surface; water; or any other object that can cause a shot to ricochet.

Samuel Colt
1814 – 1862

"God created man, but Sam Colt made them equal."

While the Colt Single Action Army Model 1873 (the Peacemaker) is arguably one of the best known Colt models, it actually wasn't developed until after Colt's death. And while other "repeating" pistols existed before Colt's time, Sam Colt gets credit for developing the first practical revolver, the Colt Patterson, released in 1836. While his Patterson plant was a commercial failure, he achieved success with subsequent models including the Colt Walker, the 1851 Navy, and the 1860 Army, which was the standard sidearm of Union officers in the Civil War.

11. Store guns and ammunition so they are not accessible to minors (that's federal law) and unauthorized individuals.

FIREARM MAINTENANCE

1. Be sure your gun is safe to operate. If you're not sure, bring it to a qualified gunsmith. This is particularly important if you've purchased or inherited a used firearm, or if you notice any cracks, or any change in the firearm's operation (for example, a failure to eject, or a higher frequency of malfunctions).

2. Clean and lubricate your firearm promptly after use. The most common reason for a firearm malfunction is a dirty gun. Plus, these are expensive pieces of equipment. Cleaning your firearm after every use will help to ensure its value is maintained.

ON THE RANGE

1. Wear eye and ear protection every time out. If you can't hear instructions on the range, do *not* crack your ear protection, instead, cup your hand over the back of your ear to indicate that the commands should be repeated.

2. Know and observe all range rules. A key range rule frequently violated is the rule to case and uncase firearms on the firing line, rather than on the shelf or table behind the firing line. This is a major safety violation. In addition, ALWAYS follow the four Universal Safety Rules, and report any individual to the range officer who is not following these rules or who exhibits any unsafe behavior.

3. Never step in front of or behind the firing line.

HOLSTER SAFETY

1. Ensure that your holster of choice completely covers the trigger and trigger guard. No exceptions.

2. Your holster should retain your firearm in place even if running or jumping. Select a rigid holster that is molded specifically for your firearm rather than a more general "one size fits all" holster.

THE "BELT PARKWAY" CASE

On July 8, 1967, a New York City police detective watched as a bright yellow Camaro crossed several lanes of traffic on the Belt Parkway before crashing into the bushes at the edge of the parkway. Detective Vito DeSerio rushed to the Camaro only to find the driver, 17-year-old Nancy McEwen, slumped over and unresponsive. McEwen was rushed to Coney Island Hospital where the doctors tried desperately to save her life. At 11:15 a.m. McEwen was declared dead. Only then did the doctors discover the cause of her death – hidden by her long blond hair, was a single, bloodless gunshot wound. Returning to the scene, detectives found that all of the Camaro's windows were closed, except for the rear passenger window. Detectives concluded that the shot must have entered that window and could only have come from the sand dunes or reeds of Plum Beach which paralleled the parkway. They immediately set out to search the area for a shell casing, yet none was found. After a ballistics check concluded that the bullet came from an Enfield Model No. 44, the police resorted to a house by house canvass of the neighborhood in an attempt to locate anyone with information about the mystery rifle. In an amazing coincidence, the third stop for the detectives was a Mobile station, where they asked the owner, 46-year-old Theodore DeLisi, whether he owned a rifle. DeLisi answered that he did indeed own a rifle, namely an Enfield Model No. 44. The story that DeLisi told spoke of an amazing series of unlikely timing, incredible ballistics, and major errors in judgment. On the fateful day that Nancy McEwen was shot, DeLisi was heading out to sea for a day of fishing for bluefish. DeLisi brought along his Enfield in case he needed to fend off any sharks that might be attracted by the bluefish bait. Before leaving the inlet, DeLisi decided to test his Enfield on a beer can floating along beside him. His first shot hit the beer can dead center, throwing it across the waves. His second shot missed. Investigators believe that the round ricocheted off the surface of the water, travelling in a ballistic arc no more than 4 feet over the ocean waves, the sand dunes, and the reeds at Plum Beach. Having traveled nearly a mile, the bullet entered the open window of McEwen's Camaro, striking her in the head. The lesson? *Never* forget Universal Rule # 4 (Always be sure of your target and beyond) and *never* shoot at a hard, flat surface; water; or any other object that can cause a shot to ricochet. Truth *can* be stranger than fiction.

From "Chief" by Albert A. Seedman
and Peter Hellman

SINGLE ACTION (SA) VS. DOUBLE ACTION (DA)

Understanding a handgun's "action" is one of the first steps toward understanding their function and in selecting one that meets your needs. Firearm engineers can argue for hours about the true definition of single action and double action, but functionally, it's a pretty simple concept. Firearms in single action mode will have a shorter, lighter trigger press, and firearms in double action mode will have a longer, heavier trigger press. Mechanically speaking, single action means that the trigger performs a single function, that is, it releases the hammer (which means that the hammer already has to be cocked), while double action means that the

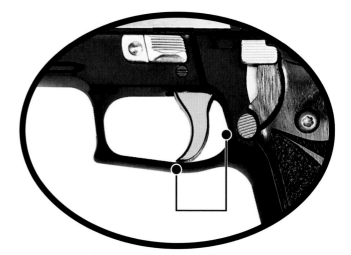

trigger press does two things – it first cocks the hammer, then it releases it. Feel free to ignore the mechanical definition and just remember that single action means a shorter and lighter trigger press and double action means a longer and heavier trigger press. Today, some pistols are single action only (SAO), some are double action only (DAO), and some can be fired in either mode, like the examples below and to the right, a SIG SAUER P229.

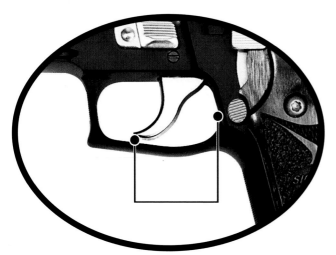

In double action, the distance of trigger press is approximately ¾ of an inch.

Weight of press is approximately 12 pounds.

In single action, the distance of trigger press is less than ½ of an inch.

Weight of press is approximately 4 ½ pounds.

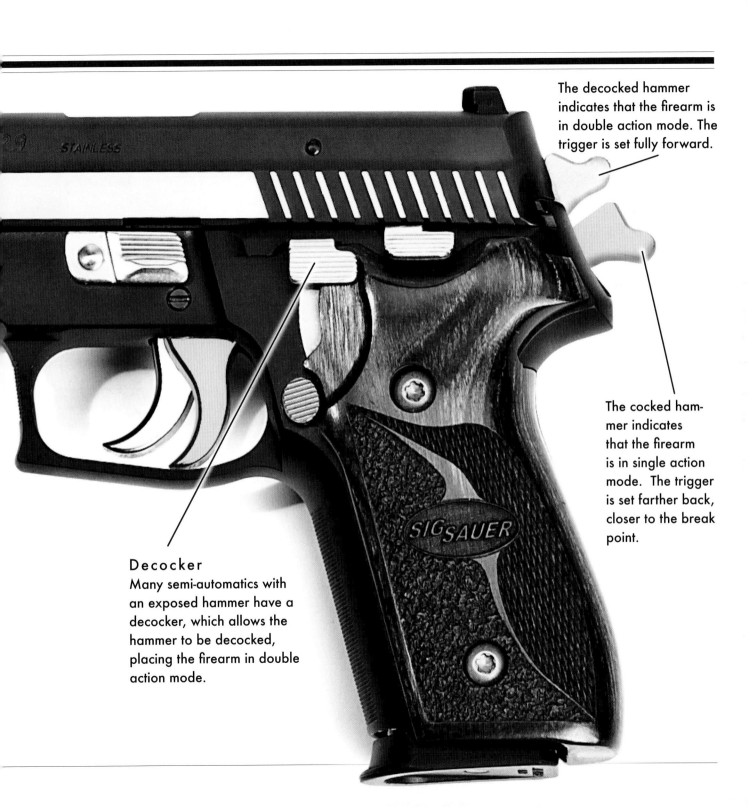

The decocked hammer indicates that the firearm is in double action mode. The trigger is set fully forward.

The cocked hammer indicates that the firearm is in single action mode. The trigger is set farther back, closer to the break point.

Decocker
Many semi-automatics with an exposed hammer have a decocker, which allows the hammer to be decocked, placing the firearm in double action mode.

UNDERSTANDING REVOLVERS

HOW DOES A REVOLVER WORK?

Revolvers operate with rounds loaded into a revolving cylinder. Pressing the trigger (in double action mode) or cocking the hammer rotates the cylinder, placing a new round in alignment with the hammer and barrel.

DA/SA REVOLVERS

Modern revolvers with an exposed hammer are designed to allow the shooter to fire in either single action or double action mode. With the hammer forward (double action mode) a longer, heavier trigger press will rotate the cylinder and cock and release the hammer. Manually cocking the hammer with the thumb puts the gun in single action mode, which might have a trigger press as light as 3 pounds, and trigger travel as short as 1/16th of an inch. Nice for accurate target shooting, but less safe for a self–defense gun. In addition, unlike most DA/SA semi-autos, there is no decocker on revolvers. Decocking a revolver requires very precise control of the hammer and trigger to lower the hammer safely.

DOUBLE ACTION ONLY (DAO) REVOLVERS

With its hammer hidden within the frame of the gun, this revolver is double action only (DAO) which provides a consistent trigger press that is longer and heavier than a similar revolver shot in single action mode. This provides an additional level of safety, since a longer, heavier trigger press requires more intent than a short, light trigger press. If you already own a revolver with an exposed hammer, a qualified gunsmith can de-horn the hammer spur.

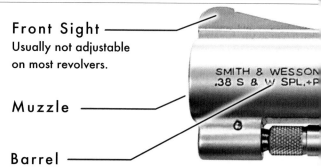

Front Sight
Usually not adjustable on most revolvers.

Muzzle

Barrel
The measured length of the barrel does not include the length of the cylinder.

Cylinder
Cylinders can hold anywhere from five to eight rounds.

Rotation of Cylinder
The teardrop-shaped indents on the side of the cylinder indicate the direction that the cylinder will rotate.

Cylinder Release
Allows the cylinder to be opened for loading and unloading.

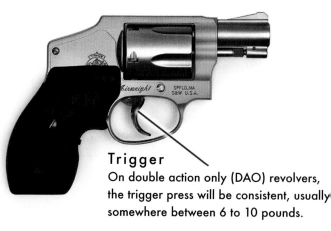

Trigger
On double action only (DAO) revolvers, the trigger press will be consistent, usually somewhere between 6 to 10 pounds.

Rear Sight

Hammer

Grips
Revolver grips can be replaced with aftermarket grips, allowing the grip size to be increased or decreased, and allowing the revolver's natural point of aim (its "pointability") to be adjusted for the individual shooter.

Trigger Guard

Trigger
The weight and distance of the trigger press is much lighter and shorter in single action mode versus double action – as light as 3 pounds in single action, and as heavy as 10 pounds in double action.

UNDERSTANDING SEMI-AUTOMATICS

HOW DOES A SEMI-AUTO WORK?

Semi-autos utilize a moving slide, which slides back using the power of the pistol's recoil (or the blowback of the expanding gases), ejecting the empty casing and re-cocking the hammer or striker. A powerful spring then reverses the direction of the slide, causing it to strip a new round off the top of the magazine, chambering it, and putting the slide back into battery.

SINGLE ACTION ONLY SEMI-AUTOMATIC

The Model 1911 shown to the right can only be fired after the hammer has been cocked, either by racking the slide or with the thumb, which makes it a single action only. The light, short trigger press necessitates that the pistol have a manual safety, which locks the slide and trigger, and allows the gun to be carried "cocked and locked."

DA/SA SEMI-AUTOMATIC

DA/SA semi-automatics are normally carried with the hammer forward, so the first shot will be a double action shot and all subsequent shots will be in single action (since the moving slide automatically cocks the hammer/striker during the firing cycle). Like most DA/SA semi-automatics, this P229 has a decocker, which allows the hammer to be lowered safely, placing the firearm in double action mode, which is considered to be a safer method for carrying.

DOUBLE ACTION ONLY (DAO) SEMI-AUTOMATIC

Like a double action only revolver, DAO semi-automatics have only one firing mode, which will consistently be a longer, heavier trigger press when compared to a similar model shot in single action mode. While this P250 looks similar to the P229, it lacks the exposed hammer, making it DAO.

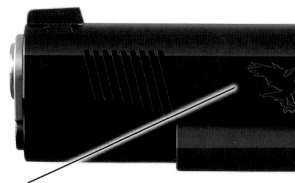

Slide
The moving part of the pistol that slides to the rear, ejecting a spent casing and loading a new round.

Slide Lock / Take Down Lever
Most semi-automatics have two separate controls to lock the slide back and to disassemble the firearm (as in the two examples below), while the 1911 combines them into a single control.

Decocker

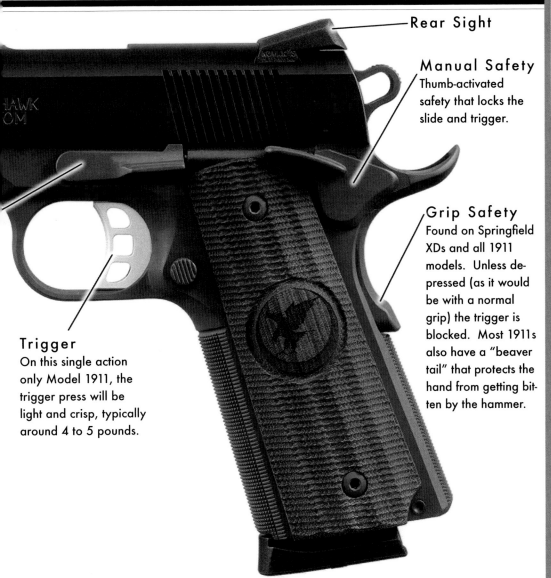

Rear Sight

Manual Safety
Thumb-activated safety that locks the slide and trigger.

Grip Safety
Found on Springfield XDs and all 1911 models. Unless depressed (as it would be with a normal grip) the trigger is blocked. Most 1911s also have a "beaver tail" that protects the hand from getting bitten by the hammer.

Trigger
On this single action only Model 1911, the trigger press will be light and crisp, typically around 4 to 5 pounds.

Grips
The grips on Model 1911s can be swapped for aftermarket grips, but for style and thickness only, not to affect the pistol's natural point of aim. Our favorites are from a Minnesota guy named Dan Cashman. Check out his work at www.stradcustomgrips.com.

Model *1911*

In 1906, Colt Manufacturing Co. submitted a Browning-designed semi-auto pistol to the U.S. Army, which adopted the design on March 29, 1911, giving the pistol the name M1911. World War I increased production to include the Springfield Armory and Remington Rand, while World War II ballooned production to include manufacture by the Rock Island Arsenal, Ithaca, and even Singer (yes, the sewing machine company). 1911s have served in every military conflict since World War I, with more than 2.75 million produced for military use. Today, the 1911 is seeing action with the U.S. Marines in Iraq and Afghanistan. More than 15 manufacturers currently have 1911s in their line-up, and nearly every semi-automatic pistol today can trace its lineage back to Browning's innovative 1911 design.

The actions described on the previous pages all have one thing in common – the firearms are all hammer operated; that is, regardless of whether or not the hammer is exposed or hidden, it's the hammer that drives the action. Hammer operated firearms fit more neatly into the "single action only, double action only, or DA/SA action" categories than do many popular firearms, including the Glock and Springfield XD shown here. Both Glocks and Springfield XDs are striker fired, and utilize a striker/firing pin held back under the tension of a spring.

SPRINGFIELD XD "ULTRA SAFETY ASSURANCE" TRIGGER SYSTEM

Internally, Springfield XDs are categorized as single action (racking the slide fully cocks the striker/firing pin mechanism), yet externally, they mimic the longer, heavier trigger press of a DAO, similar to the Glock. XD's trigger weights typically fall between 5.5 – 7.7 pounds. While the XD trigger weight and length of press are similar to the Glock, it has a longer trigger reset than a Glock.

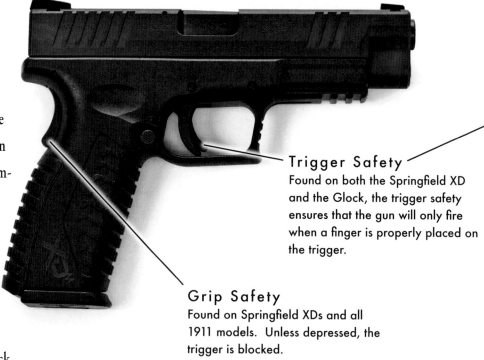

Trigger Safety
Found on both the Springfield XD and the Glock, the trigger safety ensures that the gun will only fire when a finger is properly placed on the trigger.

Grip Safety
Found on Springfield XDs and all 1911 models. Unless depressed, the trigger is blocked.

Grips

The grips on most composite pistols can't be replaced, but many newer pistols have replaceable backstraps, and ship with several backstraps of various sizes, so that users can tailor the grip size to the size of their hands. Pistols with this feature include the Walther P99, the Smith & Wesson M&P, the Ruger SR9, the HK P30, the new Glock Gen 4 shown here, and the new XD(M) from Springfield on the opposite page.

GLOCK "SAFE ACTION" TRIGGER SYSTEM

Although the BATF has categorized the Glock a DAO pistol, internally, it falls halfway between a single action and double action. When the slide is racked, the striker/firing pin mechanism is only *half* cocked. Upon pressing the trigger, the firing pin is fully cocked, then released. Like other striker fired pistols, if a round fails to fire, the Glock does not get a "second strike" capability and the slide must be racked to recock the striker.

WHAT HAPPENS WHEN I PRESS THE TRIGGER?

When the trigger is pressed on a semi-automatic, a bullet leaves the barrel and the slide cycles, ejecting the empty casing and loading a new round, all faster than the eye can see. The step-by-step operations shown here follow the mechanics of a Glock pistol in action.

1 When at "rest," the Glock's firing pin is half-cocked, and the firing pin channel is blocked by the firing pin safety (highlighted). The barrel is "locked" to the slide by the tight fit of the barrel's square chamber, and the slide's square ejection port (visible in the diagram just above the chambered round).

2 When the trigger is pressed, an extension of the trigger bar pushes the firing pin safety up, clearing the firing pin channel. As the trigger continues rearward, the firing pin (highlighted) is fully cocked, then released. The firing pin hits the chambered round's primer with enough force to cause a small explosion, creating a small shower of sparks, which ignite the round's propellant. The solid propellant rapidly turns gaseous, and the expanding gases force the bullet from the casing and accelerate it down the barrel. The barrel's "rifling" (the spiral grooves) causes the bullet to spin, which stabilizes it in flight.

3 At the same time that the bullet is accelerating down the barrel, the handgun is pushed back with an equal amount of force. When the shooter has a solid grip, the momentum of the frame is quickly stopped, but with nothing to stop the slide (and barrel which is still mated to the slide) from its rearward motion, it continues backward, extracting the empty case from the chamber. The small object highlighted in the diagram (called the locking block) unlocks the barrel from the slide, lowering the barrel into position to allow the empty case to hit the ejector, and to allow the new round to be fed into the chamber.

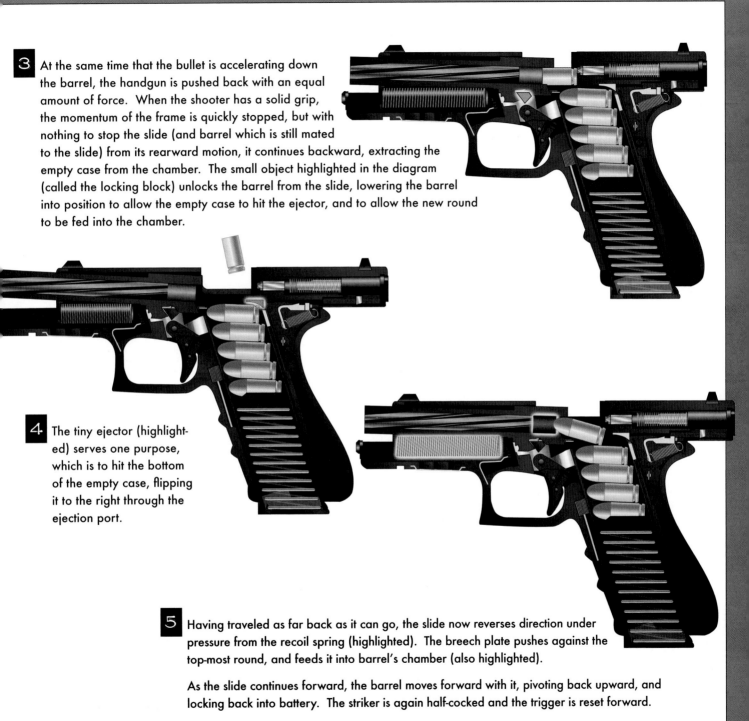

4 The tiny ejector (highlighted) serves one purpose, which is to hit the bottom of the empty case, flipping it to the right through the ejection port.

5 Having traveled as far back as it can go, the slide now reverses direction under pressure from the recoil spring (highlighted). The breech plate pushes against the top-most round, and feeds it into barrel's chamber (also highlighted).

As the slide continues forward, the barrel moves forward with it, pivoting back upward, and locking back into battery. The striker is again half-cocked and the trigger is reset forward.

SAFETY AND DECOCKER VARIETIES

The preceding pages were just a taste of the variations that exist in the marketplace. Just like automobiles, options are endless, including how the firearm's controls operate. Below and to the right are a few additional examples of how controls differ between handguns, including external safeties and decockers. Bottom line? Pick a handgun that works for you and train with it until you can operate its controls in the dark. Someday, you might just have to.

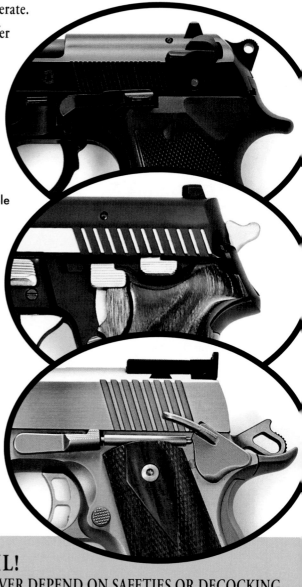

Beretta 92
The Beretta 92 has both a decocker and safety. The hammer is decocked and put on safe by lowering the decocker/safety. Many people carry the Beretta de-cocked but with the safety off, since when decocked, it is in double action mode and is considered safe to carry without the safety engaged. However, see the warning below.

SIG P229
The SIG P229 has a decocker which lowers the hammer by pushing the decocker down. When decocked, the firearm is considered safe to carry and has no additional manual safety.

1911s
The 1911's safety is engaged by pushing it up (the opposite of the Beretta 92). To fire the 1911, the safety is dropped down with a quick action of the thumb. Since the 1911 is a single action only pistol, the hammer must be cocked (either with the thumb, or by racking the slide) before it will fire. For that reason, most people carry the 1911 "cocked and locked" with the hammer back and the safety engaged.

WARNING: MECHANICAL DEVICES CAN FAIL!
The comment that we made earlier in this chapter is worth repeating: NEVER DEPEND ON SAFETIES OR DECOCKING LEVERS! MECHANICAL DEVICES CAN FAIL! Regardless of what safety measures your pistol has, including a manual safety, a grip safety, a trigger safety, or whether it's a double action only with a long, heavy trigger press, the ONLY safety that you should trust is the brain matter between your ears and your trigger finger. If you put your finger in the trigger guard and press the trigger, you should always, always, always expect to hear a BANG, and see a hole appear somewhere.

SEMI-AUTO MAGAZINES

While revolvers have a built in device to hold multiple rounds (the cylinder), semi-automatics have rounds fed from a detachable magazine. Magazine types and styles vary, but all can be categorized as single stack or double stack. Single stacks store rounds one on top of the other in a single, straight line, while double stacks store rounds in two staggered rows, allowing more rounds to be stored but resulting in a wider magazine (and larger pistol grip.)

SPRING FATIGUE?

Some gun owners are concerned that if they store magazines fully loaded, the internal spring will become fatigued and may fail to properly feed rounds when they are needed. Stop worrying – experts (and engineers) have proven that springs have no "memory" and suffer no additional fatigue when they remain in a compressed state for months or even years. Fatigue *does* occur when the spring is compressed past its design limits or after repeated cycles of compression and release. So *do* replace magazine springs if they've undergone hundreds or thousands of compressions, but *don't* replace them just because you've kept them fully loaded.

Double Stack Magazines

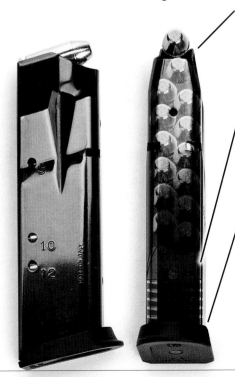

Magazine Lips
The width of the lips is slightly smaller than the diameter of the round, holding the round in place until it's stripped off and loaded into the chamber. When the gap widens on a worn magazine, double-feeds can result.

Follower and Spring
Rounds sit on top of the follower, which is pushed up by the spring. When the last round is fired, the follower pushes up the slide lock on the pistol, thereby locking the slide back.

Base Plate and Base Pad
The base plate secures the spring to the bottom of the magazine, while the pad gives more area when slapping the magazine into the magazine well and also protects the magazine when it hits the floor during a speed reload.

Single Stack Magazines

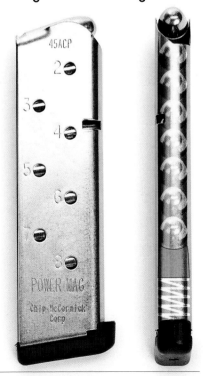

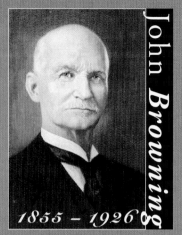

WHAT SIZE FIREARM IS RIGHT FOR YOU?

In addition to considering whether you'd like to gravitate toward a revolver or a semi-automatic (plus all of the other features such as the action and additional safety components), you'll also have to consider what size and weight of firearm is right for you, based upon:

- The caliber range that you are comfortable shooting.
- Your size and the way you normally dress.
- Holster options that work for you.
- When and where you plan to carry.
- The weather and time of year.

Trade-Offs

Lighter, smaller firearms usually mean a smaller caliber (and less stopping power) or a more punishing recoil, which might lead to less time on the range. Larger firearms, on the other hand, never get any lighter as the day goes on, which may cause you to leave it at home.

Other criteria to consider:

- **Grip size, shape, angle, and material.** Determine how well the grips allow the firearm to properly "point" for you and whether or not your knuckles properly align to the front strap. Grip material and texture are important elements to consider to ensure a solid grip that won't slip. On 1911s, it's worth the extra money to pay for front and backstrap checkering.

- **Grip Length:** Short grips are more concealable and "print" less on covering garments, but they provide less space to fit all four fingers of your support hand.

- **Proper placement of your finger on the trigger:** The trigger should rest comfortably in the range between the pad of your finger and first knuckle crease.

- **Balance:** Revolvers and composite framed semi-autos can sometimes feel nose heavy. Always test balance with a fully loaded firearm (make sure this is done on the range, and not on the sales floor).

Smith & Wesson
Model 27
Length: 9.25"
Frame Material: Steel
Caliber: .38/.357
41 Ounces

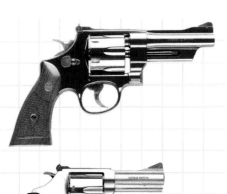

Smith & Wesson
Model 60
Length: 7.5"
Frame Material: Steel
Caliber: .38/.357
24 Ounces

Smith & Wesson
Model 36
Length: 7"
Frame Material: Steel
Caliber: .38 Special
20.4 Ounces

Smith & Wesson
Model 442
Length: 6.4"
Frame Material:
Aluminum Alloy
Caliber: .38 Special
15 Ounces

NAA Mini-Revolver
Length: 4"
Frame Material: Steel
Caliber: .22 LR
4.5 Ounces

Springfield
1911 Loaded
Length: 8.5"
Height: 5.5"
Frame Material: Steel
Caliber: .45 ACP
41 Ounces

Smith & Wesson
M&P
Length: 7.75"
Height: 5.5"
Frame Material: Composite
Caliber: 9MM/.40 S&W
30 Ounces

SIG SAUER
P229 Equinox
Length: 7.1"
Height: 5.4"
Frame Material: Steel
Caliber: .357 Sig/.40 S&W
32 Ounces

Springfield XD
Sub-Compact
Length: 6.25"
Height: 4.75"
Frame Material: Composite
Caliber: 9MM/.40/.45
26 Ounces

Ruger LCP .380
Length: 5.2"
Height: 3.6"
Frame Material: Composite
Caliber: .380 ACP
9.4 Ounces

POCKET PISTOLS

Pocket Pistols (so named because they can easily fit into a pocket) have become the new rage as more and more citizens apply for their concealed carry permits and as more states jump on the "shall issue" bandwagon. As mentioned earlier, smaller pistols do tend to offer lower calibers (usually .380 ACP and below) which historically have been knocked for their lack of stopping power, but most permit holders have discovered that carrying a pocket pistol is so *easy* that carrying becomes almost second nature, as easy as slipping a wallet into your pocket. And while a .380 caliber or below certainly does have less stopping power than a 9MM or above, it has infinitely more stopping power than that 9MM, .40 S&W, or .45 ACP that was left at home because it was too bulky or too heavy. We've highlighted a fe of our favorite pocket pistols below, including options from Kel-Tec, Ruger, Taurus, and Smith & Wesson. One last com ment – NEVER slide a pocket pistol into your pocket withou a pocket holster. Loose change, keys, or fingers can easily sli into the trigger guard unless the pistol is properly secured in holster that *completely* covers the trigger and trigger guard. Chapter Six for a couple ideas on pocket holsters.

Side Guard Holsters "Minimal Clip"

When using an Inside the Waistband (IWB) holster with a small pistol like the Ruger LCP, the pistol's grips can disappear below the belt line making it difficult to get a solid grip prior to drawing. This holster from Side Guard Holsters holds the pistol up above the belt line, giving the user easy access to the grips.

MANUFACTURER / MODEL / CALIBER	WHAT WE LIKE
Kel-Tec P-32 .32 ACP P-3AT .380 ACP	The early market leader, Kel-Tec's P-32 and P-3A1 have both developed a large fan base. With the wide distribution, a large number of holsters and accessories are available.
Ruger LCP .380 ACP	After an early hiccup that required a recall, the Ruger LCP has become one of the most popular pocket pistols in the market. Similar in design and function to the Kel-Tec, but expect to pay a bit mor
Taurus 738 TCP .380 ACP	The Taurus 738 TCP arrived on the scene after th Ruger LCP and Kel-Tec, but has already gained in popularity. While similar in size and price to the LCP and Kel-Tec, the Taurus does offer one additional function that the other two lack, namel the slide locks back on an empty magazine.
Smith & Wesson Bodyguard .380 ACP	Debuted at the 2010 SHOT show in Las Vegas, the S&W Bodyguard is one of the most innovative pocket pistols to hit the market. While more expensive than the other options mentioned, the Bodyguard comes with an integrated laser, built right into the pistol's frame. Besides that, the Bodyguard just looks really, really cool.

HANDGUN SELECTION, PROS AND CONS

TRAINING	HANDGUN	SKILL LEVEL	PROS	CONS
50 rounds per year or less	Double Action Only (DAO) Revolver	Low	• No safety or decockers to worry about, just point and shoot. • A heavier, longer trigger press requires more intent to shoot. • Disassembling this firearm for cleaning consists of opening the cylinder. • Suitable for pocket carry. • Malfunctions are almost unheard of. If a round fails to fire, you simply pull the trigger again.	• Fewer rounds, typically five on a carry-sized revolver. • Wider profile, which can be more difficult to conceal in a belt holster. • Slower to reload than a semi-auto (don't tell Jerry Miculek that though).
50 rounds every 3 – 6 months	Double Action Only (DAO) Semi-Automatic	Medium	• No safety or decockers to worry about, just point and shoot. • A heavier, longer trigger press requires more intent to shoot than those that can be fired in single action mode. • Higher ammunition capacity than a DAO Revolver (up to 20 on some 9MM).	• Probability of a failure is much higher than with a revolver. The owner MUST practice clearing these malfunctions. • More complex to break down and clean than a revolver.
50 rounds every 1 – 2 months	DA/SA Semi-Automatic	Intermediate	• Lighter trigger press on the second shot to the last shot, aiding in accuracy. • If the pistol has an exposed hammer, the shooter has the option of also shooting the first round in single action.	• The two different trigger weights and travel can cause the shooter to miss the first shot. • Decockers and safeties can be confusing in a stress situation.
50 rounds every month	Single Action Only Semi-Auto	Advanced	• Light, short trigger press aids in accuracy for experts or competitors.	• Single action trigger is less safe for those unwilling to practice.

Smith & Wesson

Smith & Wesson
Springfield Massachusetts

In 1852, partners Horace Smith and Daniel B. Wesson formed the "Volcanic Repeating Arms Company," which was eventually sold to Oliver Winchester, who at the time was a shirt manufacturer. In 1856, the partners left the Volcanic Company to form Smith & Wesson, manufacturing the newly designed revolver based upon Rollin White's patent.

Today, S&W is the leading manufacturer of revolvers and also produces a variety of semi-autos including the M&P, and a number of 1911s. S&W also jointly develops and distributes the SW99, an "Americanized" version of James Bond's new pistol of choice (the P99), with Walther of Germany.

What you see below are not bullets; they are more properly called cartridges, rounds, or ammunition. The bullet is the conical-shaped object sitting on top of the propellant (in other words, it's the part of the round that shoots down the barrel). As simple as the self-contained cartridge sounds, it wasn't until 1847 that a practical, self-contained cartridge was patented, with credit going to a French gunsmith by the name of B. Houllier. In 1855, Sam Colt made a major blunder when he rejected an employee's idea to bore completely through a revolver's cylinder, which would have allowed these new self-contained cartridges to be dropped in from the rear. Rollin White subsequently had the idea patented, and licensed the patent to Horace Smith and Daniel Wesson.

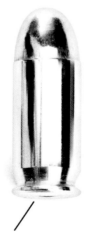

Bullet
This "full metal jacket" (FMJ) bullet shows how the copper sheath covers a lead core

Propellant
Modern propellants have a high amount of surface area to ensure a rapid, stable burn, ensuring a maximum expansion of gases.

Primer
When struck by the firing pin, the round's primer causes a small explosion, showering sparks into the round's casing, igniting the propellant.

Rimless
rounds are designed for semi-automatic handguns – the rimless design allows them to stack easily within a magazine and also allows the round to feed and extract smoothly.

Rimmed
rounds are designed for revolvers – the rim keeps the round from dropping all the way through the cylinder.

DEFINING CALIBER AND OTHER MEASUREMENTS

CALIBER

The name of ammunition is typically its caliber (the diameter of the bullet) in either 100ths of an inch or in millimeters, and some other designation such as the company that holds the original patent on the round. For example, the name .45ACP (Automatic Colt Pistol) tells us that this round is forty-five one-hundreds of an inch in diameter, and that Colt originally patented this round. The round carries the same name regardless of whether it's being shot in a Colt, a Kimber, a Springfield, etc. Caliber measurements are sometimes inexact; for example, the .38 Special has an actual measurement of 357/1000ths of an inch. That's a holdover from the days of muzzle loading firearms, when the actual diameter of a ball had to be slightly smaller than the barrel in order to allow the ball to fit.

GRAINS

Grains are a unit of weight, with 7,000 grains per pound, or 437.5 grains per ounce. That means that a 230 grain bullet is just over half an ounce.

Caliber
Caliber is a measurement of the diameter of the bullet (not the casing). The caliber designation has nothing to do with the round's power, it only defines how big of a hole it will make (see example below).

Bullet Weight
The bullet's weight is indicated in grains. There are 7,000 grains in a pound, and handgun bullet weights range from about 40 grains to 230 grains or more.

Case Volume
The relative volume of the case is a good indication of how much propellant the round has. The greater the volume, the more propellant. The more propellant, the faster the bullet will leave the barrel.

IS CALIBER ALL THAT MATTERS?

Each of the three rounds to the right is .22 caliber, that is, they'll all make *exactly* the same size hole in their target. They also happen to all have a 40 grain bullet, yet the differences in case volume (i.e. volume of propellant) makes dramatic differences in the relative velocity of each bullet, translating to dramatic differences in the "power" of each round.

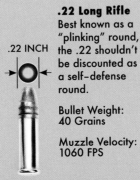

.22 INCH

.22 Long Rifle
Best known as a "plinking" round, the .22 shouldn't be discounted as a self-defense round.

Bullet Weight: 40 Grains

Muzzle Velocity: 1060 FPS

.22 INCH

5.7MM FN
Designed by FN as an alternative to the 9MM, the 5.7MM FN is blazing fast at nearly 2,000 FPS.

Bullet Weight: 40 Grains

Muzzle Velocity: 1950 FPS

.22 INCH

.223 Remington
Best known as the standard NATO round for light rifles, it has a velocity more than triple the .22LR.

Bullet Weight: 40 Grains

Muzzle Velocity: 3330 FPS

KNOCK DOWN POWER

Knock down power is a hot topic of discussion at any gun club. Some people will argue for hours that knock down power is directly related to a bullet's kinetic energy, while others will argue that a bigger hole is all that matters. Kinetic energy is measured using the following formula:

$$\text{Kinetic Energy} = \tfrac{1}{2} MV^2$$

where M = the weight of the bullet in grains, and V = the speed of the bullet in feet per second. The actual formula needs to convert the weight of the bullet from grains to pounds (there are 7,000 grains in a pound), and needs to figure in gravity (32 feet per second per second). This formula has been the standard for computing a bullet's energy, but it favors velocity over weight, which can result in some oddities. For example, it shows the 9MM bullet having more energy than the .45ACP, which tends to fly in the face of real world military, police, and self-defense statistics. That problem has caused many people to disregard the kinetic energy formula in favor of the Taylor Knockout Factor (TKOF), developed by John Taylor. In addition to using the bullet's velocity and weight, the TKOF formula also includes the bullet's diameter (the size of the hole the bullet will make). Unlike the kinetic energy formula, the TKOF also provides equal weighting to the bullet's weight, speed, and diameter. The Taylor Knockout Factor is measured using the following formula:

$$\text{TKOF} = (MVD) / 7{,}000$$

The Taylor KO Factor tends to favor heavier, larger caliber bullets when compared to the kinetic energy formula. While either formula provides valuable information, we tend to favor the TKOF measurement (which is how we've placed the rounds to the right), since it seems to better reflect real world statistics.

Feel free to ignore the debate and the formulas – our advice is to simply select the biggest caliber you can shoot well and load it with good self-defense ammunition.

Oh, and for you Dirty Harry fans, you might be wondering where the venerable .44 Magnum is on our scale to the right. We'd love to add it, but we'd have to *double* the height of our book. The .44 Magnum has a TKOF factor of 18.55, nearly double the .357 Magnum.

SELF-DEFENSE CALIBER OPTIONS

We recommend that your self-defense firearm falls within the green or yellow scale to the right (preferably the green), as long these rules apply:

Rule #1: You select a gun that you'll actually carry (that is, it isn't too heavy).

Rule #2: You select the largest caliber that you're comfortable shooting (and comfortable paying for practice ammunition!)

Remember that a .22 caliber in your holster is infinitely more valuable than a .45 left at home.

10MM
Bullet Weight: 200 Grains
Muzzle Velocity: 1300 FPS
Energy: 750 Ft. Lbs.
TKOF: 14.86

.45 ACP
Bullet Weight: 230 Grains
Muzzle Velocity: 835 FPS
Energy: 356 Ft. Lbs.
TKOF: 12.35

.40 S&W
Bullet Weight: 180 Grains
Muzzle Velocity: 990 FPS
Energy: 390 Ft. Lbs.
TKOF: 10.18

.357 Magnum
Bullet Weight: 158 Grains
Muzzle Velocity: 1235 FPS
Energy: 535 Ft. Lbs.
TKOF: 9.95

.357 SIG
Bullet Weight: 125 Grains
Muzzle Velocity: 1350 FPS
Energy: 506 Ft. Lbs.
TKOF: 8.55

9mm Luger
Bullet Weight: 124 Grains
Muzzle Velocity: 1140 FPS
Energy: 358 Ft. Lbs.
TKOF: 7.14

.38 Special +P
Bullet Weight: 130 Grains
Muzzle Velocity: 925 FPS
Energy: 247 Ft. Lbs.
TKOF: 6.13

.38 Special
Bullet Weight: 130 Grains
Muzzle Velocity: 800 FPS
Energy: 185 Ft. Lbs.
TKOF: 5.30

.380 ACP
Bullet Weight: 95 Grains
Muzzle Velocity: 955 FPS
Energy: 190 Ft. Lbs.
TKOF: 4.93

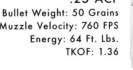

.32 ACP
Bullet Weight: 71 Grains
Muzzle Velocity: 905 FPS
Energy: 129 Ft. Lbs.
TKOF: 2.94

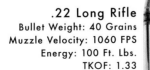

.22 Long Rifle
Bullet Weight: 40 Grains
Muzzle Velocity: 1060 FPS
Energy: 100 Ft. Lbs.
TKOF: 1.33

.25 ACP
Bullet Weight: 50 Grains
Muzzle Velocity: 760 FPS
Energy: 64 Ft. Lbs.
TKOF: 1.36

TAYLOR KNOCKOUT FACTOR

15
14
13
12
11
10
9
8
7
6
5
4
3
2
1
0

Rounds shown in actual size

WHY USE HOLLOWPOINTS FOR SELF-DEFENSE?

In 1998, the New York City Police Department became the last major police department in the United States to switch from full metal jacket ammunition to hollowpoints. Police Commissioner Howard Safir commented, "We are going to switch to hollowpoint ammunition as soon as we receive it. They are much safer than fully jacketed bullets, which will go through a person and then continue on and hit innocent victims." Commissioner Safir didn't make this statement in a vacuum. A report that year by the New York Times confirmed that in a two-year period, 46% of innocent bystanders that were struck by police bullets were hit by rounds that passed through an attacker's body, or through another object. Equally troubling, 39% of police officers struck by "friendly fire" were hit by bullets that overpenetrated the bodies of attackers the police were battling. Advocates for the switch included the Civilian Complaint Review Board, the independent agency charged with monitoring the police. In addition to the reduced chance of overpenetration, advocates of the change also observed that hollowpoints had a greater chance of stopping an attacker with fewer bullets, also lessening the chance that innocent bystanders might be injured. Today, nearly every police department in the United States issues hollowpoint ammunition as standard issue. While you'll need to make an individual decision as to whether or not hollowpoint ammunition is the right choice for you, your decision might be made a bit easier by contacting your local police department and asking them what *they* carry. Note that hollowpoint ammunition is *not* legal in all states.

HOW DO HOLLOWPOINTS WORK?

Hollowpoints operate on hydraulics – that is, the fluid contained within a body provides adequate pressure within the hollowpoint's cavity to rapidly expand the cavity, and fold back the lead core and pre-scored copper jacket. While this is occurring, the increased diameter causes a rapid deceleration of the bullet, eventually slowing and stopping it. This deceleration occurs much more rapidly in a hollowpoint bullet that has fully expanded, when compared to a bullet that is not designed to expand (such as a full metal jacket), or a hollowpoint that fails to expand because of a lack of velocity, or one that has become clogged with heavy clothing, which can cause the hydraulic process to fail.

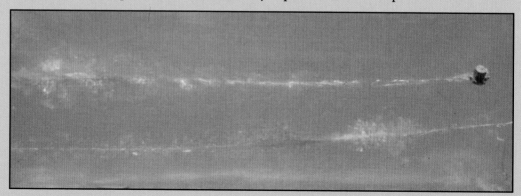

Ballistic Gelatin test showing a 9MM Hollowpoint penetrating to a depth of 12.5"
and a Full Metal Jacket (FMJ) overpenetrating and exiting the 16" block.

SELF-DEFENSE AMMUNITION OPTIONS

There are too many self-defense rounds for us to comment on, but we've described a few of the most popular below. You'll notice that we've focused on "traditional" hollow-points (the EFMJ aside), rather than more exotic rounds such as frangibles, which are designed to shatter on impact to avoid overpenetration.

ROUND	DESCRIPTION	CHARACTERISTICS
Hornady TAP FPD (For Personal Defense)	Uses "low flash" powder to protect night vision. Also has black nickel plating to provide better feeding and eliminate corrosion.	Both the low flash characteristics and nickel coating make this a great home defense round. The black case color is also pretty cool, and actually feels slick to the touch.
Federal Hydra-Shok	Copper Jacketed Hollowpoint, with unique center post to provide controlled expansion.	Until recently, the Hydra-Shok was almost universally adopted as the ammunition of choice for police departments across the U.S. Federal recently released an update to the Hydra-Shok, called the HST, which seems to offer more consistent expansion than its predecessor and is quickly replacing the Hydra-Shok as the ammunition of choice for law enforcement.
Federal EFMJ (Expanding Full Metal Jacket)	Looks like a full metal jacket, but has a scored copper jacket covering an internal rubber nose and lead core.	The full metal jacket look and characteristics allow this round to feed much more reliably than traditional hollowpoints, yet the expansion is still impressive. We've personally tested the expansion of a .45 ACP that mushroomed to .70. Unlike traditional hollowpoints which rely on hydraulics to expand, the EFMJ operates on deceleration, with the scored jacket collapsing over the rubber nose upon impact, resulting in a pancaked bullet.
Magtech First Defense & Cor-Bon DPX	Solid Copper Hollowpoint, resulting in 100% weight retention.	The Magtech First Defense and Cor-Bon DPX rounds are 100% copper, without any jacket that can tear away. This results in 100% weight retention, which means that 100% of the bullet penetrates to the full depth.
Speer Gold Dot	Copper Jacketed Hollowpoint with a wider and deeper cavity than traditional hollowpoints.	With so many "shall issue" states, firearm manufacturers have been selling more short barrel pistols than ever before. Those short barrels result in lower muzzle velocities, which can result in hollowpoints failing to open. The Gold Dot line has much larger and deeper hollowpoint cavities, resulting in positive expansion, even with short barrel handguns.

WHY DOES BARREL LENGTH MATTER?

Why does barrel length matter? A longer barrel will result in a higher velocity bullet, since there is more time for the bullet to accelerate before the gases dissipate. For the same model pistol with different barrel lengths (for example, Springfield XDs with 3", 4" and 5" barrels) velocity can vary by as much as 300 feet per second for the same weight bullet. So why does that matter? When it comes to punching holes through paper, it really doesn't matter. When it comes to us-ing a firearm for self–defense, it *does* matter. A higher veloc-ity round is more likely to stop a violent attacker because of deeper penetration of the bullet and a higher probability that hollowpoint bullets will expand. There used to be a "magic number" of about 1,000 feet per second before a hollowpoint bullet would expand, but with newer hollowpoint bullets with larger cavities, that barrier is no longer critical.

Feet Per Second

Sample Muzzle Velocities by Barrel Length

CALIBER	5 INCHES	4 INCHES	3 INCHES	2 INCHES
.38 Special	1062	1014	878	733
9MM Luger	1233	1173	1105	1019
.40 S&W	1193	1136	1071	985
.45 ACP	1047	1003	911	857

Source: ballisticsbytheinch.com

AMMUNITION CARE AND STORAGE

Taking care of your ammunition (including storing it safely) is as important as caring for your firearm. Here's what you should remember:

- Keep ammunition in a cool, dry area and store it separately from your firearm.
- Keep ammunition in its original factory box or carton.
- Do not expose ammunition to water or any gun solvents or oils. They can leak into the seam between the bullet and the casing, allowing the propellant to become damp and unreliable, possibly leading to a hang fire.
- As mentioned in our "Additional Safety Considerations" section, use only the correct ammunition for your gun, matching up the caliber on the barrel, the ammunition box, and the stamp on the bottom of the cartridge. In addition, prior to using any ammunition with a higher than normal pressure rating (indicated by a +P or +P+ designation), ensure that your firearm is rated for these pressures.
- Inspect ammunition prior to loading. Discard rounds with damaged cases, corrosion, or loose bullets.
- Avoid chambering and un-chambering the same round multiple times, which can lead to projectile set-back. Put simply, projectile set-back is when the bullet becomes jammed back farther into the case than it is meant to be, which can increase the pressure of the round, resulting in a damaged firearm (and damaged hands, eyes, etc.) This typically occurs when someone clears a firearm every night before storing it (dropping the magazine and ejecting the chambered round) then reinserting the ejected round on top of the magazine.
- Replace personal protection ammunition at least once a year (ammunition that has been loaded into your firearm, but not fired). That's not because the ammunition goes bad (we've fired .38 Specials that were found in the in-law's basement and were at least 40 years old). It's because repeated heating and cooling of your firearm and ammunition can lead to condensation, which can lead to corrosion of both.
- Understand that not all types of ammunition will feed reliably in your firearm. In particular, for self-defense ammunition, you should practice with at least 200 to 250 rounds before selecting your personal protection ammunition of choice.

MYTH BUSTED: THE STORY ABOUT THE .22 "FUSE"

Much to the dismay of story tellers everywhere, the urban myth about a .22 used as a car fuse was busted on one of our favorite shows, "Myth Busters." As told, the story has two friends returning home from a night out hunting frogs, when their car blew a fuse. Lacking a spare, they inserted a .22 long rifle cartridge in its place, which eventually "cooked off," shooting the driver and seriously injuring him. Myth Busters concluded that while it was *possible* for a round to cook off if a serious short occurred, it was unlikely to seriously injure or kill someone. During each test, the high-speed video showed the bullet and casing simply blowing apart in opposite directions with the lighter case flying away with more velocity than the heavier bullet. It was apparent that without a breech plate to rest against or a barrel to accelerate down, a cooked off round would be more likely to give a "nasty bruise" than to prove lethal.

THE DEATH OF BRANDON LEE

Squib loads are known more for blown barrels than fatalities, but that's exactly what happened to Brandon Lee on the set of his movie "The Crow." On March 31, 1993, Lee was killed while filming a scene in which his character was, ironically, shot and killed. The series of fatal errors began much earlier, when the film crew created their own "dummy" rounds by using real cartridges. The crew attempted to make the live rounds inert by removing the bullets and dumping out the propellant before reinserting the bullets, but they failed to remove the live primers. At some point in the filming, the trigger was pressed and a squib load occurred, lodging a bullet in the barrel. During the fateful scene, the same revolver was loaded with blanks, and fired at Lee. The resulting propellant charge was enough to drive the lodged bullet from the barrel into Lee's torso, resulting in his death.

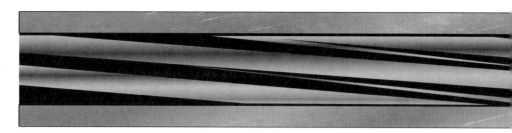

No "Pop" from the primer, no "Bang" from the shockwave, just the "Click" of the hammer falling.

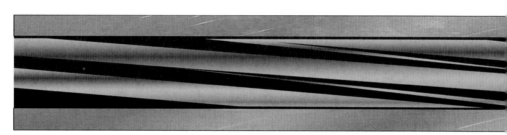

Just the "Pop" of the primer, but no "Bang" for up to a minute. Very rare.

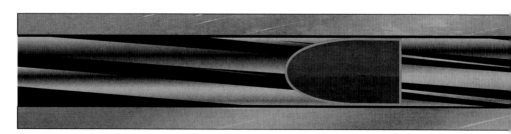

Just the "Pop" of the primer and low or no recoil. PUT IT DOWN!

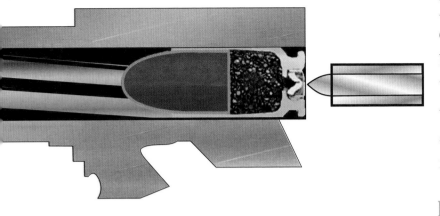

MISFIRE

Occurs when the primer fails to ignite after being struck by the firing pin. This causes a "Type One" failure and must be cleared with the procedure on the following page. The usual suspect? A dirty firearm, rather than a bad round.

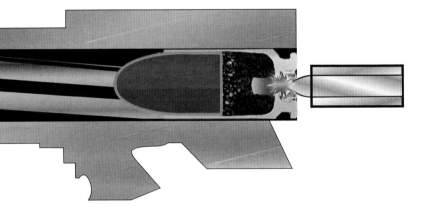

HANG FIRE

A delay in the firing of the round after the primer has been struck by the firing pin. Typically caused when moisture or oil has found its way inside the cartridge, which can cause any dry propellant to act like a fuse. If that fuse burns its way to a concentration of dry propellant, the round can fire up to a full minute after the trigger was pressed.

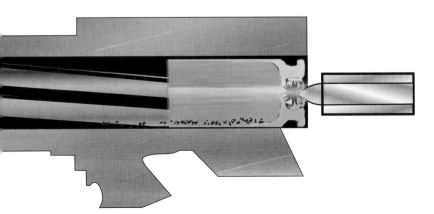

SQUIB LOAD

Often caused by a round that has no propellant – the primer's small explosion is enough to drive the bullet from the casing, but not enough to make it all the way down the barrel. If you believe you've had a squib load, stop firing immediately, or you risk a damaged barrel, damaged hand, damaged eyes, etc.

SEMI-AUTO MALFUNCTIONS & THEIR CLEARANCE

Semi-autos can have failures for a variety of reasons:

1. A round has misfired and remains chambered (also referred to as a "Type One" malfunction).

2. The ejected casing has failed to completely eject and is caught between the slide and the barrel (known as a "stovepipe" or a "Type Two" malfunction).

CLEARING TYPE ONE & TYPE TWO MALFUNCTIONS

Type One and Type Two malfunctions are cleared with a three step process:

3. The lack of a solid grip allows the entire gun to shift rearward, resulting in the slide's failure to separate from the frame far enough to eject the empty casing, and the empty casing is reloaded in the chamber.

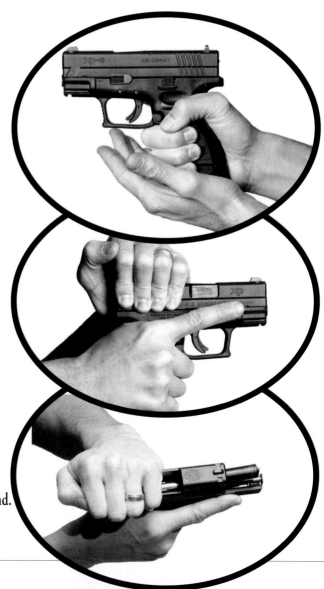

1 SLAP the bottom of the magazine to fully seat it.

2 RACK the slide fully to the rear. Notice that we're grasping the slide between the palm of the hand and all four fingers, rather than pinching the rear of the slide between the thumb and index finger which is referred to as "sling shotting."

3 ROLL the gun to the right to dump out the bad round / empty case. Releasing the slide (not easing it forward) loads a new round.

Type Three failures (which include failures to feed / feedway stoppages, and failures to eject) are usually caused by one of two culprits:

1. A worn extractor, which can leave the empty case in the chamber of the gun even after the slide cycles.

2. A bad magazine can cause two rounds to be fed at the same time.

Either failure will try to force two objects into the chamber at the same time, in effect, locking the slide in place and disabling the firearm. These failures are identified by the slide not locking into battery and an inability to rack the slide.

CLEARING TYPE THREE MALFUNCTIONS

If you've completed the three malfunction clearance steps on the previous page and discover that the slide isn't going forward, you most likely have a Type Three malfunction. To clear it, accomplish these additional steps:

4 LOCK the slide to the rear.

5 DROP the magazine (it may be necessary to pry it from the gun if a double-feed has it locked in place). Once the magazine is dropped, more often than not, you'll see two rounds hit the floor.

6 RACK the slide three times to remove any additional obstructions.

7 REINSERT the magazine (or insert a spare, since the magazine itself might be causing the problem) and rack the slide to chamber a new round.

HANDGUN OR SHOTGUN FOR HOME DEFENSE?

Conventional wisdom is that a shotgun is the best firearm for home defense when compared to a pistol, but that "wisdom" is usually based upon the incorrect theory that you can't miss with a shotgun. In the close quarters of a home, even the longest hallway might measure no more than 4 to 6 yards, and at that distance, typical shotgun chokes will open a pattern up to no more than 5 to 6 inches. That means that we still require deliberate aiming and that shooting from the hip or selecting a shotgun with just a pistol grip and no buttstock might result in a missed shot. Where shotguns *do* give us an edge is in the load that they deliver. At close

tactical shotguns can also be mounted with red dot scopes for easier point shooting, giving you the ability to look at your attacker, not the front sight. Surefire also offers mounted lights via replacement forends for Remington, Benelli, Mossberg, and Winchester models, which provide both a pressure sensitive pad for momentary activation, or a constant on/off switch. Options for home defense shotguns range from your granddaddy's old side-by-side, to auto-loaders like the Benelli M4 shown

here. Reliability counts more than auto-loading versus quarters, even #6 or #7 shot loads will stop or disable an attacker, and 00 or 000 buckshot will fire the near equivalent of 6 to 8 .380 pistol rounds, all delivered within that 5 to 6 inch pattern. Shotguns, like any long gun, also give us a much longer sight radius (the distance between the rear sight and the front sight) aiding in accuracy. If upgrading an existing shotgun for a home defense gun, we recommend that you upgrade the sights to a ghost ring or consider a TruGlo™ front sight; and many

pump, but any multi-shell shotgun has advantages over double barrels. If buying new, we recommend a 12 gauge with an 18-inch barrel and ghost ring sights or a red dot scope. On the following page, we've recommended two low recoil buckshot loads which are appropriate if you have at least 2 to 3 layers of drywall between yourself (the defender) and any loved ones or neighbors. Otherwise, we'd recommend backing up to a #4 load or smaller. Steer clear of magnum loads – you're delivering those pellets tens of feet, not hundreds.

ROUND	DESCRIPTION	CHARACTERISTICS
Federal Low-Recoil 000 Buckshot	Contains 8 .36 caliber pellets, weighing between 70 and 72 grains apiece.	The low recoil aspect allows a rapid recovery between shots, and with eight .36 caliber pellets, it's the near equivalent of delivering eight .380 ACPs all in one shot.
Hornady TAP-FPD 00 Buckshot	Designed for both pump and semi-autos, it provides very tight patterns with eight .33 caliber pellets.	TAP-FPD (For Personal Defense) buckshot is designed with home defense in mind and provides the tightest pattern on the market.

WHAT DOES "GAUGE" MEAN ANYWAY?

Unlike the unit of measurement used for bullets (caliber), shotgun sizes are measured in gauge. The gauge of a barrel is equal to the number of solid spheres of lead, each having the same diameter as the barrel, that would in total weigh a pound. For example, a solid sphere of lead weighing exactly 1/12th of a pound, would fit perfectly into the barrel of a 12 gauge, and a sphere of lead weighing 1/20th of a pound would fit perfectly into the barrel of a 20 gauge. A .410 shotgun is the exception, which is actually a caliber measurement (the barrel is 41/100ths of an inch in diameter).

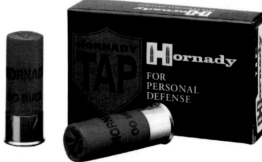

12 Gauge

Lead Ball with a Perfect Fit = 1/12th Pound

MORE ON SHOTGUNS: SHOT SIZE AND CHOKES

SHOT SIZE

Shot size ranges from #12 at .05 inches in diameter through 000 (pronounced "triple-ought") at .36 inches in diameter. For home defense, anything from #6 on up is up for the task, but our choice would be a 00 or 000 low-recoil load, which contains 6 to 8 shot, just smaller than a .380 ACP, and similar in weight to a .25 to .32ACP (at between 54 and 72 grains).

Lead Shot Size	7 ½	6	5	BB	00	000
Diameter (Inches)	.095	.11	.12	.18	.33	.36
# Per Ounce	350	225	170	50	8	6
Actual Size	•	•	•	•	●	●

HOW DOES A SHOTGUN'S CHOKE WORK?

A shotgun's choke constricts the end of the barrel to one degree or another, which affects the pattern size (the total area hit by the pellets). The tighter the choke, the tighter the pattern. Other things that can affect the pattern size are the length of barrel, shot size, and the composition of the shot, such as lead, steel, tungsten composites, etc. The pattern will open up twice the size at twice the distance, for example a pattern of 3 inches at 7 feet, will be 6 inches at 14 feet. For home defense, we'd recommend a modified or improved cylinder choke.

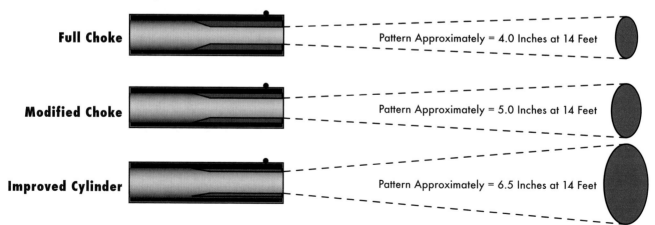

Full Choke — Pattern Approximately = 4.0 Inches at 14 Feet

Modified Choke — Pattern Approximately = 5.0 Inches at 14 Feet

Improved Cylinder — Pattern Approximately = 6.5 Inches at 14 Feet

There's a reason that police officers prefer shotguns when defending themselves in the close quarters of a home. A typical 000 load will contain the near equivalent of 6 to 8 .380 ACP pistol rounds, all delivered in a 5 to 6 inch pattern.

SHOOTING FUNDAMENTALS FOR DEFENSIVE ACCURACY

Understanding and abiding by the key shooting fundamentals will lead toward a lifetime of accurate and safe shooting. As with golf and other sports, even experienced individuals will benefit from a review of the fundamentals.

— Proper Grip —

— Stance: Body and Arm Positions —

— Point Shooting —

— Sight Shooting —

— Flash Sight Picture —

— Trigger Control —

Chapter 3

As much as we enjoy plinking at the range, the goal of this chapter is to introduce you to the shooting fundamentals required for self–defense. As you'll read in our physiological section in Chapter Five, when we're under extreme stress, our higher brain will very likely check out, and to one degree or another, automated processes will take over. Because of that, if we have a choice between a complex method of doing things and a simple method, we're going to pick simple. If we have a choice between a method that embraces those automated responses or fights them, we'll pick the method that embraces them. As you'll see in this chapter, we're going to look at the shooting fundamentals as a set of building blocks – if we can master one skill, the next skill becomes easier to accomplish. On the other hand, if we blow one of the skills, it will affect the rest. Mastering these fundamentals won't qualify you for the U.S. Shooting team or win you the Bianchi Cup, but they *will* provide the proper building blocks to work toward defensive accuracy, which we'll further define in this chapter.

Our goal when practicing these skills should be competence and consistency. Competence allows us to move on to the next major skill set discussed in Chapter Seven, which is to develop a balance between speed and accuracy. Consistency allows us to effectively bake these building blocks into our cerebellum. Whatever skill or task isn't previously hardwired in our cerebellum (what most people would call our "muscle memory") probably isn't a task that we'll be able to accomplish during a critical incident.

The great news is that there are just four building blocks to master, including grip, stance, target alignment, and trigger control.

The section on **Grip** will include the steps to achieve a proper grip and a demonstration of how the failure of a proper grip can affect your trigger control. We'll also show a couple of common incorrect grips, one of which will require band-aids once you're done shooting.

Stance (body and arm positions) will include descriptions and explanations of several "ready" positions including the "Sul" position, the "low ready" and the "high ready," as well as two shooting positions including the weaver and isosceles stance.

Our topic on **Target Alignment** will discuss **Sight Shooting, Point/Intuitive Shooting**, and using a "**Flash Sight Picture**," which are the three major options when it comes to aligning our barrel to the target. Sight shooting requires the alignment of our pistol's sights to the target; point shooting works by thinking of the handgun as an extension of our arms and hands, and "points" that imaginary line at the target (think squirt gun); while a "Flash Sight Picture," can be thought of as falling somewhere between the two previous options. We'll also discuss when one option might be preferable over the other, but we'll also discuss why the physiological reactions that we'll very likely experience might just choose the method for us.

We'll wrap up this chapter with a topic on **Trigger Control** where we'll explain how to learn to press the trigger without disrupting sight alignment, and how we can learn about our trigger's reset point.

PROPER GRIP

We often describe a proper grip as being the basis of all other shooting fundamentals. A proper grip can aid in proper trigger control and recoil management; it's a key setup component of point shooting and your stance; and it makes range exercises more relaxing and less punishing. Key things to remember: When setting up your grip, always remember Universal Rule #3 (Keep your finger OFF the trigger and outside the trigger guard until you are on target and have made the decision to shoot!). The second tip is to grip the pistol firmly, but not *too* firmly. The majority of pressure holding the firearm in place should

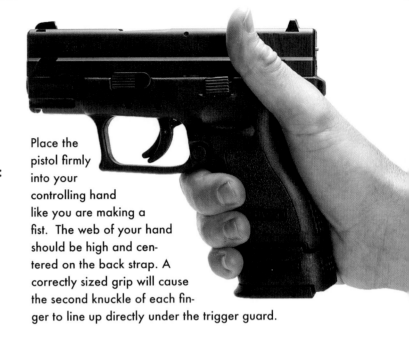

Place the pistol firmly into your controlling hand like you are making a fist. The web of your hand should be high and centered on the back strap. A correctly sized grip will cause the second knuckle of each finger to line up directly under the trigger guard.

The trigger finger is OUTSIDE THE TRIGGER GUARD and is pressed on the frame, and the middle finger is bumped up against the bottom of the trigger guard.

come from the isometric tension between the two hands (see the opposite page), rather than from trying to hold the pistol in place by finger pressure alone. Our last piece of advice is to pay attention to where your support thumb is and NEVER wrap it around the back of a semi-auto. If you're wondering what would happen, check out the example we call the "Railroad Track" grip on page 88.

ISOSCELES GRIP

When using the isosceles stance, wrap the fingers of your support hand firmly around the firing hand with the index finger pressed firmly against the bottom of the trigger guard. To create the perfect "seal" between both hands, the thumbs are stacked, with the third knuckle of the support hand nestled in the space between the first and second knuckle of the firing hand. Solid isometric pressure should be applied from the front and the rear, which will provide effective recoil management.

WEAVER GRIP

When using the weaver stance, the support hand is rotated farther to the rear when compared to the isosceles grip, and the thumbs will be slightly overlapped, rather than being stacked. From the shooter's perspective, this grip forms what is often referred to as a "baby's butt" (no, we can't take credit for that one). As with the isosceles grip, solid isometric pressure should be applied from the front and rear.

WARNING: GRIPS TO AVOID!

THE "RAILROAD TRACK"

If you plan on using this grip (with the support thumb wrapped around the back), grab a red magic marker and mark two red lines down the back of your support thumb, because as soon as you fire that's exactly what's going to appear there, just after the slide slams back and slices your thumb open. This is by far the most common error we see with new semi-auto shooters. We literally cringe when we see someone firing with this grip, because we know we're gonna see blood.

THE "TEA CUP"

Another common error is called "Tea Cupping" (named because the support hand acts like a saucer holding a cup of tea), which doesn't take full advantage of the support hand. This style of grip might have solid support with the firing hand, but the support hand can act like a pivot, forcing the muzzle up and actually increasing muzzle rise, rather than managing it.

THE "MILKING EXERCISE"

The "Milking Exercise" below is used to prove that a solid grip provides better trigger control than a loose grip. The solid grip (with fingers tightly squeezed around the pistol's grip) has the tendons and muscles in your hand and arm tightly flexed, allowing you to rapidly press your trigger finger without moving your hand, wrist, or arms. A loose grip can cause a milking action, causing you to shoot high and to the side.

1 With your fingers curled as though you were loosely gripping a pistol, rapidly move the index finger as if pressing a trigger.

2 You will see your other fingers reflexively close along with your trigger finger. This reflex is called "milking" and can cause you to shoot high and to the side.

3 Try the exercise again, but this time tightly curl your fingers as though gripping a pistol firmly. Notice the tendons in your arm will be pre-flexed.

4 When the trigger finger is pressed, the other fingers cannot reflexively contract, because they are already contracted as tightly as possible.

STANCE: "READY" AND "SAFE" POSITIONS

Once the firearm is out of the holster, its appropriate position and orientation is going to depend upon the disposition of the attacker, and the location of loved ones or other friendlies. The three "ready" or "safe" positions shown below and on the opposite page, including the "Sul" position, the "Low Ready" and the "High Ready," are designed

The slide of the firearm overlays the knuckles, with the muzzle pointed directly at the ground, between the shooter's feet. ▶

◀ **"Sul" Position**   The "Sul" position was originally developed for Brazilian police officers ("Sul" translates to "South" in Portuguese) preparing for close quarter battle (CQB), when officers would be stacked up in close proximity. The position is considered to be more of a "safe" position than it is considered a classic "ready" position, and would be appropriate for permit holders when the firearm is out of the holster, and "friendlies" are in extremely close proximity. The "Sul" position places the support hand against the solar plexus, with the fingers parallel to the ground, and the thumb pointing up. The firing hand and firearm overlay the support hand, with the muzzle pointed directly down. The thumb pads should touch, which locks the position into place, and creates a pivot point should the need arise to quickly take up a shooting stance.

for a variety of situations where it is appropriate to have the firearm out of the holster, but where it is *not* yet appropriate to take up a shooting stance, or to reholster. Regardless of the position, the trigger finger should remain *outside* of the trigger guard.

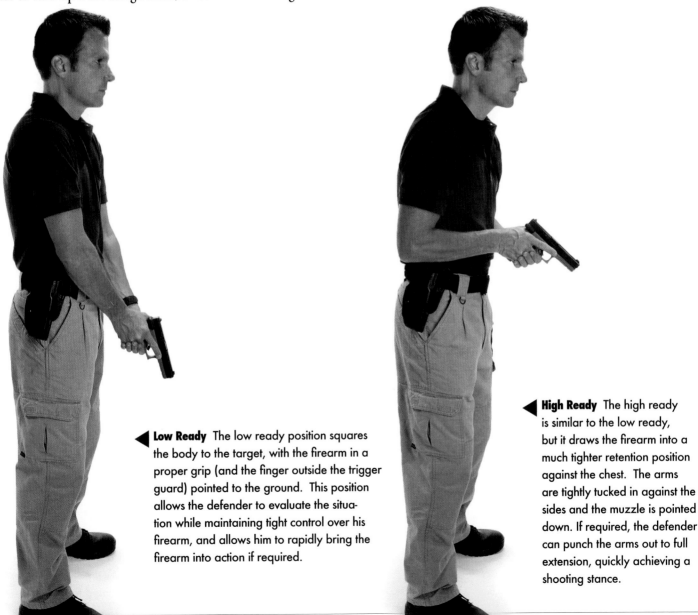

◀ **Low Ready** The low ready position squares the body to the target, with the firearm in a proper grip (and the finger outside the trigger guard) pointed to the ground. This position allows the defender to evaluate the situation while maintaining tight control over his firearm, and allows him to rapidly bring the firearm into action if required.

◀ **High Ready** The high ready is similar to the low ready, but it draws the firearm into a much tighter retention position against the chest. The arms are tightly tucked in against the sides and the muzzle is pointed down. If required, the defender can punch the arms out to full extension, quickly achieving a shooting stance.

Jack *Weaver*

The Weaver stance was developed by L.A. Deputy Sheriff Jack Weaver, in an effort to win Jeff Cooper's "Leatherslap" competition in Big Bear, California in 1959. At that time, the typical competitive shooter shot from the hip or one-handed from the shoulder, and according to Jack, "what started out as serious business soon produced gales of laughter from the spectators as most of the shooters blazed away..." and "with guns empty and all 12 rounds gone but the 18 inch balloons still standing, they had a problem: load one round and take aim or load six and blaze away again." By the time the 1959 Leatherslap rolled around, Jack had realized that "a pretty quick hit was better than a lightning-fast miss," and decided to bring the pistol up using both hands and use the pistol's sights, rather than just shooting from the hip. Jeff Cooper commented, "Jack walloped us all, decisively. He was very quick and he did not miss."

Jack died in April of 2009. One of our most prized possessions is an autographed poster of Jack, showing him at the now famous Leatherslap competition.

WEAVER STANCE

The Weaver stance, named after the late Jack Weaver, takes up a "bladed" body position, with the strong side foot placed to the rear and the body bladed at approximately 45 degrees. The arms create solid isometric pressure with the strong arm slightly flexed and pushing forward, and the support arm elbow down, and pulling back. Advocates of the weaver stance like the fact that it places the body in a traditional fighting or defensive position, and the stance mimics the same body position used for shooting a shotgun or rifle, minimizing the variables that the shooter must learn if they train with multiple guns. In addition, since the firearm is held closer to the body when compared to the isosceles, shooters may find the stance less tiring, and shooters with weaker eyes may find it easier to get a good sight picture.

◄ The shoulders and body are bladed to the target at approximately 45 degrees.

▲ The arms create solid isometric pressure with the strong arm slightly flexed and pushing forward, and the support arm elbow down, and pulling back.

◄ Knees are slightly flexed.

◄ Feet are shoulder-width apart and are bladed to the target, with the strong side foot planted to the rear.

ISOSCELES STANCE

The Isosceles (which gets its name from the perfect triangle formed by the squared shoulders and straight arms) squares the body to the target, with both arms fully extended and tensed, pointed directly at the target. Fans of the Isosceles believe that the stance better matches the body's and mind's natural reaction to face an attacker head on and to push the arms out defensively, which allows the shooter to "train the way they'll fight." In addition, since both arms are straight and tensed, recoil and follow-through are easily managed – shooters will find the firearm dropping back on target immediately after the muzzle rise. Since the arms point at the target using the Isosceles, it also provides a simple, repeatable method of point shooting in a stress situation.

◀ The shoulders are square to the target, with both arms thrust straight out, forming a perfect isosceles triangle (that's a triangle with two sides that are the same length).

▲ The firearm is elevated high enough to allow the shooter to use the sights, or the shooter can look over the top of the sights when point shooting or when using a "flash sight picture."

◀ The mid-section can act as a "turret" (picture the turret on a tank), allowing the shooter to rotate at the waist or on the balls of the heels to cover 360°.

◀ Knees are slightly flexed.

◀ Feet are shoulder-width apart and squared to the target, or the strong side foot can be planted slightly to the rear, which can provide better stability.

POINT/INTUITIVE SHOOTING VS. SIGHT SHOOTING

While we grew up learning to sight shoot (that is, we learned to shoot by aligning three indexes – the front sight, the rear sight, and the target), the more we studied actual defensive shootings including those outlined in the book "Deadly Force Encounters" (discussed in Chapter Five) and the deeper we dove into the inner workings of the brain, the more we came to believe in "simple over complex" and techniques that match the body's and mind's natural reactions rather than in methods that fought those reactions. When under attack, one of those natural reactions will very likely be the motor cortex literally *forcing* our head to face the threat and *forcing* our eyes to focus directly on the threat, making it impossible to focus on the front sight. If we've *only* trained by focusing on the front sight (the proper method to use when sight shooting) we might just find ourselves stuck in an endless feedback loop, with our eyes locked on the threat, and the coded instructions in the cerebellum (more on that in Chapter Five) screaming "don't fire until you focus on the front sight!"

POINT SHOOTING

Knowing that those reactions are possible, if not probable, we'd be negligent if we didn't at least consider an alignment method that embraced those natural reactions. Point or "Intuitive" shooting doesn't discard the idea of alignment, it simply makes the pistol's muzzle an extension of the hands and arms, and points the extended arms and hands at the target. The finger that you have aligned on the side of your handgun's slide or cylinder (before you've made the decision to fire) isn't just there for safety, it's also the end of the arm's and hand's "axis," and should point directly at the target. Think of this as no different than how you'd extend your arm and point your finger at *any* object – at the close distances that would typically accompany an attack, you'd have no problem accurately pointing at an object *much* smaller than the size of a human being.

DEFENSIVE ACCURACY

So what's the downside of point shooting? If our goal is to put the bullets through a silver dollar sized hole, then we're going to sacrifice some accuracy and we'll have a larger margin of error when compared to sight shooting. On the other hand, that shouldn't be our goal. If we *must* fire, our goal is what's called defensive accuracy. Defensive accuracy can be thought of as any round that *significantly affects the attacker's ability to continue his attack.* In one situation, if an attacker is standing directly in front of us, it might mean shots fired at his cardiovascular triangle (discussed in Chapter Five). While in another situation, if an attacker is shooting at us from behind a barrier and the only thing visible is his shooting hand, arm, and shoulder, then defensive accuracy might mean hitting that hand, arm, or shoulder.

REQUIREMENTS FOR PRECISION

When comparing the two methods, it's fair to ask whether or not the requirements for precision for a given situation might *require* us to choose sight shooting over point shooting. If our brain doesn't give us that option, then the argument between the two methods is moot. On the other hand, if our brain *does* allow us to see our gun's sights (giving us the option of using the sights for alignment) then we'll need to pick the appropriate method of alignment based upon the requirements for precision for the *specific circumstances* that we find ourselves in. An attacker charging us with a knife with a concrete wall behind him will require one degree of precision. That same attacker bending down to pick up our child will require another degree of precision entirely.

When conducting mental exercises on the range, you'll need to run through scenarios where the requirements for precision increase or decrease depending upon the scenario, and the penalty for a miss is anything from "one more second of me getting stabbed, choked, or shot" to "go to jail, go directly to jail."

Point Shooting
Violent attacks will be *fast*, and they'll be *close*. Your motor cortex will very likely lock your eyes and your focus onto the weapon in the attacker's hands.

Sight Shooting
Forcing your eyes to change focus from a six foot tall attacker to a 3 millimeter wide front sight, *may simply not be possible*.

POINT SHOOTING

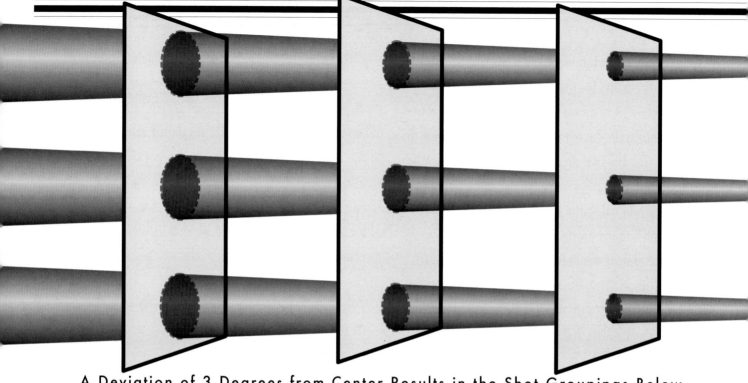

A Deviation of 3 Degrees from Center Results in the Shot Groupings Below

15 Feet
Shot grouping
9.3 inches across

10 Feet
Shot grouping
6.2 inches across

5 Feet
Shot grouping
3.1 inches across

At close distances, the Isosceles enables simple point shooting by its nature – it points the barrel of our firearm directly at the target. In other words, the firearm becomes an extension of our hands – where our hands point, the gun points. When using this method, our advice is to focus on the *exact spot* where you want your rounds to land, rather than focusing on the entire target. Just like pointing your finger at a *spot* on the wall is more specific than pointing at the entire wall, focusing on a spot on the target will enable more accurate shooting. Speaking of accuracy, the average person's arc of move-

ment with point shooting will deviate by only a few degrees from his natural point of aim, allowing for tight shot groups at 10 to 15 feet, and even tighter groups at closer distances. Check out the calculated groupings above showing shot groups at 5 feet, 10 feet, and 15 feet, with an arc of movement of three degrees (you should be impressed – we had to break out our trigonometry tables to calculate this). Finally, think about it in the same way you "shoot" a squirt gun – you don't use the squirt gun's sights and yet, more often than not, you can hit your "target" center of mass.

Whether we're pointing a finger, pointing a dart gun, or pointing a firearm, the human body is *designed* to point. With the arm, hand and finger extended, the body has a natural, straight line from the shoulder to the fingertip, and we're born with the ability to point that straight line with a high degree of accuracy. When pointing a firearm, we should train to elevate the firearm up into our line of sight (regardless of our method of target alignment), which allows even more accurate pointing than if the firearm is below our line of sight. When point shooting, the firearm's sights will be out of focus, but should be visible on our target's center of mass. Transitioning between point shooting and sight shooting (when our brain allows us) is then a matter of changing our focus from the target to the front sight.

WHAT'S ARC OF MOVEMENT?

Watch any movie where a laser sight is being used and the red dot doesn't waver a millimeter once it's on target. If you're the Terminator it might work that way, but in real life it doesn't. The body's natural movement, including heartbeat and breathing, and the effects of adrenaline on your muscles, will limit your ability to hold your firearm perfectly on target and a small amount of waver is expected. That's actually okay – at close distances (15 feet or less) a small amount of waver still allows accurate point shooting. In the calculated groupings on the opposite page, we're showing an arc of movement of three degrees, which equates to your muzzle wavering by an inch and a half in any direction, which is exactly the size of a silver dollar. Double the waver and you'll double the margin of error.

SIGHT SHOOTING

If the specifics of our situation call for greater precision and *if* our brain allows us to focus on the front sight, then sight shooting may be preferable over point shooting. When using our firearm's sights, two fundamentals matter: focusing on the front sight, and aligning three indexes – the front sight, the rear sight, and the target.

FRONT SIGHT FOCUS

When training to use our pistol's sights, it's natural to want to focus on the target, but it will result in poor sight align-ment. It's an especially common error for hunters used to a scope, where the target and the reticle are both in focus. It will take practice to refocus the eye from where it wants to focus (the target) to where it should focus (the front sight). When focused on the front sight, it will be in complete focus, the rear sight will be semi-blurred, and the target will be the blurriest thing in your sight picture.

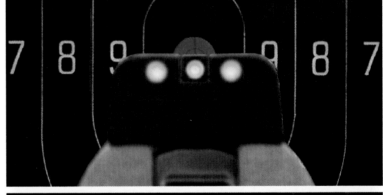

Incorrectly Focusing on Target
The target is in focus and the sights are blurry

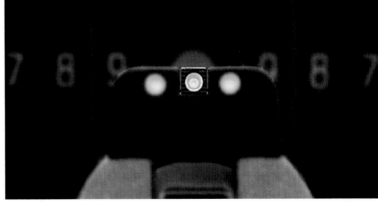

Properly Focusing on the Front Sight
The front sight is in focus, the rear sight and target are blurry

Front Sight too High or too Low

Sights Not Evenly Spaced

Proper Sight Alignment

SIGHT ALIGNMENT

During exercises where students are training to use their pistols' sights, we'll often hear comments like "What's wrong with my shooting? My shots are all over the place!" When we ask them if their sights are in perfect alignment (right after we've asked them if they're focusing on the front sight) we'll often hear "they were very close" or "the front sight was only a little bit off." Here's what you should remember: Since the end of the barrel isn't actually touching the target, the bullet will travel in a straight line (following the misaligned sights) which will place the shot even lower, higher, to the right, or to the left of where the front sight is placed. What's the best way to ensure perfect sight alignment? See the previous page.

FLASH SIGHT PICTURE

The third major option for aligning the muzzle to the target (and could arguably be described as a combination of point shooting and sight shooting) is using a "flash sight picture" to verify alignment before the trigger is pressed. Put simply, a flash sight picture occurs when the shooter is able to get a rapid "overlay" of the sights on the target, without focusing on the front sight, and without taking the time to gain perfect sight alignment. A flash sight picture will have the target in perfect focus, with the front sight and rear sight both visible (but out of focus) on the target.

Said another way, the shooter looks for a "flash" of the sights on the target to *verify* proper alignment, rather than using the sights to *attain* proper alignment.

As with all methods of alignment, it's important to look at the *exact spot* where you want the round to impact. Then, when the firearm is elevated into your line of sight, a "flash sight picture" occurs (the front and rear sights overlay the spot that you want to shoot) and the trigger is pressed.

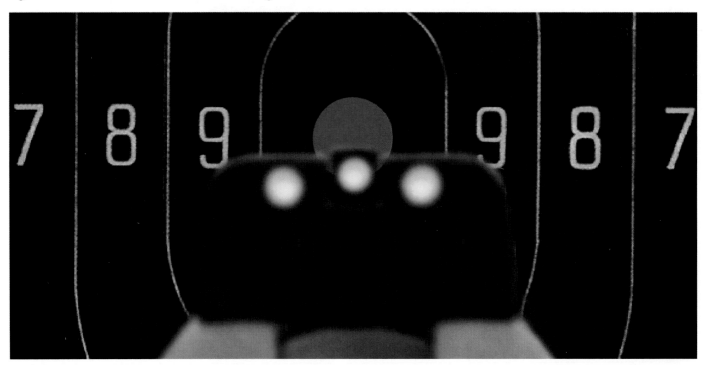

While there is no "perfect" flash sight picture (any of the sight pictures on page 99 would suffice), the example above approximates how the sights might appear when they overlay the target. Since in this example, the plane of the firearm is slightly below the sight plane (the line between the eye and the spot where you want the round to impact), an appropriate flash sight picture would have the front sight slightly above the rear sight.

TRIGGER CONTROL

When learning any new skill, the mind can typically focus on a single task at a time (it's the old "patting the head while rubbing the stomach" problem). That means that a new shooter who is focusing on trigger press, might find it difficult to maintain target alignment, and visa-versa. To solve that problem, new shooters should begin with what's known as a "surprise break" when learning proper trigger control. The theory behind the "surprise break" method, is that it forces the mind to choose which of the two actions we'll focus on, by choosing to maintain target alignment, rather than focusing on the *exact moment* that the hammer/striker will fall (think of it as focusing on patting the head, rather than rubbing the stomach). When starting out, we recommend that you begin with the "surprise break" exercise described below, before progressing to the "compressed break" exercise, which will slowly begin to pick up the speed of the trigger press, while maintaining perfect target alignment.

SURPRISE BREAK

Gently apply pressure until all of the slack (what's called "over travel") is taken out of the trigger. Counting up to five, continue to apply smooth pressure until the hammer/striker falls (it doesn't matter if the hammer/striker falls at one, at five, or anywhere in between). *One-hundred percent* of your focus should be on maintaining target alignment, and not on when the hammer/striker falls.

COMPRESS BREAK

Gently apply pressure until all of the slack is taken out of the trigger. Counting "one-one-thousand," continue to apply smooth pressure until the hammer/striker falls. As with the surprise break, one-hundred percent of your focus should be on maintaining target alignment, and not on when the hammer/striker falls. Continue practicing this drill until the compress break is reduced below .5 (or even .25) seconds.

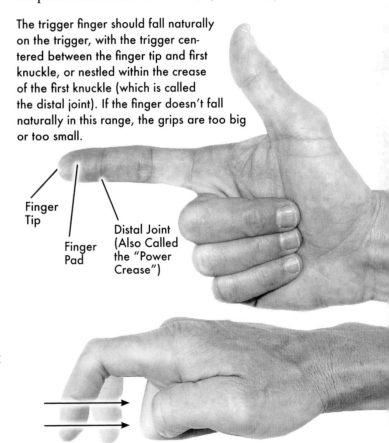

The trigger finger should fall naturally on the trigger, with the trigger centered between the finger tip and first knuckle, or nestled within the crease of the first knuckle (which is called the distal joint). If the finger doesn't fall naturally in this range, the grips are too big or too small.

Finger Tip

Finger Pad

Distal Joint (Also Called the "Power Crease")

Wherever the trigger is placed, the finger must be pressed STRAIGHT to the rear so that the muzzle alignment is not disturbed.

As important as it is to build "muscle memory" for a smooth trigger press that doesn't disrupt target alignment, it's equally important to understand how far forward your trigger must travel before the trigger is reset, and to build that reset point into your neural pathways. The reset point is easily identifiable by a tactile and audible "click" as the trigger is traveling forward. At that reset point, the trigger can once again be pressed to fire the gun. You'll find dramatic differences in how far forward the trigger must travel before it's reset when comparing different types of handgun actions, so you'll need to learn the reset point for each handgun you own. The illustrations to the right provide an example of a Glock, including the trigger position when fully at rest, at the break point, and at the reset point.

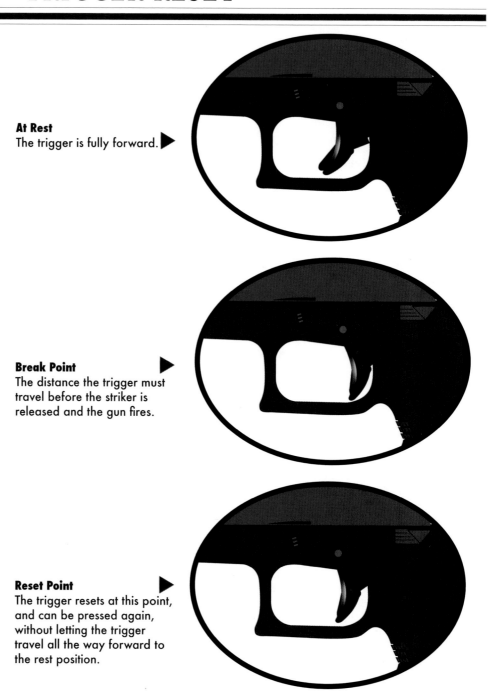

At Rest
The trigger is fully forward. ▶

Break Point ▶
The distance the trigger must travel before the striker is released and the gun fires.

Reset Point ▶
The trigger resets at this point, and can be pressed again, without letting the trigger travel all the way forward to the rest position.

Having mastered the fundamentals, competitor Ron Westberg demonstrates an emergency reload while competing at Oakdale Gun Club in Lake Elmo, Minnesota.

THE LEGAL USE OF FORCE

The right to legally use force, up to and including deadly force, is covered in detail in this chapter.

— Reviewing the Legal Definitions of
Reasonable Force and Deadly Force —

— Understanding the Use of Force Continuum —

— A Detailed Walkthrough of the Four Pillars
for Justifying the Use of Deadly Force —

— How Defense in the Home Differs from Outside the Home —

— Defending Property —

Chapter 4

Every state in the U.S. has definitions, statutes, and case law defining when civilians may legally use force (up to and including deadly force) to protect themselves, their families, and their homes. Although statutes and case law vary from state to state, most laws are based at least in part on the "reasonable person" test discussed in Chapter One. That means that whenever *any* level of force has been used, the prosecutor may second guess your decision, using 12 jurors to decide whether or not they believed your actions were reasonable under the circumstances.

We'll start this chapter by looking at our "Use of Force Continuum," which provides examples of escalating levels of force that might be used when defending ourselves from a violent attack. As you'll see on the continuum, each progressive level of force will be viewed with a higher level of scrutiny. Depending upon the circumstances, a jury might decide that it would have been reasonable for you to point your firearm at an attacker, but it was unreasonable to shoot and kill him. When deadly force has been used, in addition to the "reasonableness" test, the courts will ask the jury to ensure that you've met other requirements which we'll discuss in this chapter.

In addition to discussing your right to use force outside of your home, we'll also discuss your right to use force (up to and including deadly force) when defending your home. This aspect of the law is getting a fresh look in many states - approximately 25 states have passed what are generally referred to as "Castle Doctrine" laws, which in part, remove the obligation to retreat when you're in a place where you have a right to be; and, they make the legal presumption that someone who has entered your home or occupied vehicle by stealth or force is there to do you harm, allowing you to use deadly force to stop that individual.

We'll wrap up this chapter with a discussion on "defense of property." As with the other use of force laws, defense of property laws will vary from state to state, but regardless of your state's laws, we'll discuss whether or not we think using force to defend property is a good idea.

66 *"Among the natural rights of the Colonists are these: First, a right to life; Secondly, to liberty; Thirdly, to property; together with the right to support and defend them in the best manner they can."* 99

Samuel Adams
The Rights of the Colonists,
The Report of the Committee of
Correspondence to the Boston
Town Meeting, Nov. 20, 1772

THE USE OF FORCE CONTINUUM

The diagram below provides examples of different types of force and the level of force that they might be viewed under. It also shows the rules that must typically be followed, and the types of crimes you might be charged with if the rules aren't followed.

DEADLY FORCE

REASONABLE FORCE

NO FORCE

RETREATING - OR - DE-ESCALATING **EXPOSING FIREARM** **POINTING THE FIREARM AT ANOTHER PERSON** **SHOOTING AT SOMEONE** **SHOOTING AND KILLING SOMEON**

The Rules You Must Follow

1. Reasonably in fear of a threat against yourself or another.
2. Any force must be reasonable for the circumstances.

1. Reasonably in immediate fear of death or great/grave bodily harm for yourself or another.
2. Must be an innocent party.
3. Must have no reasonable means of retreat.
4. No lesser force will suffice to stop the threat.

If You Don't Follow the Rules

- Misdemeanor or gross misdemeanor assault.
- Terroristic threats.
- Brandishing a firearm.

- Felony assault.
- Attempted murder.

- Manslaughter in the 1st or 2nd degree.
- Murder in the 1st, 2nd or 3rd degree.

Although laws vary from state to state when defining our legal right to use force to protect ourselves, others, our homes, and our property, at their heart, most states' laws require that any use of force be "reasonable for the circumstances." That is, in addition to any specific rules outlined in statutory or case law, we must also pass the "reasonable person" test described in Chapter One. When deadly force has been used, we'll not only need to pass the "reasonable" test, we'll also need to pass other test criteria, which we'll explore on pages 110 – 115.

REASONABLE FORCE

Although laws vary, most states will define "reasonable force" as the *minimum* level of force required to end a threat, without going beyond that level. Said another way, reasonable force can be thought of as a level of force that does not *exceed* the threat. For example, if a threat to you included the possibility that you'd be bruised or receive a bloody nose, it wouldn't be considered "reasonable" for you to respond with a level of force that could break bones or permanently disfigure your attacker. That's the theory at least – you'll have seconds (or less) to decide whether or not your attacker will be satisfied with bloodying your nose, while the prosecutor gets hours or days to make the same determination.

DEADLY FORCE

Each state's laws also define when it is permissible to use what is generally referred to as "deadly force," "lethal force," or "the justifiable taking of a life." To simplify this topic,

we'll refer to this level of force as "deadly force." While specific state laws vary, a common standard for the use of deadly force exists, which is:

Deadly force may only be used when there is an immediate, and unavoidable danger of death or great/grave bodily harm to an innocent person, where no other option exists other than the use of deadly force.

As simple as that statement may sound, each state will provide further legal definitions or interpretations for each component of that statement, including what it means to be "innocent," what "immediate" means, and what "great" (or "grave") bodily harm means. To help, we've summarized what those definitions *typically* mean and don't mean, into four key rules outlined on pages 110 – 115. After any use of deadly force, the prosecutor and/or jury will get a chance to determine whether or not they agree with your interpretation of those definitions, and of course, they'll get to conduct their thought experiment over the course of hours or days, and in the relative safety of a courtroom, while you'll need to make your decision in seconds, while under attack. The phrase "deadly force" itself can also be misleading – based upon the name alone, one might assume that if the attacker didn't die, then the deadly force rules wouldn't apply, but that's actually not the case. Typically, the term "deadly force" means a level of force which is *likely* to cause, or *could* cause the death of the other person, regardless of whether or not they actually *did* die. We'll take a look at that issue in more detail on the following page.

USING DEADLY FORCE

WHERE DOES DEADLY FORCE BEGIN?

It might not be where you think, and it's usually up to the prosecutor to decide. Since most states' deadly force rules are applicable when a level of force has been used which *could* have caused the death of another person (even if the person didn't die), the prosecutor gets to decide whether or not he or she thinks death could have resulted, and whether or not the deadly force rules should apply. (Hence the extension of the "Deadly Force" bar on the continuum beyond "Shooting and Killing Someone.") That fact alone causes us to strongly recommend against warning shots. Prosecutors can easily refer to your warning shot as a "miss," and they can make a case to the jury that you actually *did* attempt to kill the alleged attacker, even if you claim that you only fired into the ground (a bad idea) or into the air (an even worse idea since you'll have responsibility for wherever your bullet eventually lands.) If the judge instructs the jury to view your case under the deadly force rules rather than just the reasonable force rules, you'll suddenly have a much, much steeper hill to climb, since you'll need to prove that all of the deadly force rules were true, in addition to the reasonable force rules. Finally, it's important to understand that for us to be legally authorized to use deadly force, each of the deadly force rules must be in place and must remain in place at *every single moment* when we use, or attempt to use deadly force. As an example, in the opening stages of an attack we may have no ability to retreat (rule #3) because the attack may have occurred so quickly and at very close quarters. But, if we are able to wound the attacker such that an opening to retreat suddenly becomes available, we must retreat at that point, rather than continue our use of deadly force. On the following pages, we're going to look at each of the deadly force rules in detail, including what the rules typically mean and don't mean. We'll also use a real life scenario to illustrate how each rule might be followed or broken.

SUMMARY OF THE RULES GOVERNING THE USE OF DEADLY FORCE OUTSIDE THE HOME

1 Reasonably in immediate fear of death or great/grave bodily harm for yourself or another. The threat must be immediate and must be so serious that a reasonable person would fear death or great/grave bodily harm. Great or grave bodily harm is a significant or life-threatening injury.

2 Must be an innocent party. You cannot be seen as the person who started or escalated a conflict. This does not mean that you cannot come to the defense of another person, it simply means that you did not start the conflict and you are reluctantly entering it.

3 Must have no reasonable means of retreat. If you can retreat, you must. However, you are not required to place yourself or a loved one in greater danger by retreating.

4 No lesser force will suffice to stop the threat. If you can stop a threat with something less than deadly force, you are required to.

The four deadly force rules must be in place during *every single moment* when you attempt to use deadly force. As scary and as threatening as this individual looks, count on the prosecutor to second guess your decision *whenever* deadly force is used.

SCENARIO #1

Pulling into your apartment complex, you notice a neighbor standing on his third floor balcony.

You exit your vehicle and head toward the front door of your first floor apartment.

Leaning over his balcony, your neighbor (who has threatened you in the past) pulls a knife from his waistband and shouts "You're a dead man!"

Fearing death or great bodily harm, you shoot your neighbor.

While you could claim that you feared death or great bodily harm, you'd fail on the "immediate" portion of this rule. Since your neighbor was on the third floor and you were on the first, the threat most likely would not be perceived as "immediate" by the prosecutor.

1 REASONABLY IN IMMEDIATE FEAR OF DEATH OR GREAT/GRAVE BODILY HARM FOR YOURSELF OR ANOTHER

What it Usually Means:

- You must pass the reasonable person test. The prosecutor must agree that a "reasonable person" would have also felt that he or she would have been in immediate fear of death or great/grave bodily harm in the same situation.
- This rule applies whether protecting yourself or another person.
- The threat must be immediate. The attacker must have the immediate means and opportunity to carry out his threat. A verbal threat to injure or kill you is not enough.
- Great or grave bodily harm is a legal measurement that implies injuries so great that death is likely or possible, or that you'll be disfigured or crippled permanently or for a significant period of time.
- The condition of the victim matters. For example, in most cases, if a smaller man is punching a larger man in the chest, it would not be considered great/grave bodily harm. However, if the larger man had a pacemaker, the criteria might be met, even though the attacker had no knowledge of the condition.

What it Usually Doesn't Mean:

- It is not necessary that the attacker(s) have a weapon. Depending on the relative number, size and/or strength of the attacker(s) and the victim (what would be called a "disparity of force") the measurement of great/grave bodily harm might be met even though the attacker is unarmed.
- Distance is not critical. If you cannot retreat, you are not required to wait until an attacker is close enough to injure or kill you before you are authorized to use deadly force. Remember the "Tueller Drill" (and remind your lawyer about it).

2 MUST BE AN INNOCENT PARTY

What it Usually Means:

- In a deadly force situation, you must be the innocent party – you *cannot* be seen as the aggressor. That is, you must not be the person who started or escalated the conflict.
- Shoving someone at a bar obviously violates this rule, but how about flipping someone off on the freeway? If the situation escalates, don't be so sure what the prosecutor will think.
- The prosecutor will not only analyze the timeline of the incident itself, he'll also want to go back in time before the incident occurred to understand whether or not you knew the attacker, whether there was bad blood between you, and if there are any witnesses or evidence (prior arrests, etc.) to suggest that you're not as innocent as you claim to be.

What it Usually Doesn't Mean:

- It doesn't mean that you are barred from everyday disagreements, but it does mean that if you see the situation escalating, you must disengage, allowing the situation to de-escalate.
- You are not barred from coming to the defense of another, but unless you can clearly identify who is the attacker and who is the innocent victim, a prudent course of action would be to call 911 and be a good witness. Don't assume that the guy who has the upper hand in the fight is the bad guy.

SCENARIO #2

After entering a bar, another individual steps on your toe.

You failed the "innocent party" rule.

You mutter "asshole" under your breath.

The individual bumps into your shoulder, knocking you back.

You failed the "innocent party" rule again.

You shove the individual to the floor.

At this point, you are in immediate risk of death or great bodily harm, but since you've broken rule #2, you should expect to be charged with a crime.

The individual jumps up from the floor and charges you with a knife.

You shoot the individual charging you with the knife

SCENARIO #3

On your way home from work, a dog runs in front of your car on the freeway. You slam on your brakes and are rear ended.

Your car is fine, so you continue on until you can pull onto the shoulder, but the other car is out of commission, and pulls over several hundred feet behind you.

The other individual jumps out of his car with a machete, and charges your vehicle, screaming that he's going to kill you.

You exit your vehicle, and take up a position behind your driver's door. You shout commands continuously for the 40 seconds it takes the other individual to reach you.

You shoot the individual as he gets within 20 feet of you.

At this point, you are in immediate risk of death or great bodily harm, but you had plenty of time to drive off (remember that your car was fine in this scenario), leaving the deranged individual behind.

3 NO REASONABLE MEANS OF RETREAT

What it Usually Means:
- Most state's laws requires that if you can do so safely, you are expected to retreat from a potential confrontation, rather than stand your ground and defend yourself. As mentioned in the chapter introduction, a number of states have updated their laws removing the obligation to retreat, but our recommendation is that even in those states, if you can retreat, you should retreat. Nothing in the law is black and white, and prosecutors are adept at threading the needle in their arguments to jurors.
- The obligation to retreat never ends. For example, if you are able to wound an attacker such that it opens up an opportunity to retreat safely, you MUST retreat at that point.

What it Usually Doesn't Mean:
- You are not expected to retreat from a bad situation to a worse one. For example, if your only means of retreat is across a busy road, you are not expected to put yourself in greater danger by retreating.
- You are not expected to retreat and leave behind a companion in the dangerous situation. That is, if you can outrun an attacker, you are not expected to if it means leaving a companion behind.

4 NO LESSER FORCE WOULD SUFFICE. DEADLY FORCE WAS THE ONLY OPTION

What it Usually Means:

- If you can stop a threat with something less than deadly force, you are required to. For example, if a reasonable person would have expected that you could have stopped an attack with your hands (or the pepper spray that you chose to carry) the prosecutor may not agree that deadly force was authorized.
- You are required to stop using deadly force as soon as the threat of death or great/grave bodily harm has ended. If three bullets stop an attack, the fourth bullet could be considered a crime.
- Relative size and strength of the attacker(s) and/or victim matter. For example, a large man being attacked by an unarmed, much smaller woman, may have lesser-force alternatives rather than resorting to deadly force. In the reverse scenario, the disparity of force may mean that the smaller woman might have no alternative other than immediately resorting to deadly force.

What it Usually Doesn't Mean:

- You are not required to try other methods before using deadly force, you are simply expected to consider alternatives, and to only use deadly force when no other option is reasonably sufficient.

SCENARIO #4

You leave a busy city street and turn down an alley to take a short cut to your car.

An individual approximately half your size steps from behind a dumpster and pulls his shirt aside, while reaching for a semi-automatic tucked into his waistband.

Your first mistake. While you haven't broken one of the rules yet, you've put yourself in a risky situation that could have been avoided if you'd stayed with the crowds.

You shout "don't hurt me!" and draw your firearm from the holster. You leave your pepper spray in your pocket.

The individual draws his firearm from his waistband, and elevates it in an effort to shoot you.

At this point, you would probably get most prosecutors to agree that you had no alternative other than to immediately resort to deadly force, and that you would not have been expected to try your pepper spray first.

You fire two rounds at him and one strikes him in the shoulder. He immediately drop his firearm and it slides under the dumpster.

Bleeding, the individual stumbles toward you.

However, at this point, the individual no longer had control of his firearm (and was injured) and your pepper spray would most likely have sufficed to have stopped the continued threat. In addition, a prosecutor might argue that you've also broken rules #1 and #3 as well.

The individual refuses your further commands to stay back, and he steps into what you consider to be your "danger zone" so you shoot him again.

HOW WILL THE PROSECUTOR EVALUATE YOUR CASE?

As discussed in Chapter One, when deciding whether or not to file charges against an individual claiming self-defense, the prosecutor is going to care about more than just who was shot and who did the shooting. As outlined in our scenarios, the prosecutor will analyze each time slice of the incident in an attempt to understand exactly what occurred, including whether or not you started the ball rolling or kept it rolling. The prosecutor might also back up to the hours, days, and even years before the incident, in an attempt to understand the entire story.

The prosecutor will want to know:

- Does the timeline include *anything* that shows you as the aggressor (even if it happened after an initial move by the other individual)? Did you start the ball rolling, or give it a good kick to keep it rolling?
- Did you know the other individual, and was there any history of bad blood? How far back does the timeline extend?
- What kind of individual are you? What do your friends, ex-friends, neighbors, and co-workers say about you?
- What's on your Facebook or MySpace pages, including pictures, philosophy, and behavior? Is there any indication of aggressiveness, a belief in vigilantism, or gang activity?
- Are you considered a bully or aggressive? Are there any witnesses, prior arrests, or documentation (including anything you've ever written, posted, emailed, blogged, texted, or tweeted) that would substantiate that categorization?
- Did you pass or fail the "reasonable person" test, including whether or not you used a reasonable level of force based upon the circumstances?
- Do they believe that you met all four deadly force crite-

ria during *every single moment of the timeline* where you threatened deadly force?
- Was any alcohol in your blood, and if so, does that affect your "reasonable person" argument?
- What statements did you make to the police immediately after the incident? (The answer to this question better be nothing.)
- What did the police uncover during a search of your car or home? (Any search better have been conducted with a warrant, rather than your passive agreement.)

Based upon the answers to those questions, you may not be viewed as the innocent victim. You might be viewed as a hot-headed bully that got the ball rolling, even if the "ball" got rolling months in advance. Here's the reality – in the end, it truly doesn't matter what really happened. What matters is what the prosecutor can get 12 people to believe. If your past behavior leads the jury to agree with the prosecutor's version of events, even an incident where you did everything right might result in your conviction, since your attacker will have his own version of events which might include "this crazy dude pulled a gun on me, so I had to pull my knife to defend myself!" Who will the prosecutor and/or jury believe?

Our best advice? Be nice to everyone; be smart about alcohol use; and don't ever say, email, text, or post anything that could help a prosecutor's case. To quote Mother Teresa, "Treat people with more kindness than is required." While you can't get Mother Teresa to testify on your behalf, her philosophy might help you in the end.

If the prosecutor isn't buying your story, he's going to give you a chance to sell it to 12 jurors, who most decidedly will not be your peers. Don't count on any permit holders or lifetime NRA members to sit on your jury.

USING DEADLY FORCE TO DEFEND YOUR HOME

State laws governing the use of deadly force in defense of our homes (or defense of ourselves or our families while in our homes) generally provide a lower threshold when compared to the lawful use of deadly force outside the home. That difference is derived from the belief that "our home is our castle," and laws making that distinction are often referred to "Castle Doctrine" laws. While the generally accepted rule for the use of deadly force outside the home is to prevent "death or great/grave bodily harm," most state laws authorize a use of deadly force inside the home when the occupant is attempting to end or prevent a felony in the home. (What exactly a "felony" is will vary from state to state, and of course, the prosecutor gets to apply his or her interpretation after the fact). Most states also make a distinction between inside and outside the home when it comes to the requirement to retreat. Outside the home, it is generally an obligation of the victim to retreat if retreat is safe and practical; inside the home, that is generally not a requirement.

When it comes to the applicability of "defense of home" laws versus the general use of force laws, state laws also vary when it comes to defining exactly what the "home" is. Some states will only include the physical structure of your home or apartment, while other states may include detached buildings (such as garages or storage sheds) and others will include any location where you spend the night, such as a hotel, motel, tent, camper, etc.

Because of the variety of state laws, and the fact that the "reasonable person" test will usually apply in any defense of home claim, we recommend that you do the following when defending your home:

- If an intruder is in the home, do *not* attempt to locate him. Barricade yourself and your family in a safe location, call 911, and defend that safe location.
- If an intruder is outside of your home, in your garage, in your storage shed, or attempting to steal your car, do *not* leave your home in an attempt to stop him. Call 911 and only use force to defend your life or the lives of your family.
- One additional tip is to keep an extra set of keys in your bedroom attached to a cyalume glow stick. When the police arrive, alert them that you'll be throwing the keys out a window to allow them to gain entry to the home without kicking down a door.

Now that this burglar has left the home, the rules for "Defense of Dwelling" no longer apply. The four rules governing the use of deadly force are back in place.

WHAT ABOUT USING FORCE TO DEFEND PROPERTY?

While most states' laws allow a use of force to protect property (or to keep it from being stolen) they typically do *not* allow us to use deadly force. The problem is, if you voluntarily step into a situation (i.e. there was nothing reluctant about your decision) with the intent to use force to protect property, and it escalates and deadly force results, you'll find yourself in trouble.

Because of that, our recommendation is that you *not* use force to protect property; instead, we recommend that you get to a safe location or stay in a safe location, and dial 911.

To illustrate the differences between a "defense of property" and a "defense of person," many instructors use the "shark tank" analogy. The analogy asks us "What would it take for me to jump into a shark tank?" "How about if my child fell in?" For most parents, it wouldn't even be a question – they'd jump into the tank in an attempt to rescue their child, even if they knew it could mean their death. The analogy goes on to ask, "Would I jump in to save an expensive watch?" You get the difference? If it isn't worth dying over, then it isn't worth killing over. Dial 911, and stay safe.

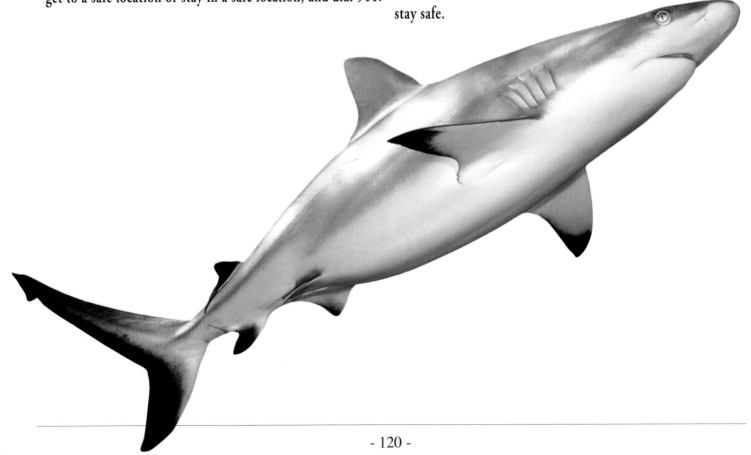

Although most states' laws allow a use of force to stop property crimes, they typically do *not* allow deadly force. If it isn't worth dying over, and if it isn't worth going to jail over, then it isn't worth using (or threatening) deadly force. Call 911 and be a good witness instead.

VIOLENT ENCOUNTERS AND THEIR AFTERMATH

In this chapter, we'll explore the amazing physiological reactions that we should expect to undergo if we're ever involved in a critical incident. We'll also review the steps we should take and the options we might have if we're confronted by a violent criminal. We'll also discuss what we should know about the immediate aftermath, including phone calls we should make and how to deal with the police.

— Understanding Fight or Flight —

— The Physiological Reactions Associated with Extreme Stress —

— Stress Inoculation and Muscle Memory —

— Action versus Reaction —

— Issuing Commands and Reviewing Our Options —

— When We're Left With No Other Choice —

— When the Right to Use Deadly Force Ends —

— The Immediate Aftermath —

— Dealing With the Police —

Chapter 5

If we ever have to use force to defend ourselves, whether we've exposed our firearm or have fired our gun to stop a violent attack, we can expect a rapid series of events to occur prior to, during, and immediately after the incident. The first topic we'll cover in this chapter focuses on the amazing physiological (physical and psychological) reactions that we'll most likely experience in what is generally termed a "critical incident." Within that section, we'll take you on a guided tour of the brain and nervous system, and we'll help you to understand not only *what* kind of reactions you'll most likely experience, but we'll explain *why* they happen as well. As you read the detail surrounding the remarkable transformations that we'll undergo during critical incidents, pay particularly close attention to the "Training Tips" that we've outlined for each topic. These tips are designed to help you embrace each of the physiological effects into your training plan so they'll be expected, rather than come as a surprise.

Also in this chapter, we'll review what we should do in the opening stages of an attack, including a review of our options, and the type of language and commands to use (and not to use). We'll also address the very difficult topic of exactly what we'll need to know if we have *no other choice* but to use deadly force to stop an attack.

Finally, we'll explain what we should do in the immediate aftermath of an attack, including what phone calls we should make, how to deal with the police when they arrive at the scene, and what we should and shouldn't say to the police. It's unfortunate, but the reality is that if we've used our firearm in any capacity, however justified we believed it to be, the police are no longer there to serve and protect us. They are there to serve the prosecuting attorney and protect the case. For that reason, we need to prepare for how to interact with the police after such an incident, including preparing for our arrest.

Finally, we'll also discuss the legal and emotional aftermath that we should be prepared for if we're ever involved in a critical incident. It's an unfortunate reality, but once the incident has ended, the real trouble is just getting started.

" *"Arms discourage and keep the invader and plunderer in awe, and preserve order in the world as well as property... Horrid mischief would ensue were the law-abiding deprived of the use of them."* "

Thomas Paine,
Thoughts On Defensive War, 1775

UNDERSTANDING FIGHT OR FLIGHT

It's been long known that when under extreme stress (including when under attack) the human body will undergo a series of involuntary changes as part of the "fight or flight" mechanisms built into our systems. Anecdotal evidence from the last five wars (including the current two) plus a number of law enforcement studies, have all confirmed that these effects happen, yet very few delve into *why* they happen. Some of the most interesting research we've seen on the topic comes from three of the leading researchers in this field, including Alexis Artwohl, Bill Lewinski, and Bruce Siddle. We've highlighted studies from all three researchers in this section of the book.

In her book "Deadly Force Encounters" (written with co-author Loren Christensen) and subsequent research papers, Dr. Alexis Artwohl provides incredible insight through in-depth interviews with 157 police officers involved in deadly force shootings. The many quotations you'll see in this section are from Dr. Artwohl's interviews, and a summary of her findings are shown in the chart to the right, which shows that approximately 80% of the officers interviewed experienced the most well-known physiological effects, including tunnel vision and diminished sounds, and that more than 50% experienced time distortions or memory loss. Most surprising, more than one in five experienced false memories; that is, they remembered something that *never actually happened.* These and other physical and psychological effects have long been attributed to adrenaline or other natural chemicals that flood our bodies during extreme stress, but the "fight or flight" mechanisms that are part of our systems go well beyond a simple chemical dump by our adrenal glands. They exist as a true survival mechanism that is hardwired into our brains, as surely as an electronic fuse will trip when a short occurs. In this section of the book, we're going to go well beyond explaining *what* kind of physiological effects you're likely to experience during a critical incident; we'll explain *why* these effects occur and how you can work them into your training regimen. To do that, we're going to explore the inner workings of the brain and nervous system, as well as offer a visual explanation for each for these amazing effects.

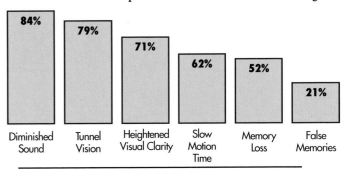

Source: Deadly Force Encounters, Paladin Press
Based on Surveys from 157 Police Officers involved in Deadly Encounters

SUMMARY OF PHYSICAL AND PSYCHOLOGICAL EFFECTS

Effects of the Brain's "Alarm Circuits"
- Reflexive Crouch.
- Hands Elevated to Protect the Face.
- Head Turned and Eyes Locked on Threat.

Effects of Brain's Signals Being Prioritized or Filtered
- Tunnel Vision.
- Heightened Visual Clarity.
- Diminished Sounds.
- Slow Motion Time.
- Memory Loss.
- Memory Distortion or False Memories.
- Inability to Count.

Effects of Adrenaline and Endorphins
- Increase in Strength.
- Heightened Pain Threshold.
- Decrease in Fine Motor Skills.

THE BRAIN AND CENTRAL NERVOUS SYSTEM

The brain is made up of a variety of interconnected structures, but the ones we'll concentrate on are those involved in sensory input and sensory processing, reasoning and planning, movement, and the brain's "alarm circuits." We'll also take a look at a key component of the nervous system called the sympathetic nervous system. To make it a bit easier to understand, we're going to use everyday descriptive terms (such as "the Switchboard") in addition to using the technical term (such as "the thalamus").

THE "SWITCHBOARD"

Our senses (things like sight, sound, and touch) provide sensory and emotional input to our brains, which is routed through a structure called the **thalamus**. The thalamus used to be thought of as nothing more than a relay station, simply passing signals from the senses to the sensory cortex. Now, scientists think of the thalamus as more of a "switchboard" within the brain, making determinations about where input is routed, and which information is filtered or blocked. As it receives sensory input, the thalamus routes that input to the cortex (the long route) and the amygdala (the short route). Under periods of extreme stress, scientists believe that the thalamus can block any sensory input that it doesn't consider necessary to the situation.

THE "THINKER"

The **cortex** not only allows us to plan and reason, it also contains sub-structures to interpret sensory input that has been routed from the thalamus. Like the thalamus (the "Switchboard"), the sensory cortex will selectively process or ignore input based upon the task at hand. For example, when we're focused on a TV program (visual input) we don't always hear our spouse's request to take out the garbage; or, when we're focused on a radio program in the car (audio input), we might ignore the visual input of a stop sign and blow right by it. When we're under extreme stress, this selective processing and prioritization becomes pronounced.

THE "ENGINEER"

The **motor cortex** receives most of its instructions from the thinking and planning part of our brain, but the amygdala also has a direct connection to the motor cortex for those times when it's necessary for us to do something *right now*, such as freezing, ducking, raising our hands, or crouching.

THE "FIRE ALARM"

Sitting next to the **thalamus** is a tiny, almond-shaped structure called the **amygdala**. The amygdala contains most of the brain's alarm circuits designed to react to any imminent threat passed on by the thalamus. When its alarm circuits are tripped, the amygdala has a direct connection to the motor cortex (that is, it skips the reasoning and planning part of the brain) in order to take *immediate* action (such as making us duck if something is thrown at our heads), and to the hypothalamus, to kick our endocrine system into gear. "Evolved" alarms are contained within the amygdala, such as a fear of large, roaring carnivores, while "learned" alarms are accessed by the hippocampus (the "Scrapbook") such as a fear of snakes with rattles.

THE "SCRAPBOOK"

The **hippocampus** provides access to our memories and personal experiences, including any "learned" threats. That recall will include more than just a visual snapshot of the learned threat, it will also recall information about the context and situation surrounding the object. For example, if an individual had been attacked by a thug wielding a baseball bat, the sight of another individual carrying a baseball bat might fire the alarm circuits if the rest of the context met other stored criteria, such as an aggressive facial expression on the part of the person with the bat. On the other hand, a baseball bat in the hands of a smiling little leaguer most likely would not fire those circuits.

THE "PHARMACY"

The sympathetic nervous system involves two additional structures in the brain, namely the **hypothalamus** and the **pituitary gland**, as well as the **adrenal glands**, situated on top of the kidneys. Upon hearing the alarm bells fired by the amygdala, the hypothalamus signals the pituitary gland to release ACTH and endorphins. ACTH alerts the adrenal glands to release adrenaline (also known as epinephrine) into the bloodstream, and endorphins act as a natural pain killer by blocking the body's pain receptors.

THE BRAIN'S LONG ROUTE AND SHORT ROUTE

Of the components described on the preceding page, the amygdala (the "Fire Alarm") is responsible for initiating the body's "fight or flight" defenses whenever it receives sensory input that matches predefined alarm circuits. Sensory input reaches the amygdala from the thalamus (the "Switchboard") along two paths. One path is a direct connection, while the second path is first routed through the sensory cortex (the "Thinker").

The route through the cortex is known as the long route and the direct connection is known as the short route. The components along the long route are often referred to as the higher brain while the components along the short route are often referred to as the lower brain or reptilian brain. Although input is passed from the thalamus along both paths, in most cases, the lower brain remains passive, and our movement and other activity is

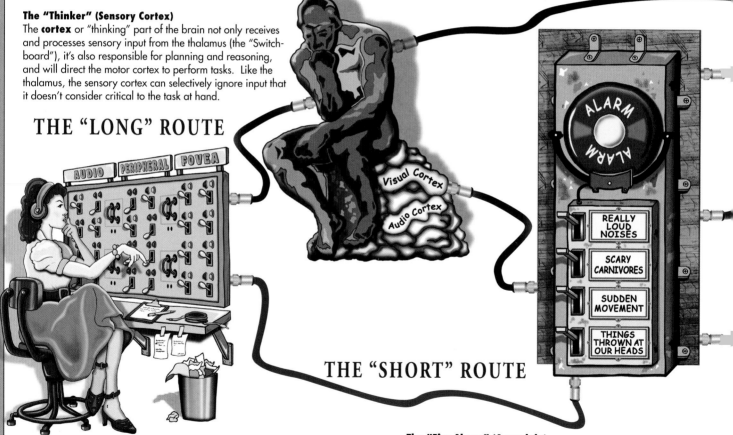

The "Thinker" (Sensory Cortex)
The **cortex** or "thinking" part of the brain not only receives and processes sensory input from the thalamus (the "Switchboard"), it's also responsible for planning and reasoning, and will direct the motor cortex to perform tasks. Like the thalamus, the sensory cortex can selectively ignore input that it doesn't consider critical to the task at hand.

THE "LONG" ROUTE

THE "SHORT" ROUTE

The "Switchboard" (Thalamus)
The **thalamus** can be thought of as the switchboard of the brain, responsible for routing, blocking, or filtering sensory input. In the illustration above, the thalamus has blocked nearly all audio and visual input other than the high resolution fovea at the center of the retina.

The "Fire Alarm" (Amygdala)
The **amygdala** contains the brain's hardwired alarm circuits which will fire if matching input is received from the thalamus, such as a really loud noise (watch any video of soldiers ducking when a mortar shell goes off, and yo just saw the amygdala in action) or when something is thrown at our head

driven by our higher brain as it processes and "thinks about" the input that it's receiving. In cases where the information flowing along the paths matches a predefined alarm circuit, the amygdala effectively throws a switch, and within microseconds, it executes a series of tasks that may include signaling the motor cortex (the "Engineer") to duck into a crouch, rotate toward the perceived threat and lock our eyes on that threat; and it might send a message to the hypothalamus (the "Pharmacy") to get adrenaline moving into the system. Much faster than it would take to think through the situation, the short path through our brain has already prepared us for fight or flight, and it might have already saved us from serious injury or death if it froze our motor cortex before we stepped in front of a speeding bus or ducked our head to protect us from a flying rock.

The "Scrapbook" (Hippocampus)
The **hippocampus** provides access to our memories and experiences, including any "learned" threats and the context surrounding those threats. For example, the hippocampus could access the fact that coiled objects are threats if they're alive and have rattles, but that coiled objects that look like rope are not threats. When matching threat information is identified by the hippocampus, the amygdala will fire its alarm bells.

The "Engineer" (Motor Cortex)
The amygdala has a direct connection to the **motor cortex** for those moments when we need to do something *right now*, such as: freezing; raising our hands to protect our head from a flying rock; or ducking into a crouch, orienting toward a threat, and locking our eyes onto that threat.

The "Pharmacy" (Hypothalamus, Pituitary Gland & Adrenal Gland)
Upon hearing the alarm bells fired by the amygdala, the **hypothalamus** signals the **pituitary gland** to release ACTH and endorphins. ACTH alerts the **adrenal glands** to release adrenaline (also known as epinephrine) into the bloodstream, and endorphins act as a natural pain killer by blocking the body's pain receptors.

THE EFFECTS OF ADRENALINE & ENDORPHINS

As mentioned in the introduction to the structures of the brain and nervous system, the sympathetic nervous system is responsible for releasing adrenaline into the system. Adrenaline immediately prepares the body for "fight or flight" by increasing blood, oxygen, and glucose to the major muscles including the heart; it increases heart rate and oxygen consumption by the lungs, and it dilates the pupils. Side effects will include a loss of manual dexterity in our extremities (most importantly, our hands) and our hands may shake from the loss of blood and the influx of adrenaline. In addition,

the lack of blood on the surface of our skin and the effect of endorphins released by the pituitary gland will provide us with an elevated pain threshold. This can allow us to fight long after we might have given up from injuries, but it also means that we'll need to immediately check ourselves and loved ones for injuries in the immediate aftermath.

Under Stress
Adrenaline forces a constriction of blood vessels to force blood, oxygen, and glucose to the major muscle groups and away from the skin and extremities to allow us to run faster than we've ever run, or fight harder than we've ever fought.

No Stress
When relaxed, the muscles have an equal distribution of blood, oxygen and glucose. The major muscle groups have normal strength and the minor muscle groups have high dexterity.

The manual dexterity that we'll lose under the effects of adrenaline just happens to be the same dexterity required to manipulate holster retention devices, safeties, and slide releases.

TRAINING TIP

Learn to manipulate your firearm's controls as though you were missing your fingertips. That means ignoring your slide release, and racking (or releasing) the slide by grasping it between the palm and four fingers of your support hand. If you want a taste of what your hands might actually feel like under the affects of adrenaline and extreme stress, try this: run through our "Slap, Rack, and Roll Drill" in Chapter Seven, after soaking your hands in a sink full of water and ice cubes for a minute or two. The resulting hand shake and lack of feeling will give you a small taste of the real thing.

THE STRUCTURE OF THE EYE

To understand why visual side effects occur, it's necessary to understand the structure of the eye itself. As shown in the diagram below, the human eye can be thought of as similar to a digital camera. In a camera, the lens focuses the image onto a CCD chip containing millions of light sensitive cells. In the human eye, the lens focuses the image onto the eye's retina which contains more than 100 million photosensitive cells called rods and cones. Rods and cones convert the incoming light into signals which are sent into the visual cortex for processing, via the thalamus (the "Switchboard"). Rods and cones serve different purposes. Rods are designed to operate in low light and they're sensitive to movement, but they see in black and white and are low resolution. Cones provide a much higher resolution image and they see in color, but they are less beneficial in low light. While the majority of the retina has a mixture of rods and cones, the exact center of the retina contains a tiny area called the fovea, composed entirely of the higher resolution cones. Interestingly, the area of the visual cortex that's mapped directly to the fovea is disproportionately large when compared to the area mapped to the remainder of the retina. Said another way, not only does the fovea provide a much higher resolution image when compared to the rest of the eye, but the brain also sets aside a much greater amount of power to process that input. Although the entire retina provides as much as 200 degrees of peripheral vision, the higher resolution fovea provides no more than a few degrees of vision. Don't believe it? Try this test – stare at any word on this page and try to identify any other word at least three to four words away. You'll pretty easily see that the word you're focused on looks high resolution, while every other word appears low resolution and is most likely illegible.

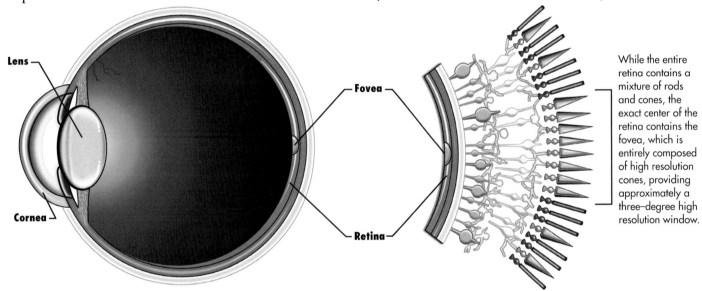

While the entire retina contains a mixture of rods and cones, the exact center of the retina contains the fovea, which is entirely composed of high resolution cones, providing approximately a three-degree high resolution window.

VISUAL DISORTIONS

TUNNEL VISION AND HEIGHTENED VISUAL CLARITY

So why does tunnel vision and heightened visual clarity occur? As shown in our brain schematic, the thalamus acts as the brain's switchboard, not only deciding *where* to route signals, but also *if* it should route a signal at all. Under extreme stress, the thalamus filters out what it considers to be non-critical sensory input, which may include filtering out visual input other than the information from the eye's high resolution fovea. That means that our visual input might be reduced to no more than a few degrees (which equates to about a 12-inch circle at 20 feet) but the input that is processed, is *extremely* high resolution. That corresponds with reports from survivors of violent attacks who experienced tunnel vision and who often couldn't describe their assailant, but could describe their assailant's weapon in detail, as though they were reviewing a high resolution picture.

DISTANCE DISTORTION

Survivors of critical incidents have also reported distance distortion, either believing that their attacker was much closer or much farther away than he actually was. Tunnel vision can cause us to believe that an attacker was farther away than he actually was, since we're losing most of our stereoscopic vision, which is required for depth perception. The "high resolution effect" or "heightened visual clarity" can lead us to believe the attacker was *closer* than he actually was, since under normal circumstances, we know the difference between how clear and well-

focused a person or object is at different distances. Under the effects of extreme stress, when the brain is limiting the visual input to the high resolution area at the center of the retina, a person who is actually at 20 feet may look like he has the same clarity and detail as a person at, say, 10 feet. Our replay of the incident would incorrectly conclude that the person was closer than he actually was.

> " *I told the SWAT team that the suspect was firing at me from down a long dark hallway about 40 feet long. When I went back to the scene the next day, I was shocked to discover that he had actually been only about 5 feet in front of me in an open room. There was no dark hallway.* "

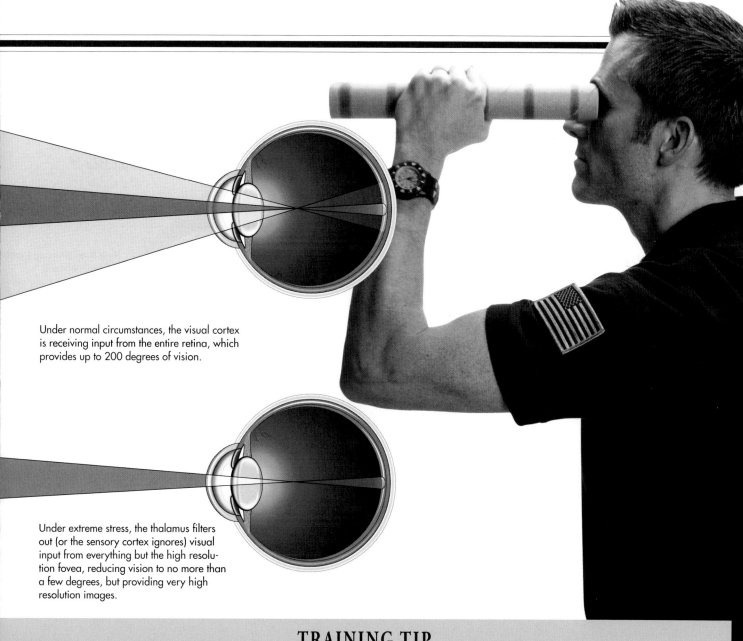

Under normal circumstances, the visual cortex is receiving input from the entire retina, which provides up to 200 degrees of vision.

Under extreme stress, the thalamus filters out (or the sensory cortex ignores) visual input from everything but the high resolution fovea, reducing vision to no more than a few degrees, but providing very high resolution images.

TRAINING TIP

Take a look through a paper towel tube to get a sense of what the scene will look like with just three degrees of visibility. With that mental picture, train yourself to elevate your firearm up into that three–degree window and physically move your head, rather than just your eyes, when engaging multiple targets. When running drills on the range, practice lowering your firearm to a low ready once the drill is complete, and perform a 360° scan of the area by physically moving your head. In a critical incident, this head movement can reset the filtering that occurs within the thalamus or sensory cortex.

DIMINISHED SOUND (AUDITORY EXCLUSION)

Selective auditory exclusion happens all the time (just try to get the attention of a six-year-old when he's watching SpongeBob). This is nothing more than the sensory cortex's prioritization of one signal over another, which also explains why we can hold a conversation in a crowded room full of noise. During non-critical moments, we can easily change our sensory focus by listening to a different conversation or temporarily ignoring audio input while we focus on visual input. This is an everyday function of our sensory cortex – it allows us to selectively process sensory input to accomplish the task at hand. However, once the brain's alarm circuits have been fired, the thalamus (the "Switchboard") appears to literally halt the flow of audio signals to the cortex. This corresponds with interviews from the Artwohl research, where police officers who experienced auditory exclusion *knew* their firearms should be going "bang," they were *listening* for their firearms to go "bang," yet all they heard was a "pop" or no sound at all. Interestingly, while the thalamus appears to halt the flow of audio signals along the "long route," it appears as though the signal flow along the "short route" is uninterrupted. In a study conducted by Bruce and Kevin Siddle of PPCT Management Systems in 2004, researchers put 49 police officers in an enclosed trailer, and ran the officers through an intense force-on-force drill, where the officers were fired on from three different "attackers." During the 30 second "attack," the researchers sounded an air horn, which in the enclosed space, should have been deafening. During the debriefing, when the officers were asked if they heard the air horn, fully 97% replied that they *never heard it*. The video tape, however, told a different story – 39 percent of the officers who said that they never

heard the air horn still reacted to it by flinching, or by briefly orienting toward the sound. That indicates that the thalamus-to-amygdala connection remained in place, which allowed the amygdala to continue its automated processes, even though the "thinking" part of the brain was left out of the loop.

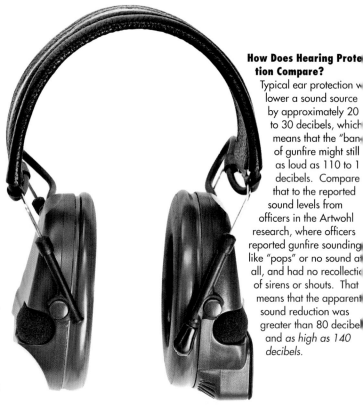

How Does Hearing Protection Compare?

Typical ear protection will lower a sound source by approximately 20 to 30 decibels, which means that the "bang" of gunfire might still as loud as 110 to 1 decibels. Compare that to the reported sound levels from officers in the Artwohl research, where officers reported gunfire sounding like "pops" or no sound at all, and had no recollection of sirens or shouts. That means that the apparent sound reduction was greater than 80 decibels and *as high as 140 decibels.*

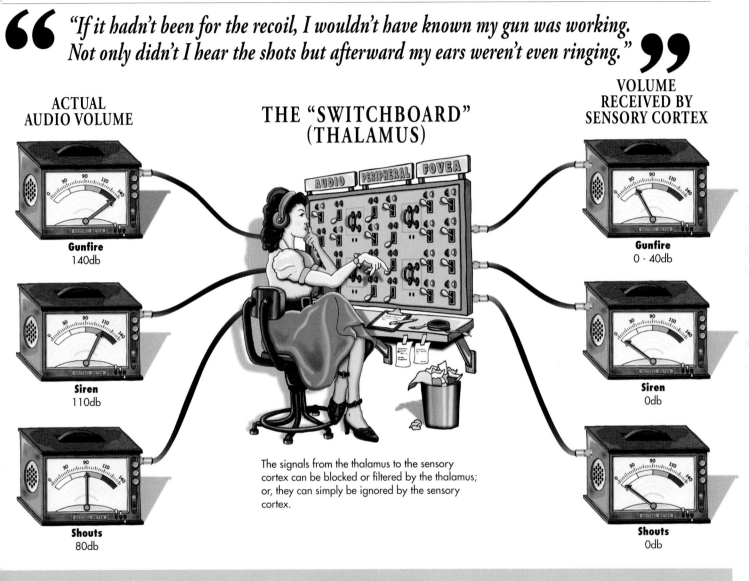

"If it hadn't been for the recoil, I wouldn't have known my gun was working. Not only didn't I hear the shots but afterward my ears weren't even ringing."

ACTUAL AUDIO VOLUME

THE "SWITCHBOARD" (THALAMUS)

VOLUME RECEIVED BY SENSORY CORTEX

AUDIO   PERIPHERAL   FOVEA

Gunfire
140db

Siren
110db

Shouts
80db

Gunfire
0 - 40db

Siren
0db

Shouts
0db

The signals from the thalamus to the sensory cortex can be blocked or filtered by the thalamus; or, they can simply be ignored by the sensory cortex.

TRAINING TIP

With a buddy's assistance, try our "Slap, Rack, and Roll Drill" in Chapter Seven, with live stereo ear pieces inserted under your normal hearing protection. Turn up the volume loud enough so that the combination of music and hearing protection drowns out all other sounds. This will teach you to recognize your firearm's proper operation and failures by feel alone. You'll learn to trust that your firearm actually fired even though you didn't hear the "bang," and you'll learn to identify failures through a lack of recoil, rather than a lack of sound. During this exercise, your buddy can alert you to any range commands that you'll be unable to hear.

SLOW MOTION TIME

Processing the input of sensory information requires processing power, no different than a computer requires processing power to run applications. During non-stressful situations, our sensory cortex must balance the processing of a variety of sensory input, including sound, touch, smell, and about 200 degrees of visual input. Under periods of extreme stress when the thalamus has shut down all sensory input except for the high resolution fovea, we'll suddenly have throughput and processing power to spare. So what does that have to do with the "slow motion effect" reported in the Artwohl research? In part, it's due to the fact that most of our perception of time is based upon the sensory input that we receive. Under extreme stress, the unusually high volume of visual information that's passed to and processed by our cortex can be interpreted by our conscious self as time slowing down, rather than the "processing" or "throughput" speeding up. To use another computer analogy, let's assume that a computer is running ten applications, including a video processing application that

normally processes one gigabyte of video per second. If the other nine applications were suddenly shut down, the computer might suddenly jump to processing 10 gigabytes per second. the computer's clock was based upon how many gigabytes we processed, it would now record that ten seconds had passed for each real second, which from the computer's perspective, is the most logical conclusion (rather than concluding that its processing power had somehow magically increased). That's over simplification, but it paints an easy picture to understand

5 Seconds at Twice the Volume of Visual Input Can be Interpreted by the Mind as 10 Seconds
During periods of extreme stress when the thalamus is blocking virtually all sensory input other than the high resolution fovea, we'll not only have a much wider stream of high resolution visual input, but we'll suddenly have the processing power to handle it. Continuing the analogy to film, it's like jumping from 24 frames per second to 48 frames per second or more. The result can be like something straight out of "The Matrix," such as the amazing quote from the Artwohl research on the opposite page.

> *"During a violent shoot-out I looked over, drawn to the sudden mayhem, and was puzzled to see beer cans slowly floating through the air past my face. What was even more puzzling was that they had the word Federal printed on the bottom. They turned out to be the shell casings ejected by the officer who was firing next to me."*

5 Seconds of Real Time

Although light enters the eye as a continuous stream and not as individual "frames," the analogy to film helps to explain why slow motion time occurs. During normal, non-stressful situations, the cortex will process a balance of sensory information in order to accomplish the task at hand. Visual processing might be comparable to traditional motion picture film at 24 frames per second. That's enough visual input to walk without tripping over our feet, and to catch a ball without getting hit in the face, yet it's slow enough to cause motion blur. For example, empty shell casings flying by our face will appear as a blur.

TRAINING TIP

Build the knowledge of "slow motion time" into your mental scenarios and practice your drills at a measured, not frenzied, pace. The best training tip is to simply be aware that it exists so that if you find yourself in a critical incident, you can tell yourself "here it is," rather than "what's happening to me?!?" There are 100,000 years of human evolution behind this capability – take advantage of it.

In order to recall a memory, our hippocampus (the "Scrapbook") actually reconstructs it by integrating elements of that memory scattered in various locations of our brain. For example, for us to recall a camping trip from the previous summer, the brain doesn't open a "file" the same way a computer file is opened; instead, the hippocampus reconstructs the memory by recalling separately stored memories connected via pathways of what we did, saw, smelled, tasted, and heard on that trip. Memories are also associative, which means that newer memories are more easily recalled if we can associate them with previously acquired knowledge. For example, if the camping trip reminded us of an earlier trip we'd been on, it would be easier to recall the details of the more recent event. Under extreme stress, we're lacking both of those fundamental "recall" operations. Instead of a variety of elements stored for that memory, we might have only a single element captured (visual) and we most likely have no previous memories to associate it with. In addition, in order to be recalled in the first place, memories must have been transferred to long term memory (also managed by the hippocampus), which required them to be transferred from "sensory memory" (which might last less than a second) to short term or "working" memory (which might last less than a minute), to long term memory. Under extreme stress, the hippocampus may simply discard information that it doesn't consider necessary to survival, never moving the input past sensory or short term memory. The Artwohl research includes multiple incidents where officers blacked out on one or more parts of the incident, including their own actions, such as forgetting phone calls they made, how many rounds they fired, or even whether or not they fired their own gun.

> " *When I got home after the shooting, my wife told me that I had called her on my cell phone during the pursuit of the violent suspect just prior to the shooting. I have no memory of making that phone call.* "

EVENT

Input passed through the thalamus will first reside in "sensory" memory. If it is passed on, it will next reside in short term or "working" memory.

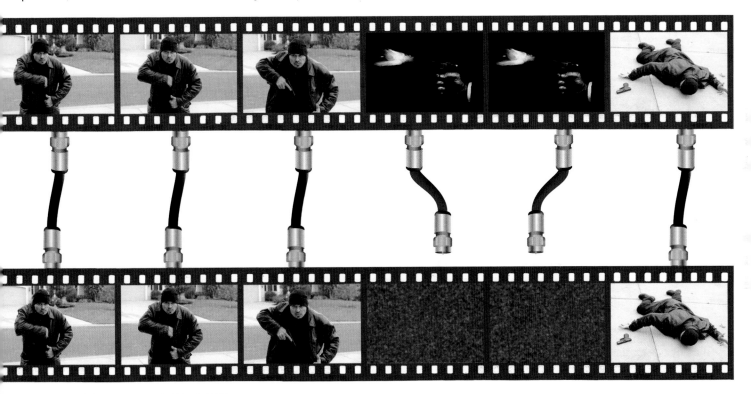

LONG TERM MEMORY

Only memories that have been passed to long term memory are available for recall. If the thalamus blocked the input, or the hippocampus failed to move it to long term memory, it simply *will not be there for recall.*

TRAINING TIP

Build the aftermath into your mental scenarios to include the phone calls and limited statement to the police described later in this chapter. In the Artwohl research, more than 50 percent of police officers involved in critical incidents had memory loss for at least some part of the critical incident. You *must* speak with your lawyer and have him or her review any evidence before you and your lawyer review the incident with the police.

MEMORY DISTORTION OR FALSE MEMORIES

At any given moment, the information that's within our short term or "working" memory can be anything. It can include sensory input such as what we're looking at or listening to; or it can simply be thoughts or imagination, such as imagining what we'll have for dinner, picturing a loved one, or replaying a tune in our head. When we're in the middle of a critical incident, those "thoughts" might include imagining what it would be like if we or our companion were shot with the attacker's gun; or it could be vivid thoughts of loved ones; or, it could be a tune replaying in our head. Unfortunately, when we're under the extreme stress of an attack, those random thoughts can be transferred to our long term memory as though they actually occurred. Whether or not this is a survival mechanism (for example, the image of a gravely injured loved one might force us to fight even harder) or whether it's simply a "bug," the Artwohl research confirmed that the phenomenon occurred in more than one in five officers interviewed, including the vivid, yet false memory described in the quote below.

Working Memory (or the Subconscious)
Our working memory can include not only input that's been passed on from the thalamus, it can also contain thoughts, fears, and imagination.

> 66 *"I saw the suspect suddenly point his gun at my partner. As I shot (the suspect), I saw my partner go down in a spray of blood. I ran over to help my partner, and he was standing there unharmed. The suspect never even got off a shot."* 99

EVENT

Input passed through the thalamus will first reside in sensory memory. If it is passed on, it will next reside in short term or working memory.

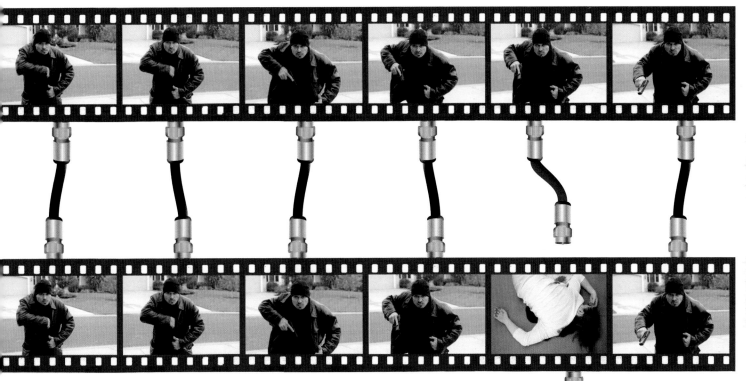

LONG TERM MEMORY

Under extreme stress, the hippocampus might not only store actual events into our long term memory, it might also "log" into long term memory images that had resided within our subconscious, as though they had actually occurred.

TRAINING TIP

Build the aftermath into your mental scenarios to include the phone calls and limited statement to the police described later in this chapter. In the Artwohl research, nearly one in five police officers involved in critical incidents recalled events that never occurred. You *must* speak with your lawyer and have him or her review any evidence before you and your lawyer review the incident with the police.

Incredibly positive things result from the automated processes described on the previous pages, including the ability to find strength to escape, evade, or fight beyond what we believed possible. However, these involuntary reactions are evolutionarily designed to help us fight off attacking wolves more than they're designed to fight off 21st-century rapists, robbers, and murderers. So what does that mean to 21st-century humans who want to properly train to survive a critical incident? It means we need to understand these involuntary reactions, and rather than fight them (or pretend that we can train hard enough to override them), we need to embrace them and make them part of our training.

STRESS INOCULATION

To a point, learned behavior will affect the routing of signals controlled by the lower brain. As an example, if the average person were plucked off the street and dropped in the middle of the Serengeti to face a charging elephant, the amygdala would fire all alarm bells and route all signals necessary to prepare the person to run faster than he's ever run in his life. This includes routing blood into his lungs, heart, and major muscles, and voiding his bowel and bladder (sorry to break it to you, but it happens). On the other hand, if a seasoned elephant hunter were dropped into the same situation, the amygdala would know from learned experiences recalled by the hippocampus that it can limit its signals to increasing the heartbeat and requesting that the adrenal glands give the hunter a quick shot of adrenaline (just in case he or she *also*

needs to run really, really fast). Despite this, no one knows just how much "learning" we'll need, to have even a hope of inoculating ourselves against the natural inclination of the brain to follow its hard-wired instructions. It would be fair to say that individuals who have trained extensively in force-on-force scenarios, virtual simulation, and other reality-based training (which we'll discuss in Chapter Seven), and who have mentally conditioned themselves to expect surprises, will recover more quickly from the automated responses than individuals who shoot only casually (or not at all) at their local range. But it's also fair to say that the vast majority of permit holders don't train extensively in force-on-force scenarios, and it would be foolish to pretend that an hour a month at the local range, or even a 5-day session once a year at an advanced school, will override the brain's hardwiring. It's better to assume that it exists and to build a training regimen (and statements to the police) around it. To hear more about "stress inoculation," check out the introduction to Chapter Seven.

WHAT EXACTLY IS MUSCLE MEMORY?

When a certain skill or movement is practiced repeatedly, pathways are actually modified in the cerebellum to store the learned memory of movements for near automatic playback (what's commonly referred to as "muscle memory"). As an example, new students learning to draw from the holster will learn that there are four steps involved, and they'll practice those movements in four distinct steps. But after thousands of repetitions, those four movements have become fluid, and the "experts" may not even be able to answer the question, "How many steps does it take to draw the handgun from the holster?" To them, the process is fluid and automatic (they might even say, "It takes just one step.") No one knows just how many times a task or series of tasks will need to be repeated before it's ready for "automatic playback," but suffice to say, it's going to be more than plinking at the range a couple times a year. Dry firing and drawing from the holster with a cleared firearm are both ways that these pathways can be built, all without a shot ever being fired.

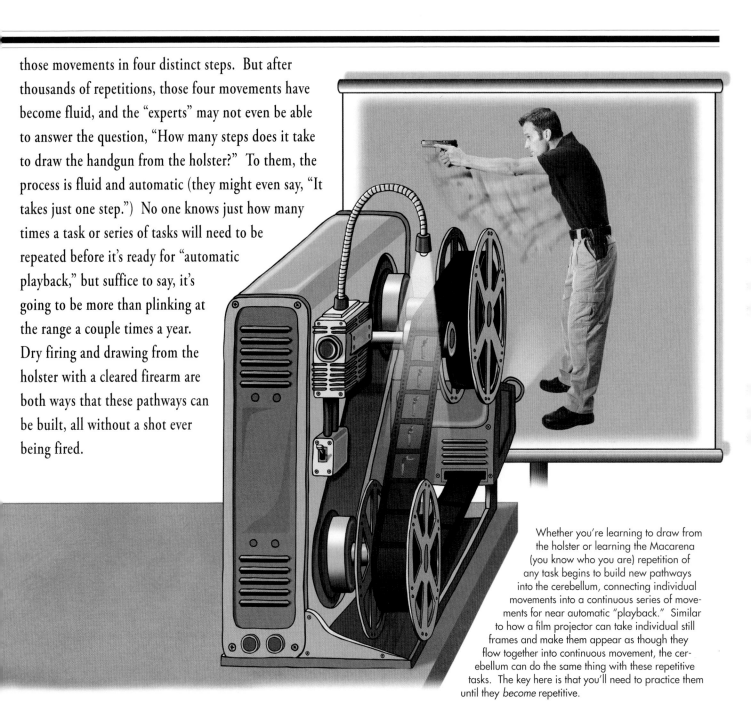

Whether you're learning to draw from the holster or learning the Macarena (you know who you are) repetition of any task begins to build new pathways into the cerebellum, connecting individual movements into a continuous series of movements for near automatic "playback." Similar to how a film projector can take individual still frames and make them appear as though they flow together into continuous movement, the cerebellum can do the same thing with these repetitive tasks. The key here is that you'll need to practice them until they *become* repetitive.

IS ACTION FASTER THAN REACTION?

If an attacker unexpectedly lunges at you with a knife, can you draw your firearm in time to stop him? Can you "out draw" an attacker if he already has a firearm pointed at you? When the threat ends, how quickly can you stop shooting? Is there any plausible explanation for why an attacker might be shot in the back? These hypothetical situations all beg the question, "Is action faster than reaction?"

If we're going to prepare ourselves for the reality of shooting in self-defense, and the reality of defending our actions in court, it's critical to understand the limitations of human reaction time, and how those limitations should affect our preparation and training, as well as our defense in a court of law.

To help prepare ourselves for those realities, we're going to take a look at two studies which analyzed reaction times to visual stimuli. The first study analyzed braking reaction time, while the second study analyzed the reaction time required for shooters to start shooting, and to stop shooting. The results of both studies will help to answer the questions posed earlier.

BRAKING: HOW LONG DOES IT TAKE TO STOP?

Before we delve into reaction times of law abiding citizens defending themselves from attack, let's take a look at a study analyzing the reaction times of drivers to a braking maneuver. In the article "How Long Does It Take To Stop? Methodological Analysis of Driver Perception-Brake Times" published in 2000, researchers concluded that "reaction time" was actually a sequence of multiple stages. For our purposes, we'll group

We've all tried the "dollar bill" trick, where one individual drops a dollar bill without warning, and a second person tries grabbing it. The question is, why is it so difficult to catch the dollar, even though we're expecting it to be dropped? As shown in the studies outlined in this section, researchers know that even when a stimulus is expected, humans require between one-quarter and one-half of a second to perceive and process the input, and on average, another .06 seconds to complete even the simplest movements such as pressing a trigger, or pinching our fingers to catch a dollar bill. In the "dollar bill" trick, gravity beats reaction time, since even the fastest reaction time of .31 seconds results in the dollar bill falling just over a foot and a half before the brain can process the input, and the fingers can pinch closed.

them into the following components:

- *Perception/Cognitive Processing Time.* This is the time required for the individual to receive, recognize, and process the sensory signal (auditory, visual, etc.), and to formulate a response. Referring back to our brain schematic, it's the time required for the sensory input to pass the "Switchboard" (the thalamus) and get processed by the "Thinker" (the sensory cortex).

- *Motor Reaction Time.* This is the time required for the individual to perform the required movement, such as lifting the foot off the accelerator and applying the brake. In other words, it's the time required for the "Engineer" (the motor cortex) to request movement, and the muscles to respond.

In this study, researchers tested braking reaction times under three scenarios: when the braking maneuver was expected, when it was unexpected, and when it came as a surprise. The results are summarized in the chart below.

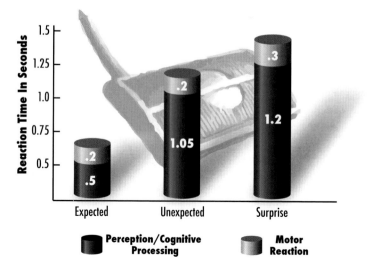

Perception/Cognitive Processing — Motor Reaction

As shown in the chart, when a braking maneuver was unexpected or came as a surprise, the perception/cognitive processing time that occurred before movement began ranged from just over one second to 1.2 seconds. Even when the maneuver was expected, the perception/cognitive processing time was .5 seconds before movement began. Before analyzing these numbers further, let's take a look at the Tempe study, which analyzed police officer reaction times to start and stop shooting.

THE TEMPE STUDY

In 2003, 102 police officers from the Tempe, Arizona Police Department underwent a series of tests conducted by Dr. Bill Hudson and Dr. Bill Lewinski, to measure their reaction time to start and stop shooting based upon visual stimuli. In these experiments, the officers were expecting the stimuli; they knew they should start and stop shooting based upon the stimuli; and they began the experiment with their trigger finger already in the trigger guard (that is, perception/cognitive processing time, and motor reaction time were kept to an absolute minimum).

Experiment #1: Time to Press the Trigger

The first test was designed to determine the officers' average response time to press the trigger based upon the visual stimulus of a light. Results indicated that the officers, on average, took 25/100ths of a second to react to the light, and another 6/100ths of a second to press the trigger, for a total response time of 31/100ths of a second.

Experiment #2: Time to Stop Pressing the Trigger

In this experiment, the officers were intentionally misled as to the basis of the experiment. During the briefing, they were

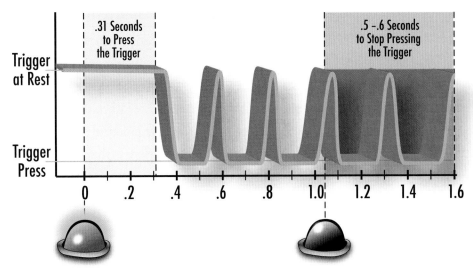

The chart to the left illustrates a "trigger pull plot" collected during the Tempe Study. The peaks and valleys indicate the actual trigger presses, with the upper boundary showing the trigger at rest, and the lower boundary showing the trigger fully pressed. The start of the plot shows the perception/cognitive processing time that occurred before the initial trigger press (the start of the first valley). The end of the plot shows two additional trigger presses after the light went out.

informed that the test was to measure how quickly they could press the trigger – the trigger press was to begin when the light went on, and end when the light went out. The officers were also informed that they would lose points if they fired after the light went out – that is, they had extra motivation to react quickly, and to *not* fire the gun after the light went out. During this test, the researchers determined that when multitasking, the average officer required between 5/10ths and 6/10ths of a second to react to the light going out, and to stop pressing the trigger. Since the trigger could be pressed much faster (6/100ths of a second) than the officers could react to the changed conditions (at least 5/10ths of a second), each officer pressed the trigger at least twice, and sometimes three times after the light indicated they should stop shooting.

MULTI-TASKING AND ITS EFFECT ON REACTION TIME

In both studies, researchers concluded that the more an individual was multi-tasking or the more complex the required movement was, the longer the reaction times would be. That conclusion is echoed in a summary of multiple driving studies compiled by the National Safety Council, where the NSC concluded that driver multi-tasking added an average of .6 seconds to the response time required for braking. During the Tempe study, multi-tasking was limited (the officers were only focused on the light and trigger press), however the researchers pointed out that during critical incidents, officers were very likely "moving, pointing, ducking, seeking cover, shooting, processing, reacting emotionally, etc.," which would affect their overall ability to start and stop shooting.

CONCLUSION

Based upon the results of both studies, it's clear that "reaction time" is more than just the time required to draw a firearm, press a trigger, or press a brake – reaction time also includes at least one-quarter of a second, and as much as 1.2 seconds of perception/cognitive processing before *any* movement takes place (and that's in ideal, controlled conditions). Taking those numbers and placing them in the context of self-defense, let's try to answer the questions first posed in this section:

If an attacker lunges at you with a knife, can you draw your firearm in time to stop him? That depends on how close the attacker is. Since attacks are almost always a surprise, we should assume that we'd need 1.2 seconds to perceive and process the fact that we're under attack, plus the time required to draw our firearm and align it with the attacker. Let's assume the motor reaction time takes two seconds (the time to orient toward the attacker, and draw our firearm from concealment). That means that our full reaction might take 3.2 seconds or more, which is enough time for an attacker to cover more than 50 feet. So the answer to the question is, "Are you more than 50 feet away from the attacker?" or better yet "How closely were you observing your surroundings?"

Can you "out draw" an attacker if he already has a firearm pointed at you? No. Based upon the results of the Tempe study, we can conclude that an attacker will require just 6/100ths of a second to press the trigger, while we'll need as much as 1.2 seconds of perception/cognitive processing time, before any movement can begin, including drawing our own firearm, or ducking behind cover. Our best bet in this situation is to count on Jeff Cooper's description of an inadequate or inept attacker.

When the threat ends, how quickly can you stop shooting? Based upon the Tempe study, the answer is at least 5/10ths of a second when multi-tasking, and longer when engaged in multiple tasks simultaneously, such as moving, seeking cover, etc. Asked another way, "Once the trigger press has started, if the attacker throws down his weapon, can the defender stop himself in time?" The answer is no. The test indicated that the time required to react to the changed condition was more than *eight times* the time required to abort a trigger press – once the trigger press began, it was simply impossible to stop it, even if the situation had changed.

Is there any plausible explanation for why an attacker might be shot in the back? Yes. An attacker, who has already made the decision to turn around, could complete that simple movement in as little as 2/10ths of a second, while the defender would require 5/10ths of a second or more to stop shooting. In the Tempe study, officers pressed the trigger twice, and sometimes *three times* after the conditions indicated they should stop shooting.

In summary, the short answer is that action *always* beats reaction. While automated responses (responses governed by the "short route" through the brain) can be near instantaneous (such as ducking into a crouch when a loud noise occurs), the cognitive responses discussed here (responses governed by the "long route" through the brain) are not instantaneous. Because of that, we must compensate by:

- Being hyper-aware of our surroundings and the individuals within our protective bubble.

- Preparing for a possible attacker *before* it occurs by increasing distance, orienting toward the possible threat, taking cover, and/or preparing to access our firearm.

- Making intelligent decisions about our equipment and carry techniques – for example, too many holster retention devices, or too many layers of clothing, can slow a response.

RECOGNIZING A THREAT & "GETTING OFF THE LINE"

Now that we've addressed the physiological reactions that are likely to accompany any violent attack, let's talk about the attack itself. While it's fair to say there is no "typical" attack, it's also fair to say that an attack will not begin with the bad guy 300 feet away, screaming "Give me your wallet!" and waving a knife. Instead, it might occur with an individual angling toward us on the street pretending to talk on his cell phone before he pulls a knife inches away from us; or, stepping out of the shadows when we're already upon him. Because of this, we need to be constantly aware of our surroundings and we must *live* the color codes of awareness described in Chapter One. We also need to be prepared to shift from Yellow to Orange to Red, without finding ourselves paralyzed by thinking "this can't be happening" or "this can't be what I think it is." Once our "mental trigger" has been tripped, we must *immediately* throw our plan into action, which may include engaging the threat. If we do find ourselves facing an immediate threat and there is no possibility of escape, two things should immediately occur. First, we should quickly take a large lateral step to move off the "line of attack." Stepping laterally not only throws off our attacker's advance, it also drops us into a crouched position, preparing us to take up a shooting stance if required. Second, we should forcefully issue commands in a "command voice."

If we find ourselves facing an attacker from any direction, we need to immediately disrupt his momentum by taking a large lateral step off the line that the attacker is approaching on, and turn to face the attacker. This lateral move combined with issuing forceful commands (as well as sweeping back our covering garment if the situation requires it) may cause even the most determined attacker to break off his attack. If not, it orients our body toward the attacker, and puts us into a crouched position in preparation to draw our firearm.

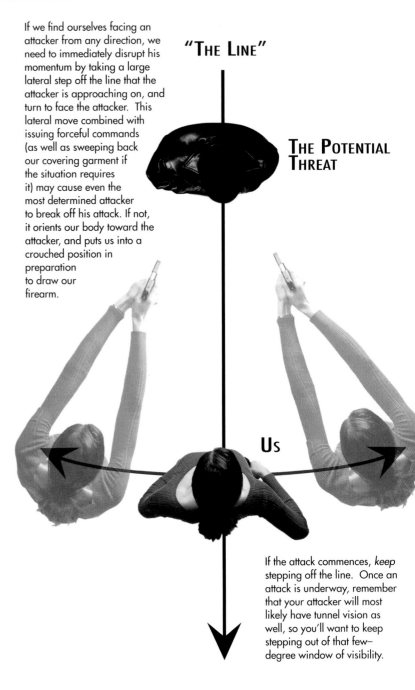

"THE LINE"

THE POTENTIAL THREAT

US

If the attack commences, *keep* stepping off the line. Once an attack is underway, remember that your attacker will most likely have tunnel vision as well, so you'll want to keep stepping out of that few-degree window of visibility.

MORE ON LATERAL MOVEMENT

In Chapter One, we discussed Dennis Tueller's experiments which demonstrated that an attacker could cover 21 feet in approximately 1.5 seconds, the same amount of time an experienced shooter could draw his firearm and place two rounds on target. Experts have observed that an attacker who can cover 21 feet in 1.5 seconds can cover 32 feet in 2.25 seconds, and that even if an attacker is hit by your defensive rounds, he may have enough oxygen and adrena-line to be in complete control for another 5 – 15 seconds. Those experts suggest that you NEVER stop thinking about increasing the distance between you and the attacker, and that in addition to moving backward, you also move laterally as well, giving yourself precious seconds to act. The Tactical "T" drill described below is used by police officers during tactical training to instill the idea of lateral movement, in addition to rearward movement.

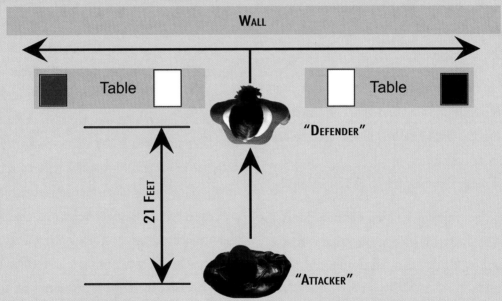

THE TACTICAL "T" DRILL

1 The drill is initiated by the "defender" drawing the top card from a pile that's on her strong side. As soon as the defender breaks eye contact with the "attacker," the attacker charges.

2 If the defender has drawn a black card, she must take a step or two back while drawing her replica firearm, and move laterally toward the black poster; if she's drawn a red card, she moves toward the red poster.

3 The goal is to reach the end of the table while maintaining distance between the defender and attacker, all while moving backward and laterally, and maintaining the firearm on the attacker. Extra credit for being able to round the table back to where you started without being touched.

Materials Needed:
- Two rectangular tables.
- One standard set of playing cards.
- One red and one black poster board.
- Red or blue replica/dummy firearm only!

ISSUING COMMANDS & EVALUATING OPTIONS

Issuing commands during a violent encounter does two things. Most importantly, it immediately identifies us as someone who will not be an easy victim, which may cause the attacker to break off his attack. As mentioned in Chapter One, the average criminal is hoping to find an easy victim in "condition white." Imagine his surprise if his potential victim suddenly takes a large lateral step and shouts "Stay back! Get away from me!" while raising a hand in a stop gesture. Secondly, issuing commands alerts anyone within the immediate vicinity that an attack is underway and that we're the non-aggressor.

When we do issue commands, we need to bark them out in a command voice, deep from the diaphragm. Even the smallest individual can pack a verbal punch when he or she practices commands such as:

"Stay back! Get away from me! Drop your weapon!"

You'll notice that the language we used was non-threatening and identifies us as the victim. Remember that witnesses may repeat everything that you say, so avoid language like this:

"If you come any closer, I'll kill you!" – Or – "I'm going to blow your %*$@ing head off!"

Our advice is to work these verbal commands into the mental scenarios discussed in Chapter One, as well as into your range or virtual exercises. In fact, you'll have the opportunity to practice using these commands and moving "off the line" during the realistic virtual simulations available at Gander Mtn. Academy. Training consistently with this method gives us the confidence that commands and movement will be an automated part of our defense in a critical incident.

WHAT ARE OUR OPTIONS?

So we've found ourselves in the middle of a situation that we didn't start and we couldn't avoid. What should our goal be at this point? Besides the obvious answer of survival, our goal should be to do *anything that affects our attacker's ability to commence an attack.* It's important to remember that in most violent attacks, we have options – finding cover, putting barriers between us and the attacker, or choosing a less–than–lethal level of force such as exposing our firearm or even pointing it at the attacker. *Anything* that causes our attacker to break off his attack before it begins is a good thing. Finally, it's important to realize that our decision to use *any* level of force will be second-guessed by the police, the prosecutor, and possibly a jury. We'll have to meet the "reasonableness" test, and if a prosecutor believes that we used excessive force, we're going to have to try to convince a jury that we're right, and the prosecutor is wrong.

Escape
Even after a violent attack has commenced, if we can escape, we *should* escape.

Cover and Barriers
We should place *anything* between us and the attacker that can protect us from the attacker's weapon(s) or that can disrupt his attack.

Verbal Commands
Forcefully barking out commands such as "Stay back! Get away from me!" will give your attacker a chance to change his mind before it's too late. As mentioned in Chapter One, the average criminal is hoping to find an easy victim in "Condition White," and verbal commands will indicate that you are anything but.

Drawing Our Firearm
It's a big jump up on the "Use of Force" continuum, but drawing our firearm immediately indicates to a determined attacker that we're not going to be an easy victim. Forcefully barking out commands such as "Stop!" also gives him a chance to change his mind before it's too late. Remember that just because you've drawn your firearm does *not* mean that you need to press the trigger.

Using Our Firearm
When we have *no other choice*, we need to be prepared to stop the threat with any force necessary.

WHEN WE'RE LEFT WITH NO OTHER CHOICE

Up to this point in the book, it's fair to say that everything we've discussed has been fairly academic, including the deadly force scenarios that were discussed in Chapter Four. On this page, we're going to need to discuss the most serious topic in the book, namely, shooting at another human being. We truly wish this topic never had to be discussed, but we also wish that criminals didn't murder, rape, assault, and rob. While we'd be the first in line to buy a Star Wars blaster that could be set on stun (seriously, we'd buy one) we're not lucky enough to have that option. Until that day, if we *do* find ourselves in a situation that we didn't start and we can't escape from, where all four rules governing the use of deadly force have been met, then we have no choice but to *stop the threat with any force necessary.*

WHERE DO WE SHOOT?

As discussed in Chapter Three on shooting fundamentals, if we must use our firearm, our goal is "defensive accuracy." Defensive accuracy is any round that *significantly affects the attacker's ability to continue his attack.* The illustration to the right is a fair approximation of the human body, internally and externally. Where would you shoot to meet the goal of defensive accuracy? Would you shoot for the arm or shoulder? How about the attacker's hand? If those shots hit, they might affect the attacker's *desire* to continue an attack, but probably not his *ability.* Remember that your attacker will also be under the effects of adrenaline and endorphins, and he'll have a heightened pain threshold. If he's consumed illicit drugs such as Methamphetamine, his pain threshold will be even higher. It's very pos-

sible that he wouldn't even *feel* a bullet if it passed through one of the areas on the diagram that contains no bone or organs. How about if you missed those small, moving targets? Remember that under the physiological effects that you'll undergo, your accuracy is likely to suffer, and the penalty for a miss can range from lost seconds and one less bullet, to the death of an innocent bystander. Keep in mind that we've moved beyond the academic and we're now talking about what it would take to stop an attacker who is seconds away from (or is already) stabbing you, shooting you, choking you, raping you, or beating you. It's a cold reality, but the fastest, surest, safest way (safest to innocent bystanders, not safest to the attacker) to significantly affect an attacker's ability to continue an attack, is to use the method taught to every police agency in the U.S., which is to aim for the attacker's "cardiovascular triangle." When the cardiovascular triangle isn't visible, police are taught to shoot at the "center of exposed mass," which is the center of the largest part of the attacker's body that's visible.

HOW LONG DO WE SHOOT?

As tempted as you may be to prematurely end your defense to see what effect your bullets have had, it's important to continue your defense until the attack has ended. It won't be like the movies, where one moderately sized bullet throws the bad guy through a plate glass window – odds are, you won't be able to tell where your bullets impact, or even *if* they have impacted. The only information that you'll be receiving will be whether the attack is continuing or whether it's ended. The moment it ends is the moment you *must stop using deadly force.*

Shooting at an attacker's head presents a number of problems, including the likelihood that a bullet might miss this relatively small (and moving) target. The skull is also extremely hard compared to the protection of the vital organs contained within the "cardiovascular triangle." Bullets risk simply ricocheting around the exterior of the skull, unless a fairly small target area of the skull (as small as 3 inches in diameter) is hit with a moderate to large caliber bullet (something within the "green" zone from our page on defensive calibers).

Cardiovascular Triangle
When no option remains other than the use of deadly force, police are taught to shoot at the attacker's "cardiovascular triangle" which is the part of the body which contains a number of vital organs as well as the spinal column. In addition to having a higher likelihood of stopping an attacker as quickly as possible, shots fired to this area are also much less likely to overpenetrate and injure innocent bystanders.

Remember that the right to use deadly force ends the moment any one of the rules governing the use of deadly force is no longer true. Some examples of this might include:

- The attacker has given up or he's run away. If he's run away, let him go. Protect yourself and your loved ones, tend to the wounded, and be a good witness.
- The attacker has been wounded and can no longer threaten us with death or great bodily harm.
- An opportunity to retreat safely has suddenly become available, such as after the attacker has been injured or has dropped his weapon.

Any use of force out of anger, retribution, or a misplaced sense of justice is a crime. Once the attack has ended, you can no longer continue to use deadly force, no matter how badly you or another individual might be injured. Picture this horrific scenario – walking through a parking garage, you come upon a rape in progress. You shout a warning and give chase when the attacker flees. You corner him at the end of the parking garage and when he charges you, you shoot and kill him. Your friends and family might call you a "hero," but you'll have to hear about it from jail.

◄ If your attacker ends the attack, your right to use deadly force ends as well. Regardless of how badly injured you or a loved one may be, or how angry you might feel, any harm that comes to the attacker at this point will be on your head. Come to think of it, any harm that came to your attacker *before* this point will also be on your head. Don't make the situation worse by continuing to shoot after the attack is over.

AFTER THE THREAT HAS ENDED

After you have determined that the threat has ended, visually scan to the left and the right of the initial threat, while keeping your firearm on target. Then lower your firearm to a low ready position (pointed down to the ground in front of you with your finger OUTSIDE of the trigger guard) and perform a 360° scan for other threats.

These scans will not only help to identify any other threats, they will also help to break tunnel vision and auditory exclusion (see the yellow box below). Once you've determined that there are no further threats, immediately perform the tasks discussed on the following pages.

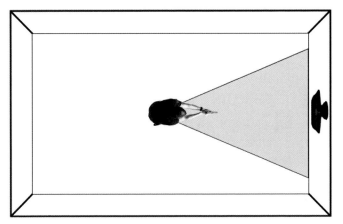

After the threat has ended, scan to the left and right to look for other threats and to break tunnel vision and auditory exclusion.

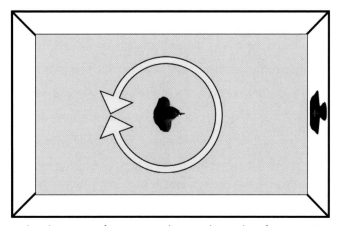

Then lower your firearm to a "low ready" and perform a 360° scan to ensure there are no other threats.

RESETTING THE BRAIN'S "FILTERS"

As discussed in the section on the "Physiological Reactions" that typically occur during an attack, you can expect to have tunnel vision and auditory exclusion, which means that you may not see threats beyond the one to your front and you may have diminished hearing. Hunters appreciate auditory exclusion because it means they don't "hear" the shot as it's being fired, but in a defensive situation, auditory exclusion might cause you to ignore a loved one's shouts or the police shouting at you to drop your firearm. Physically moving your head (rather than just moving your eyes) to scan for other threats can break both tunnel vision and auditory exclusion. The brain seems to perceive this scan as a search for new threats and the selective filtering that occurs within the thalamus or sensory cortex is reset to normal.

THE IMMEDIATE AFTERMATH

Once we've confirmed that the immediate threat has ended, we'll want to quickly complete several important tasks. First and foremost, if we believe that we're still in danger, we'll need to immediately retreat to a safe area. Once there, we should closely check ourselves and others for any injuries that might be masked by the effects of adrenaline and endorphins, and we should begin emergency first-aid to control any bleeding. Next, we'll need to make several important phone calls, including a call to 911, even if no one (including the attacker) is injured, or even if he's run away. These phone calls are CRITICAL. Even in this stressful moment, we'll need to remember that we've just used a firearm (even if it was just to expose it to end a threat), and we need to begin laying the groundwork for our defense in the event that we're charged with a crime. The phone calls to 911 and to our lawyer are the first steps in establishing this.

IF NO ROUNDS WERE FIRED, MAKE TWO CALLS

1 **Call your attorney.** If you can't reach your attorney, leave a message and contact information for where and how he or she can reach you.

2 **Call 911.** Do not let the attacker (or alleged attacker) or witnesses report the incident differently than it happened. This phone call is CRITICAL. Keep the call short and to the point:

A My name is _____ and I need to report (an attack / a possible attack) at (address, intersection, etc.).

B The individual (give a brief description of the attacker) and (ran off / drove off, etc.).

C I do have a concealed carry permit, and did expose my firearm to the attacker, but I did not use it.

D I've called my attorney and (he or she) will contact you to schedule time to make a statement. Here is my number.

E Be prepared to answer any questions related to the alleged attacker or your contact information, but do NOT answer any questions about your actions. Be prepared to hang up if the questioning gets persistent.

HOW TO CONTROL SEVERE BLEEDING

If not treated immediately, bleeding can quickly lead to shock or death. Until emergency personnel arrive at the scene, it's up to you to control severe bleeding. While performing these steps, you or a companion should call 911.

The simplest way to stop severe bleeding is to put direct pressure on the wound with any cloth available, which might include a towel, a shirt, or gauze. Fold the cloth to achieve several layers of thickness and place it directly on the wound – apply direct pressure until the blood flow stops.

If the cloth soaks through with blood, add another layer – never take off the underlying layer no matter how blood-soaked it becomes. Pulling it off the wound effectively removes the clotting that's already begun and can cause bleeding to resume.

Once bleeding is controlled, take the appropriate steps to treat the victim for shock.

IF ROUNDS WERE FIRED, MAKE THREE CALLS

1 **Call 911.** It is your obligation to seek medical attention if someone is injured! Remember that you are being recorded! Keep your 911 call short and to the point:

A My name is _____ and I need to report an attack at (address, intersection, etc.).

B The attacker (ran away / is injured / needs an ambulance).

C I'm wearing _____ and I do have a concealed carry permit so let the police know that I'll place my firearm (on the front seat of my car / on my hood / back in my holster) before they arrive.

D I need to (go help my family / watch the attacker / get to a safer place) so I'm going to hang up now.

E Hang up.

2 **Call your attorney.**

3 **Call your family.** Inform them that you've been involved in a defensive situation and instruct them to speak with no one — not the police, not the media, no one! Tell family members to inform the police that they DO NOT CONSENT TO A SEARCH OF YOUR HOME OR PROPERTY and that they will answer no questions unless your attorney is present. If you are calling them from jail, do NOT give them any details, as the call may be recorded. Simply tell them where you are and that they should call your attorney.

WHEN THE POLICE ARRIVE AT THE SCENE

After a violent confrontation where force may have been used, the police will not know exactly what has occurred. They will only know that a firearm has been used and that the armed person remains at the scene. Remember, the police will be nervous, they'll be concerned for their own safety, and their adrenaline will be flowing as well. They will most likely believe that a bad guy has just shot another bad guy, or a bad guy has just shot a good guy.

Because of the perceptions the police will have when they arrive at the scene, here's what you should do:

- Place your firearm back in its holster or off your body BEFORE the police approach. *Where* you place it will need to be based upon the current disposition of the attacker. If he's given up and is sitting on the ground in front of you, you'll need to keep ready access to your firearm, so reholstering may be the best idea. If he's run away or is incapacitated, placing the firearm on the hood or top of a car or on the ground in front of you may be a better idea.

- Put your hands high in the air as the police approach. Don't even *twitch* if your firearm is back in the holster.

- Comply with all instructions from the police and keep your hands where they can see them. This is not the time to explain that "you are the good guy."

- Don't argue, and be prepared to be pushed to the ground, handcuffed, and placed in the back of a squad car.

DIGGING YOURSELF A HOLE

After a confrontation where a firearm has been used, the police are no longer there to serve and protect you, they are there to serve the prosecutor and protect any case he or she may choose to file. Like they say in the movies, anything you say will be used against you in a court of law. Many police officers carry digital recording devices, which will be rolling the moment they arrive at the scene, and any statement, no matter how innocent (such as "I was mad") can come back to haunt you. Although the police at the scene may legitimately sympathize with you, if the incident results in a trial, the police will be testifying on behalf of the prosecutor, not on your behalf. Finally, it's fair to say that the fatal error of nearly every criminal *and* every law abiding citizen involved in an altercation is that they *want* to talk. In fact, they *love* to talk – to the police, to their family, to the media, and their family even likes to talk to the media. While that may be a natural reaction when you want to shout "I'm Innocent!" from the rooftops, you must resist that urge during the immediate aftermath of the incident; during intense pressure by the police to make a statement; when walking through a gauntlet of media when leaving jail; or when the media calls the attacker "the victim" and dredges up every questionable incident in your background. You *must* trust your lawyer to get you to the other side intact.

A FIVE PART STATEMENT TO THE POLICE

There is no upside in speaking with the police without your attorney present, and any statement you make, however true you may believe it to be, is fraught with risk (review our physiological section as a reminder on the distortion that can occur to your memory during an attack). Because of that and other risks, we recommend that you stick with this five part statement to the police and do NOT go beyond it:

1 My name is _____ and I live at _____.

2 I was attacked (by that person / by a person who ran in that direction). Note: If the attacker is no longer present, be very careful about giving a description to the police since you may be suffering from memory loss or false memories, and you may not provide an accurate description.

3 There is the evidence (point out anything that the police may miss or may not realize was used as a weapon).

4 That person / those people were witnesses.

5 I've spoken with / left a message with my attorney and I'm going to wait until (he or she) arrives to give a statement and sign a complaint.

Note: If your mind goes blank, at least remember #1 and #5 above and do *not* be embarrassed to read the above statement if you choose to photocopy this page and keep it in your wallet or purse.

WHEN PRESSED TO MAKE A STATEMENT

Once you've informed the police that you'd like to wait to make a statement until your lawyer arrives, they'll leave you alone, right? Wrong. They'll say things like "That's fine, I just need you to answer a few questions for my report." That is, they'll try to get you to make a statement, without *asking* you to make a statement. The police *know* that you have the right to consult your lawyer and they *know* it's the smart thing for you to do. That's why they *want* you to talk and possibly incriminate yourself before your lawyer is present. So no matter how many times you're asked by the police to answer questions, and no matter how many times they try to imply that asking for your lawyer makes you look guilty (it doesn't) you should repeat this statement as many times as necessary:

"I WANT MY LAWYER PRESENT BEFORE I ANSWER ANY QUESTIONS."

Keep in mind that it's never too late to stop talking. If adrenaline is making you stupid, you need to get unstupid very quickly and stop talking. Said another way, if you're digging yourself a hole, *stop digging*.

WHEN ASKED IF YOU CONSENT TO A SEARCH

When asked if you consent to a search of your person, your vehicle, or your home, state very clearly:

"I DO NOT CONSENT TO A SEARCH OF MY PERSON OR MY PROPERTY."

Repeat as often as necessary. Experts have agreed that there is zero upside in agreeing to a search. That said, do NOT interfere with the police if they choose to go ahead with a search anyway, without your consent. Police will frame their question to you in a way that makes it sound as though it's a foregone conclusion – for example, they won't ask "Do you give up your rights under the Fourth Amendment of the constitution?" Instead they'll say "It's okay if we look through your car, right?" Your answer needs to be "No."

IF I HAVE NOTHING TO HIDE, WHAT'S WRONG WITH CONSENTING TO A SEARCH?

One of the hardest things that most law abiding citizens will have to do, is to say "no" when asked by the police whether they can search our vehicle, our belongings, or our homes. The problem with consenting to a search isn't just what will happen if the police find something illegal. In the hands of the prosecutor, even legal items can taint a jury. For example, a box of ammunition found in your home or car becomes "The defendant had enough ammunition to kill 50 people!" That pain pill found under your front seat that was prescribed to you three years ago becomes "The defendant was found with illegal prescription drugs!" As our friend Marc Berris says, "The laws protecting us from illegal search and seizure are designed to protect the innocent, not the guilty."

WHEN ARE YOU UNDER ARREST?

Unfortunately, it won't be as obvious as when Horatio Cane says "Take him!" on CSI Miami. When investigating any suspicious activity (which would include the use of a firearm) the police have the right to perform what is referred to as a "Terry stop," which allows the police to temporarily detain individuals to request that they identify themselves and to question them about the suspicious activity; and to conduct a limited pat down search for weapons. Whether you've moved from a Terry stop to being under arrest may only be ascertained if you are not allowed to leave. To determine that, after you've made the five part statement, you'll need to ask "Can I leave?" If the answer is no, you should assume that you're under arrest.

WHEN DO I GET READ MY MIRANDA RIGHTS?

In most jurisdictions in the United States, Miranda Rights will be read only upon the *actual arrest and formal interrogation of a suspect.* Prior to that time, especially during the detention time allowed as part of a Terry stop, the police will be more than happy to let you run your mouth, and anything you say may not have the same protections under the Fifth Amendment as you would have after your arrest. Don't assume that just because you haven't been read your rights that you're free to say anything you want. Police and interrogators take classes to get you to spill your guts. Even if the police are acting like your best buddy, assume that you will be placed under arrest at any moment and stick with the two key statements.

WHAT SHOULD YOUR LAWYER KNOW?

1. Delay any interview with the police for as long as possible, but for at least 48 hours. Refer them to the IACP guidelines that the police themselves will follow if involved in a critical incident.

2. Your lawyer should read the physiological section in this book so he or she can understand the distortions that occur during critical incidents. He or she should also review the police interviews by Dr. Alexis Artwohl.

3. Your lawyer and his or her investigator must review the scene of the crime; they must analyze all evidence; and they must conduct their own interviews of all witnesses.

4. Your lawyer may need to seek out expert testimony from professionals who have testified at (and won) multiple self-defense trials.

WHAT SHOULD YOUR FAMILY KNOW?

They should allow you to decompress for 48 hours. No alcohol, no family interviews, no talking to the police or the media.

HOW ARE POLICE TREATED WHEN THEY'RE INVOLVED IN A SHOOTING?

Most law enforcement organizations in the United States have adopted policies similar to one outlined by the International Association of Chiefs of Police, which provides 20 guidelines for dealing with a police officer who has been involved in a shooting. These guidelines are designed to have the officers avoid a "second injury" by insensitive treatment and to allow the officer to "avoid legal complications."

One of the guidelines states: "If possible, the officer can benefit from some recovery time before detailed interviewing begins. This can range from a few hours to overnight, depending on the emotional state of the officer and the circumstances." It goes on to say, "Officers who have been afforded this opportunity to calm down are likely to provide a more coherent and accurate statement."

If that advice is good enough for the police, it's good enough for us.

In the euphoria of the aftermath, you might think that the situation is a slam dunk in your favor and that you'll be hailed as a hero. We hate to burst your bubble, but it isn't, and you won't. When you run through the mental scenarios in Chapter One, don't forget to include your arrest.

THE LEGAL AND EMOTIONAL AFTERMATH

So you've survived a critical incident – what's next? Just as you protected yourself or your family from a violent attack, you'll now need to take charge of protecting your emotional, legal, and financial interests. Remember that no one will look out for your interests – you *must take charge*.

THE EMOTIONAL AFTERMATH

The emotional aftermath will leave you dealing with more than just the incident itself – you must also deal with the resulting media attention, the effect the incident will have on your job and relationships, and the possibility of criminal or civil proceedings. It would actually be out of the ordinary for you not to have sleepless nights, anxiety, or depression. Remember that you won't be the only one dealing with the fallout – your spouse and family will be dealing with it as well. Their feelings may range from being thankful that you survived, to resentment that you didn't try harder to avoid the conflict in the first place (it wouldn't be unusual for their feelings to move from one extreme to the other, after they discover the incredible negative impact that the event has had on their lives). Police officers involved in lethal encounters have reported a high rate of alcoholism and divorce – you *must* treat the emotional aftermath for both you and your family no differently than if you had sustained a physical injury. While you don't need to speak openly about the incident itself, you must speak openly with your family about their feelings, and you must consider getting family counseling. As difficult as it will be for your family to deal with you being called a "killer" by the media, it will be harder for them to deal with your job loss, your alcohol abuse, or the breakup of your mar-

riage. As hard as it is to read the traumatic stories of aftermath in "Deadly Force Encounters," it's also reassuring to know that many of the officers involved in shootings ultimately survived the incident through the strength and support of their families, their peers, their legal advisors, and their spiritual advisors.

THE LEGAL AFTERMATH

In addition to possible criminal proceedings, you must be prepared for the possibility of civil proceedings as well. Although many states make it illegal for the attacker or his family to sue you for damages, try telling that to a lawyer. If the attacker or his family does decide to sue you, the first hearing will be for their lawyer to explain to the courts why the law prohibiting civil suits doesn't apply in your case. In other words, even in those states where you can't be sued, you might spend tens of thousands of dollars in an attempt to prove *why* you can't be sued.

FINAL LEGAL ADVICE

In addition to the legal advice suggested earlier, we'll also recommend that you not seek out advice from anyone other than your legal representative. That includes staying away from internet "experts." Be very wary of anyone proclaiming to have your best interests at heart, and do not appoint anyone your formal or informal spokesperson. In addition, it's very important that you not share your story with anyone but your lawyer. That includes staying off message boards, staying away from the media, and not revealing details to friends or relatives. From this point forward, your lawyer is your only spokesperson. If your lawyer likes the cameras, find a new lawyer.

After using force to protect yourself or your family, you might feel as though you're all alone. You *must* seek out support from your family, your legal advisor, and your spiritual advisor.

Photo courtesy of Kimber

One of the greatest things about getting your concealed carry permit is all of the great gear you'll get to buy! This chapter helps to prioritize those gear purchases and of course, you can find this gear and more at your local Gander Mtn. retail store, by catalog, or on-line at www.gandermountain.com.

— Explaining Holster Retention —

— Types of Holsters Including Belt, Pancake, Inside the Waistband, and Holsters for Concealment —

— Holster Styles we Don't Recommend —

— Other Gear Including Belts, Tactical Flashlights, Mounted Lights, Night Sights, and Lasers —

Chapter 6

The incredible amount of gear available to concealed carry permit holders can be a bit overwhelming, so we'll do our best to explain your options. Within this chapter, we'll not only help you to understand the options available for the most obvious piece of support equipment you'll need – namely a holster – we'll also explain additional pieces of gear including night sights, tactical flashlights, lasers, and more.

In our section on holsters, we'll start by explaining how holster retention devices work (and which levels of retention work for permit holders, versus what law enforcement might require) as well as explanations of the most common types of holsters including belt, pancake, paddle, pocket, and others. In our examples, you'll see a number of holsters made with leather and a number made with Kydex, which is a fancy way of saying plastic. Both have advantages – leather can be more comfortable and is usually more kind to your handgun's finish, while Kydex typically has much more of a positive "click" when the firearm is holstered. We have lots of each.

We'll round out the chapter with discussions on other important pieces of equipment, including gear to allow you to operate in low-light or no-light situations. Night sights, tactical flashlights, mounted lights, and mounted lasers have all undergone a dramatic transformation in the last three to five years, and we'll provide a detailed explanation about what you should consider when selecting these pieces of equipment. We've also included a couple of commentaries on handheld flashlights versus mounted lights, and things to know if you're considering adding a mounted laser to your gear line-up.

Before jumping into the chapter, we want to provide you with additional help and guidelines on selecting that first piece of gear; your holster. When selecting your method of carry, you'll want to focus on five key traits: concealment, access, retention, comfort, and safety.

Concealment – Holsters that offer superior concealment include pancake holsters (which hold the firearm more closely to the body than standard belt holsters), inside-the-waist-band holsters, and pocket holsters.

Access – Access includes more than just getting your hand onto the grips, it also means the ability to clear that firearm from its holster as quickly as possible. As you'll see in our "levels" topic, access to your firearm can be hindered by too many retention methods.

Retention – We like holsters that are molded to the specific firearm of choice (rather than soft–sided holsters) to ensure that the firearm will remain in the holster even if you are running or jumping. If you choose to carry openly, you'll also want to consider the additional retention available with a "Level I" holster.

Comfort – Seemingly the least important of holster traits, but believe us, if your holster is uncomfortable, you'll quit wearing it, and you'll find yourself in public, unprepared.

Safety – The number one safety criteria of any holster is that it must completely cover the trigger and trigger guard. No exceptions.

> *"Laws that forbid the carrying of arms. . . disarm only those who are neither inclined nor determined to commit crimes. . . Such laws make things worse for the assaulted and better for the assailants; they serve rather to encourage than to prevent homicides, for an unarmed man may be attacked with greater confidence than an armed man."*
>
> *Thomas Jefferson's*
> *"Commonplace Book"*

LEVELS OF HOLSTER RETENTION

Modern holsters come with a variety of methods and devices to ensure that your handgun remains in the holster until you're ready to use it. The most common retention method that holsters provide is nothing more than a snug fit. Selecting a holster that's molded to your specific firearm make, model, and size usually means that the firearm will remain in place even when you're running, jumping, or bending, but it allows your firearm to be quickly retrieved without an extra step, something you'll appreciate during an attack when your manual dexterity can go to mush. These holsters are typically referred to as "Level Zero" or "Concealment Holsters." For an extra level of retention, a variety of holsters are available with top straps, or some type of release lever usually activated either with the index finger or with the thumb. These holsters are typically referred to as "Level I" holsters, and can provide an extra level of confidence that your gun will remain in the holster until you need it.

LEVEL ZERO: FIREARM HELD IN PLACE BY TENSION ONLY

Retention by Tension
Both leather and plastic Level Zero holsters hold firearms in place by being specifically molded to a particular firearm.

Tension Screws
Some Level Zero holsters may add a tension screw (or two) that allows the holster's retention to be tightened or loosened.

LEVEL I: FIREARM HELD IN PLACE BY TOP STRAP OR RELEASE LEVER

1 **Top Strap**
Usually unsnapped by pushing the thumb toward the body while drawing.

1 **Release Lever**
A release lever is embedded within the holster and is released with either the index or middle finger. A solid "click" should be heard when reholstering.

SO WHAT ARE LEVEL II AND LEVEL III HOLSTERS?

Law enforcement officers are often required by their departments to use what are called Level II or Level III holsters, which have multiple retention methods that must be de-activated before the firearm can be drawn from the holster. Our advice is that you leave these holsters to the police. Since police typically carry exposed and have the unfortunate task of getting their hands on bad guys, the extra retention makes sense. Approximately 8% of police officers killed between 1994 and 2003 were killed with their own guns, so whether the extra retention works or not may be in the eye of the beholder.

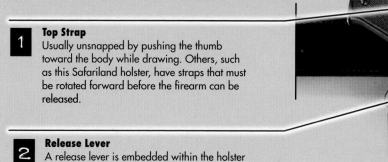

1 **Top Strap**
Usually unsnapped by pushing the thumb toward the body while drawing. Others, such as this Safariland holster, have straps that must be rotated forward before the firearm can be released.

2 **Release Lever**
A release lever is embedded within the holster and is released with either the index or middle finger.

3 **Rocking Release**
Once the top strap is released and the release lever is pushed, the firearm can only be drawn after rocking it back.

HOLSTERS OPTIONS

HIP HOLSTERS

Hip holsters are designed to be worn on the belt, outside of the waistband. "Belt loop" holsters are usually attached by a single loop behind the holster, while "pancake holsters" typically have two widely-spaced slots, allowing them to be held very tightly to the body for extra concealment. Most pancake holsters are designed to be worn on the strong side, but several (such as Side Guard Holsters "Cross Guard") are designed to be worn on the weak side with a cross draw cant. Each style has pros and cons. Belt holsters can sometimes ride too far from the body, while some leather pancake holsters can occasionally fit too close to the body, causing them to collapse when the firearm is drawn, requiring two hands to re-holster.

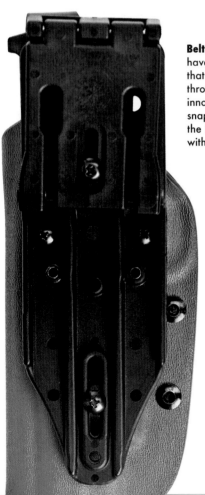

Belt loop holsters typically have a single loop in the back that the belt is threaded through. Blade-Tech offers this innovative clip that can be un-snapped and threaded through the belt, then re-snapped without removing the belt.

**Blade-Tech WRS
Duty Holster with TEK-LOK
(Back View)**

Side Guard Holsters "The Slide"

Pancake holsters typically have two belt slots, which holds the holster and firearm closer to the body for better control and concealment.

PADDLE HOLSTERS

Paddle holsters are so easy to attach and remove that they can offer some incentive to carry when you might rather not take the time to remove your belt to attach a through-the-belt holster. Find one that has a secure "tooth" that will bite into your pants, below your belt. This will ensure that the holster will not tear off your pants during a draw, which would be dangerous and really, really embarrassing.

Paddle holsters do tend to stand farther away from the body than belt or pancake holsters, which can be a plus if you prefer not to feel the holster, but a negative if you are carrying a heavier pistol (which can flop around) or are looking to conceal the outline of your firearm.

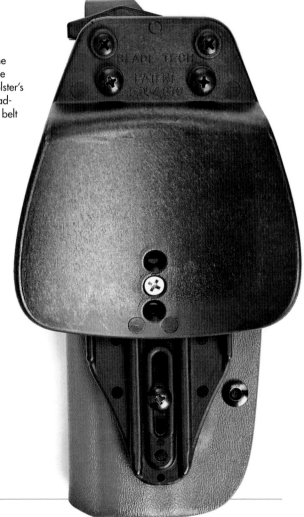

Blade-Tech Paddle Holster
This model from Blade-Tech not only allows you to adjust the cant of the holster, you can also adjust a lug in the back (the center screw in the picture) allowing you to fine tune the holster's fit for your belt of choice. A tooth on the other side of the adjustable lug will cause the paddle to lock in underneath the belt for positive retention.

CONVERTIBLE HOLSTERS

Blade-Tech offers a number of options to allow you to convert your holster from one style to another, such as converting the paddle holster on the far right to a belt holster or pancake holster.

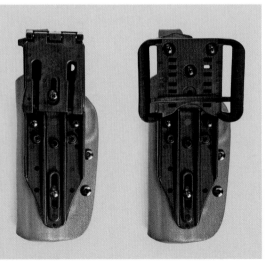

CONCEALMENT HOLSTERS

FRONT POCKET HOLSTERS

Pocket Pistols are small enough for alternate carry options, including sliding them into the front or back pocket. This pocket holster is designed to be carried in the front pocket – that additional piece of leather under the grips is designed to hook on your pocket while drawing, leaving the holster in your pocket and the gun in your hand.

Side Guard Holsters
"Rough Out"

Side Guard Holsters
"Minimal Clip"

INSIDE THE WAISTBAND HOLSTERS

Like they sound, inside the waistband holsters are tucked inside the pants, usually secured to the belt with a loop or hook system. IWB holsters are appropriate when deeper concealment is desired, and it allows the holster to be concealed even when a golf shirt or t-shirt is worn, rather than a longer outer garment. We recommend that if you decide on an IWB holster, you select one that's rigid and molded for your specific firearm of choice. This ensures that the holster doesn't collapse after drawing, allowing you to re-holster using a single hand.

OTHER HOLSTER STYLES

ANKLE HOLSTERS

Regardless of how light a gun is that you might carry in an ankle holster, it's going to feel like you've strapped on

Galco Ankle Glove

an exercise weight. We tend to steer clear of them, but for deep concealment or a backup gun, this may be your best option.

HOLSTERS FOR THE CAR

The seatbelt has a habit of lying in a perfect position to block access to your firearm when using a hip holster. So when carrying in your vehicle, a better option might be to invest in a holster *designed* for

DeSantis Kingston Car Seat Holster

automobile carry, like the DeSantis Kingston holster (we have one and love it). Like the other "off the body" holsters, you must ensure that your firearm *never* leaves your immediate control.

FANNY PACK HOLSTERS

Fanny Pack holsters allow the firearm to be carried in an easily accessible location, without giving away the fact that you happen to be carrying. Next time you see some-

Galco Elite

one wearing a fanny pack, look to see if his wallet is in his back pocket. If it is, it's a good bet that he's carrying a gun in the pack. On the other hand, if you can't see a wallet and he's also wearing Zubaz, then there's a good chance he's just stuck in the '80s.

PURSE HOLSTERS

Purse holsters hold a firearm more securely than dropping it into a normal purse, and are completely concealed. Dedicated purse holsters are also superior to normal purses in that they do have this dedicated pocket, which should carry NOTHING else besides the handgun. We were tempted to put this holster on our "not recommend-

Patricia Day Bag

ed" page, since a purse is the most likely object to be grabbed during a robbery, but we realize that a purse holster might be the best option for certain individuals. To avoid the "grab" problem, *always* loop the purse around your neck, and never allow it to leave your direct control.

HOLSTER STYLES WE DON'T RECOMMEND

SMALL OF THE BACK HOLSTERS

While "Small of the Back" holsters might look cool, we recommend against them because they make drawing the firearm more difficult, and they put significant strain on the back if it's necessary to sit while wearing the holster.

HOLSTERS LEAVING THE TRIGGER AND TRIGGER GUARD EXPOSED

This holster is an example of a bad design because the trigger guard and trigger remain exposed. This particular holster was designed as a Level I holster for hammerless revolvers, which was a great idea in theory, but poor in design. In order to fasten the strap on this holster, the operator is required to actually put his fingers THROUGH the trigger guard, which could lead to a negligent discharge.

SHOULDER HOLSTERS

Pretty cool if your name is Crocket or Tubbs, but somewhat impractical otherwise. Shoulder holsters always require that an outer garment be worn, and tend to be more difficult to draw from versus holsters worn on the belt.

One exception is for individuals of sizable girth (who are less comfortable with a belt or IWB holster), another is for individuals who spend most of their time in a vehicle. Shoulder holsters can make drawing while seatbelted easier than a holster worn on the belt.

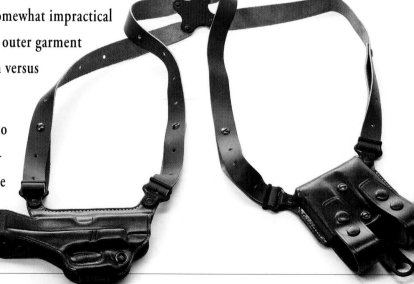

DON'T FORGET THE BELT!

Typical dress belts are not nearly stiff enough (and are rarely wide enough) to support the weight of a firearm. A number of manufacturers (including 5.11, Gould & Goodrich, Galco, and Bianchi) offer dress, casual, and tactical versions. If fitting to a belt holster, ensure that the width of the belt matches the belt loop slots in the holster. A proper belt can also make a common function a little bit easier and a little bit safer. Using the restroom while holstered presents challenges, so we recommend that you invest in a very rigid belt so that your holstered firearm doesn't drop to the floor, or you can un-holster and put the firearm in your pocket. If your belt is long enough, you can re-fasten your belt with your pants in the lowered position. DO NOT set your firearm on the floor, or hang your firearm on the coat hook on the stall door. That leaves it in a perfect position to be forgotten or grabbed while you're busy doing other things, and it can lead to a negligent discharge, and a lot of embarrassment.

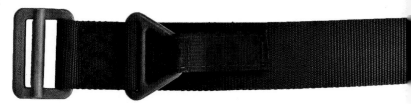

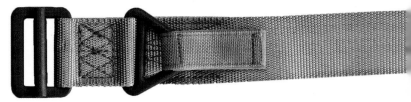

BELTS AND BATHROOMS
(AP) Faribault, MN. A trip to the restroom resulted in a trip to the hospital for a Bloomington, MN man who accidentally shot himself in the hand over the weekend at a gun show. Faribault Police Sgt. Richard Larson said the 59-year-old man shot himself while removing his gun from a hook in a bathroom stall while attending the 31st annual Faribault Rifle and Pistol Club gun show on Sunday morning. The man apparently hung his holstered Glock on the stall hook by the trigger guard. When retrieving his Glock, he set off the firearm several times, shooting himself in the hand.

TACTICAL FLASHLIGHTS AND NIGHT SIGHTS

After selecting a good handgun and holster, we recommend that you add two additional pieces of equipment to your line-up in the following priority:

Priority #1: A good, tactical flashlight. You should train using the various flashlight holds outlined in Chapter Seven, and keep this flashlight stored with your home defense gun. Check out the following page for our favorites and an explanation of what exactly makes a flashlight "tactical."

Priority #2: Night sights. 70% of shootings occur in low light situations. Without night sights, your handgun might just be useless. Most new handguns either come with night sights or offer it as an option. Aftermarket night sights are available for nearly every make and model.

The traditional "baton" style flashlight of the 70s has made way for smaller, higher intensity flashlights like the one pictured above. We recommend that you select a flashlight with a minimum of 60 lumens. Better yet, get one in the range of 125 lumens which can blind an attacker. Our favorites by far are anything from Surefire, Blackhawk, or First Light.

In addition to being used as a component in the triggering mechanism of nuclear bombs, Tritium gas also has the useful property of glowing in the dark. Night Sights use glass inserts filled with Tritium to allow easy acquisition of the sights in low light situations. Our favorites include Trijicon (pictured), Novak, and Meprolight. The squared style of the sample above allows the slide to be racked one-handed against a fixed object if your support hand has become disabled.

OUR FAVORITE TACTICAL FLASHLIGHTS

WHAT MAKES A FLASHLIGHT "TACTICAL"?

It's more than just marketing – there are major differences between flashlights that should be part of your self–defense line-up, versus what you'd pick up at your local hardware store for $10. Here's what you should look for in a tactical flashlight:

#1: High Output Beam. A minimum brightness should be 60 lumens (the average 2-AA light is about 15 lumens). 60 lumens is bright enough to momentarily blind an attacker even in daylight, while 125 lumens is like staring into the sun. Surefire has lights up to 500 lumens. We'd personally rather be tasered than have one of those hit us in the face.

#2: Lithium Batteries, which have a shelf-life as long as ten years, and have a much higher energy output for their size, versus alkaline batteries. In addition, they aren't affected by cold, so feel free to leave the light in your car.

#3: Tail-cap On/Off Switch, rather than a switch on the side. This allows the flashlight to be flashed on and off with various flashlight holds. We'd also recommend LED lights over traditional tungsten bulbs. You can hammer nails with an LED light without it breaking, while tungsten bulbs can break if the flashlight is dropped or banged on a barrier.

Surefire 6P LED Defender

Surefire is arguably the leader in tactical flashlights, and has more options than any other manufacturer. One of our favorites is the 6P, which is 80 lumens, and has a sharp "strike bezel" on the face that can be used as a defensive striking weapon of last resort. Not quite as effective as a firearm, but hitting an attacker in the face or arm while he's trying to reach into your vehicle would make him think twice. It's always present in our truck.

Blackhawk Gladius

The Gladius from Blackhawk is 90 lumens, more than enough to blind an attacker. It also has an innovative selectable tail switch, allowing the user to operate in full power, strobe, and a mode where the user can set the brightness and lock it in. We like it so much, we bought two.

First Light Liberator

The Liberator, by First Light, is a unique design that offers the best compromise between hand-held and mounted flashlights. The Liberator's handle loops through the support hand and allows a proper grip on the firearm (and also allows magazines to be changed and malfunctions to be cleared without dropping the light). It also allows the user to scan the area independent of the direction that the muzzle is pointed, something not available with mounted lights. The Liberator ST is a blazing 120 lumens and is thumb activated with 3 switches on the support bar (momentary, strobe, or constant). We absolutely love it.

LOW LIGHT SHOOTINGS

Statistically, more than 70% of defensive shootings occur in low light or no light situations (see our analysis of NYPD shootings in the section on Lasers) which would indicate that training with a light source should become part of our personal protection plan. However, an important debate has raged in the firearms training community (and countless articles have been written) as to whether a handheld light or a light that mounts to the front of a firearm is best for the average person interested in preparing for self-defense in these low light situations. The debate centers around the fact that when using a mounted light, the firearm's muzzle, by design, is *always* pointed in the direction of the light. This means that if the mounted light is our *only* source of light, Universal Rule #2 might be violated until the "target" is identified as friend or foe. Those who knock mounted lights also describe the light as acting as a "bullet magnet" on our center of mass, implying that the bright light is a perfect target for a bad guy to shoot at. On the other hand, manipulating a handheld flashlight with the support hand and a firearm with the strong hand, means that the key fundamentals of accurate and safe shooting (including proper grip) described in Chapter Three are being thrown out the window. Even highly trained individuals see their accuracy and concentration suffer when manipulating a handheld light and firearm simultaneously, especially when in the grips of an adrenaline rush. A handheld light also makes it more difficult to perform additional tasks, such as clearing a malfunction, opening a door, assisting loved ones, etc. We're happy to weigh in on the debate. To begin with, let's make one thing perfectly clear. We don't care who you are – the average individual (who, let's be honest, will never, ever, train in low light situations) or someone with extensive hours in low light training environments. We've yet to see anyone who shoots as well while holding a flashlight in their support hand, as they do with a proper two handed grip (okay, except for those guys at SureFire Institute – those guys are really, really good). We've seen individuals with more than 60 hours of low light training have a complete mental freeze when trying to manipulate a handheld flashlight and firearm simultaneously. We've seen these experienced shooters track their muzzle with their flashlight (resulting in the same complaint against mounted lights), or do the opposite and *not* be able to place the light where they need to shoot. We've even seen one of these experienced individuals actually squeeze his flashlight, when he meant to squeeze the trigger. We'll come back to our recommendations on how a handheld flashlight can fit into your personal protection plan, but let's first take a look at dispelling a few of the complaints against mounted lights.

CLEARING ROOMS?

A common argument against mounted lights is that when it is necessary to clear a room or rooms in our homes, we run the risk of pointing the muzzle of our firearm at a loved one. First of all, there is one time and one time *only* that you should even *consider* advancing through your home to clear a room or rooms, and that's when a bad guy is between you and a loved one. Otherwise, morally, and in many cases legally, you should hole-up and defend your safe zone until the police arrive. This posture helps us to avoid the problem in the first place – anyone who ignores our commands and enters our safe zone should be prepared to walk into our beam of light, and the end of our muzzle. Next, if the situation dictates that we *must* search an area, many mounted lights, such as the Surefire X300, cast a very bright, very wide beam that allows us to carry the firearm at a low ready position (pointed toward the floor) while still casting a bright enough beam to scan an area with the muzzle in a safe direction, yet quickly bring the firearm up on target if we've identified a threat. When using this method, it's important to recognize that a mounted light is actually part of our firearm

system, not a separate light that should be used to peek into corners. In addition, whether we're on the range or in our homes defending ourselves from a threat, we need to consistently live within the guidelines of Universal Rule #3.

UNIVERSAL RULE #3 ISN'T JUST FOR THE RANGE

Universal Rule #3 (Keep your finger OFF the trigger and outside the trigger guard until you are on target and have made the decision to shoot) is about more than just avoiding the embarrassment of putting a round through the ceiling at your local range. It is a fundamental rule that is intertwined with our legal right to use force, and when used consistently, it will ensure that we never fire our gun at another person without properly identifying the threat. When using a mounted light *and* following Universal Rule #3, we can avoid tragedy, even if we momentarily violate Universal Rule #2. On the next page, we've suggested a drill you can practice in your home to test out your light's peripheral brightness, while abiding by Rule #3.

A

A "BULLET MAGNET"?

Detractors of mounted lights also argue that because the light is centered on our body, the light becomes, in effect, a "bullet magnet," giving an attacker a perfect target to shoot at. We'd agree that's true in a no-light situation, which is rare. Inside or outside the home, some amount of ambient light is almost always present, from street lights, house lights, and stars outside, to electronics, smoke detectors, and alarm clocks inside the house. That means that we're almost always partially or fully silhouetted anyway, and a bright light centered on our body makes our silhouette less visible, not more. The truth is, if we're going to blind a bad guy to any place at all, we'd rather blind him to our center of mass, rather than blinding him high and outside (which is what we'd get if we used the FBI hold).

OUR ADVICE

If you are willing and able to prepare for defending yourself in a low light situation, our recommendation is that your first priority be a mounted light, since they do minimize the number of variables and allow us to consistently use the key fundamentals of shooting safely and accurately. Mounted lights require that the firearm have a light rail installed, which will be in front of the trigger guard and below the barrel on handguns, or on the forestock on shotguns and rifles. When mounting the light to the firearm, ensure that you have cleared the firearm first. When practicing with a mounted light, we'd suggest two stages. First, it's important to practice shooting with the mounted light, both in lighted and in low light situations (low light shooting should be in-structor led). Practice manipulating the light's controls prior to and during your shooting drills so that you can consistently and comfortably turn it on and off. Second, we'd recommend that you confirm your light's operation and performance in your home, after *triple-checking* that your firearm has been cleared. Practice with your firearm at a low ready and your finger OUTSIDE the trigger guard (as you should also do in a threat situation) to confirm for yourself that it is possible to check hallways, rooms, and corners, without ever bringing the firearm up above a low ready position.

FINAL THOUGHTS

While it's clear that we're fans of mounted lights and the benefits that they offer (and the importance of following the Universal Safety Rules), we're also big fans of options. If you are willing to invest further, both in time and money, we'd recommend that you add one of the tactical handheld flashlights profiled in our flashlight section, and that you practice with the different methods of flashlight holds described in Chapter Seven, including the FBI hold, the Harries hold, and the Surefire/Rogers hold. In a perfect world, we'd recommend that you operate and train using both handheld and mounted light options. This allows you to hold your firearm at a low ready, while scanning an area with your handheld flashlight. Adding a lanyard to your handheld (and looping it around your wrist), allows you to momentarily "drop" the light, while performing another task such as opening a door, clearing your firearm, or bringing your firearm up to engage a threat. In our opinion, there is no such thing as "too many flashlights."

WHY USE LASERS?

Ask any group of seasoned shooters, and odds are, they might just roll their eyes when you ask about using laser sights on your handgun. In response, you may want to quote a Crimson Trace advertisement: "Don't let your ego obscure your target, because as good as you are with a gun, a laser sight makes you better." Crimson Trace might just have a point. Looking at a summary of shootings by the New York Police Department in 2005, two things jump out. The first is that 72 percent of the reported shootings occurred between dusk and dawn.

That high percentage of shootings in low light situations calls into question a training regimen that relies solely on the traditional method of "indexing" on a target by aligning the front and rear sights. The second surprising statistic from the NYPD shootings was that the accuracy of the involved officers was well below what would have been expected, since most officers train frequently with their firearms. To paraphrase Crimson Trace, something is turning these officers from 90 percenters on the range, to 5 – 50 percenters in the field. Is it because of the extreme stress? Is it the low light? Is it a lack of realism in the officer's training program?

Light Conditions

LIGHT CONDITION	PERCENTAGE
Outdoors	40%
Artificial Light	60%

LaserLyte has produced a ground-breaking new laser design that incorporates the laser itself into the pistol's rear sight. The on/off switch at the back of the laser is easily activated by the thumb while drawing from the holster. A single press of the button activates the laser in a constant on mode, while a second press activates a pulse mode, and a third press turns the laser off.

NYPD Accuracy by Distance   Source: NYPD 2005 Firearms Discharge Report

DISTANCE	SHOTS	HITS	HIT PERCENT
0 – 2 Yards	127	65	51%
3 – 7 Yards	155	68	44%
8 – 15 Yards	205	14	7%
16 – 25 Yards	93	5	5%
Total	580	152	26%

We'll address the last topic in Chapter Seven, but let's hit those first two issues here. As discussed in Chapter Five, we know that our higher brain is going to check out during periods of extreme stress and that automated responses will take over to one degree or another. So if there's a complex way of doing things and a simple way of doing things, we need to pick simple.

TIME OF DAY	SHOOTINGS	PERCENTAGE
Midnight – 8AM	42	34%
8AM – 4PM	34	28%
4PM – Midnight	47	38%
Dark, Dawn or Dusk	89	72%

If there's a method that embraces those natural responses or fights them, we need to embrace them. Let's take sight alignment as an example. A traditional sight plane requires that three objects be aligned – the rear sight, the front sight, and the target. In addition, it fights the mind's natural inclination to focus on the threat, and forces us to change our focus to the front sight.

Point/Intuitive shooting takes a massive step in the right direction by reducing the indexes from three down to just one (the target) and it embraces our natural instinct to focus on the target, but the "margin of error" might be greater than we can allow. Point shooting also relies on an ability to make the firearm an extension of our arms; that is, we need to know where the firearm is pointing, which requires the arms to be extended as far as possible. When we're unable to use that proper arm extension – for example, when rapidly retreating, when prone, after being knocked over, or with our firearm in a tight retention position (drawn back to our side, rather than extended out straight), the margin of error can be dramatically increased.

Like point shooting, using a laser simplifies the traditional sight picture from three indexes down to one, and it allows us to embrace our body's natural reaction to focus on the threat. The edge that a laser provides is that it allows us to become indexed on the target much more rapidly, and with a much smaller margin of error. While there's no such thing as laser guided bullets, it's fair to say that if we've followed just two of the building blocks of shooting fundamentals (a solid grip and proper trigger press) our margin of error can be dramatically reduced, even when shooting from those awkward positions described above.

A laser also allows us to combine indexing strategies. If we've trained using the point/intuitive shooting method, then we've already trained ourselves to elevate the firearm into our sight plane. We can then easily move from instinctive aiming, to focusing on the red dot, to focusing on the front sight.

WHY TRAIN WITH ANYTHING ELSE?

It's possible to draw the conclusion that since the physiological reaction that we'll experience will force us to look at the threat rather than the sights, why train with anything but a laser? There are several reasons. First, like all technologies, lasers can fail and batteries can run out. Second, there are environments that are inhospitable to lasers, such as bright light situations, situations where the attacker is wearing a red shirt, or a situation where more than one defender is using a laser on the same threat (that is, how do you know which red dot is yours?) Combining training and technology is a better way to use the laser as a tool, without becoming dependant.

COMBINING TRAINING AND TECHNOLOGY

Used properly, lasers can actually help us to become more proficient at point/intuitive shooting *and* sight shooting. It can even help us to improve our trigger control. Here's how:

Point/Intuitive Shooting. Using a side mounted laser (such as those available from Crimson Trace) start from a low ready or high ready position, with your index finger blocking the laser. Fully extend your arms (elevating the firearm up into your sight plane) and point at the center of the target. Once indexed on the target, move your finger to identify where the firearm's barrel is actually pointing. This method will help you realize when your arms are too high, too low, etc. Repeating this drill dozens of times per day will begin to build in the proper pathways into the cerebellum, all without a shot being fired.

Sight Alignment. For new shooters who are having difficulty grasping the idea of sight alignment, the use of a laser can help them understand exactly what it means to align the front sight, rear sight, and target. Using a handgun with a laser which has been calibrated to align with the sights at a target 21 feet away, start from a low ready, and then extend your arms, bringing the firearm up into your sight plane. Concentrate on the position of the laser dot, and slowly move your focus to the front sight. Place the red dot on top of the front sight, and then slowly adjust the firearm until the front sight is centered between the rear sight. Many new shooters will have an "Ah ha!" moment using this simple technique.

Trigger Control. During a traditional dry firing exercise, pay close attention to what happens to the red dot prior to and immediately after the hammer/striker falls. If the red dot dances up, down, or off the target, you should revisit the topics on proper grip and trigger press. Check out Chapter Seven for an additional laser based exercise.

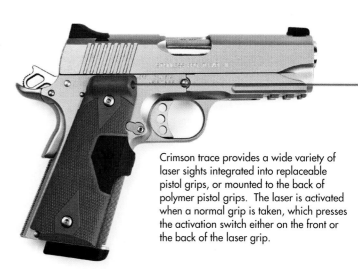

Crimson trace provides a wide variety of laser sights integrated into replaceable pistol grips, or mounted to the back of polymer pistol grips. The laser is activated when a normal grip is taken, which presses the activation switch either on the front or the back of the laser grip.

GUN SAFES AND STORAGE

Any gun shop or sporting goods store will have multiple options for firearms storage, including options for completely enclosing a loaded firearm. Our favorites are biometrically operated safes (you'll pay extra for that option though) or electronically operated safes which are opened by placing your fingers into finger impressions, and pressing the keypads in the appropriate sequence. Biometric safes allow you to store multiple fingerprints, including multiple versions of the same finger. Most small safes come with an option to anchor the safe to the floor via a mounting plate or cable. Ours contains our home defense firearm, our carry gun (when not being carried), spare magazines and a tactical flashlight or two.

GunVault MicroBioVault

The MicroBioVault and MicroVault from Gun-Vault are perfectly sized to hold a single handgun along with a spare magazine or tactical flashlight. Add a security cable and it can be permanently affixed in your home or vehicle. The thing we love about the MicroBioVault is that it has three fail-safes. If the safe doesn't open biometrically, you can open it with the proper combination of pressing the finger impressions. If that fails, you've always got the key backup. You'll just want to practice those three techniques *quickly*.

Sequiam BioVault 2.0 Biometric Gun Safe

The Sequiam BioVault stores up to 50 fingerprints, which allows multiple individuals in your household to store multiple fingers or multiple entries of the same finger. For example, storing 10 versions of the same finger ensures a higher probability that the vault will open, even with an awkwardly placed finger. The BioVault is HUGE. It's big enough to fit several pistols, along with extra magazines, and a couple tactical flashlights.

ACCIDENTAL DEATHS

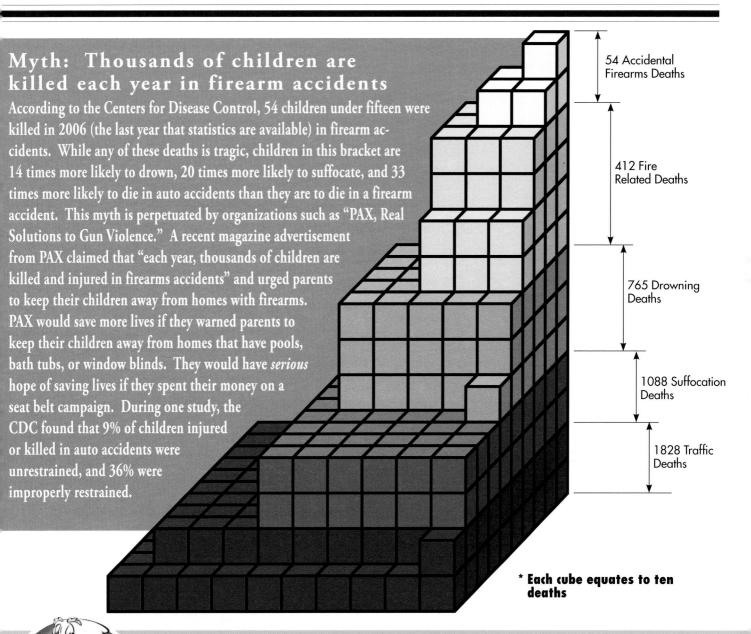

Myth: Thousands of children are killed each year in firearm accidents

According to the Centers for Disease Control, 54 children under fifteen were killed in 2006 (the last year that statistics are available) in firearm accidents. While any of these deaths is tragic, children in this bracket are 14 times more likely to drown, 20 times more likely to suffocate, and 33 times more likely to die in auto accidents than they are to die in a firearm accident. This myth is perpetuated by organizations such as "PAX, Real Solutions to Gun Violence." A recent magazine advertisement from PAX claimed that "each year, thousands of children are killed and injured in firearms accidents" and urged parents to keep their children away from homes with firearms. PAX would save more lives if they warned parents to keep their children away from homes that have pools, bath tubs, or window blinds. They would have *serious* hope of saving lives if they spent their money on a seat belt campaign. During one study, the CDC found that 9% of children injured or killed in auto accidents were unrestrained, and 36% were improperly restrained.

54 Accidental Firearms Deaths

412 Fire Related Deaths

765 Drowning Deaths

1088 Suffocation Deaths

1828 Traffic Deaths

* Each cube equates to ten deaths

NRA'S "EDDIE EAGLE" Since the establishment of the lifesaving Eddie Eagle® Gun Safety Program in 1988, more than 21 million pre-kindergarten to sixth grade children in all 50 states have learned that if they see a firearm in an unsupervised situation, they should "STOP. DON'T TOUCH. LEAVE THE AREA. TELL AN ADULT."

Eddie Eagle says, if you see a gun:
**Stop!
Don't Touch.
Leave the Area.
Tell an Adult.**

BASIC AND ADVANCED SKILLS & SELF-LED AND INSTRUCTOR-LED RANGE DRILLS

Ongoing education and training is critical to developing and maintaining your skillset. In this chapter we'll review the skills that you should develop through self-led exercises and instructor-led drills. Exercises include drills for speed, accuracy, or both. Included in each exercise description are instructions on set-up and scoring, as well as the relative skill level recommended prior to attempting the exercise.

— Properly and Safely Conducting Dry Fire Exercises —

— Drawing from the Holster —

— Flashlight Hold Options —

— Self-Led and Instructor-Led Range Exercises
from Beginner to Expert —

Chapter 7

In Chapter Three, we introduced you to the building blocks of defensive shooting fundamentals. Of course, it's fair to say that simply *reading* about those skills from any book won't do a thing for you; it's repeated and consistent practice that will build those skills into your neural pathways. The variety of exercises in this chapter are designed to help you gain the competence and consistency that we mentioned in the introduction to Chapter Three. Once you've developed competence and consistency with the basics, the next major challenge is to advance your accuracy and speed, which will constantly be in balance. Many of the exercises in this chapter will work toward speed, others toward accuracy, and some will work toward a balance of both, including three of our personal favorites called the "SEB Drill," the "Colored Number Drill," and the "Push Your Limit Drill," which were developed by Rob Pincus and his staff at the I.C.E. Training Company. While most of these exercises can be accomplished through self-led training, others require the guidance of an instructor or the assistance of a friend.

Speaking of building those neural pathways, we've started this chapter with an exercise that all shooters should be familiar with, namely, dry firing. Dry firing is one of the best practical exercises that we can run to hone the fundamentals (and write them into the pathways of our cerebellum), including proper grip, stance, target alignment, and trigger control, and it doesn't cost us a dime. Dry firing can also be used to eliminate many common shooting errors, including the habit of anticipating the recoil. You will notice though that our dry firing exercise treats safety no differently than we do for range exercises; in fact, our dry firing exercise requires *additional* setup when compared to the range.

We'll also introduce you to the concepts of drawing from the holster, low light shooting techniques, and the use of lasers, but keep in mind that this chapter is an *introduction* to these topics. If you'd like to dramatically increase your skill sets in speed and accuracy, drawing from the holster, low light shooting, and other advanced techniques, you'll need to train with skilled instructors like those at Gander Mtn. Academy. On that note, we should mention something else that can't be taught solely through visits to the range, and that's the "stress inoculation" that's a major goal of programs that provide reality-based training (RBT) through force-on-force scenarios and virtual simulations. Police departments that have undergone extensive reality-based training have seen their accuracy in critical incidents surpass 90%, including the California Highway Patrol, the Toledo Police Department, and the Salt Lake City Police Department. Despite those impressive statistics, quality RBT has not been widely or affordably available to civilians. That is, until now. As described in the book's introduction, Gander Mtn. Academy's stunningly realistic virtual simulations utilize technology previously available only to the military, government agencies, and police departments. These virtual simulations enable you to experience *first-hand* the effects of adrenaline, tunnel vision, auditory exclusion, and the other automated responses discussed in Chapter Five, so that you not only learn to recognize the automated responses as they occur, you can also learn to *compensate for their effects*.

None of us can say with absolute certainty what will occur if we become involved in a critical incident. What we *can* say with certainty is that ongoing training will help us to survive an incident when compared to someone with little or no ongoing training. Ongoing training on the fundamentals; repetition of skill, speed and accuracy drills; and participation in reality-based training, are the best methods of moving toward becoming a 90-percenter rather than a 10-percenter when it counts. Fundamentals, Repetition and Simulation – these are the cornerstones of the FRS Learning System developed exclusively by Gander Mtn. Academy.

Finally, as we mentioned in Chapter One, when you run the drills in this chapter, don't just shoot. During each drill, you'll need to create a hypothetical problem requiring a solution. Your solution should include the checklist items on page 33, including evaluating your options, determining the requirements for speed versus accuracy, and what to do in the aftermath.

DRY FIRING

WHY DRY FIRE?

Dry firing is one of the most effective exercises that we can use away from the range because it allows us to build the pathways in our brains to consistently follow the four Universal Safety Rules (and range rules). It also gives us an opportunity to practice the building blocks of safe and accurate shooting, including those outlined in Chapter Three, without spending hundreds of dollars in ammunition. Dry firing itself is not inherently dangerous but it can become dangerous if performed in a manner that ignores the Universal Safety Rules, or when done without a specific set of steps from beginning to end.

Dry firing by its nature may sound as though it is a direct violation of the "rules" but in fact, it's the opposite – it allows us to live within the Universal Rules, and to make those rules instinctual in our lives. Let's take the rules one at a time.

Treat all guns as though they are always loaded and always perform a clearance check every time you pick one up! When dry firing, we treat our firearm (which we've cleared) with *exactly* the same respect as one that we've just loaded – we don't treat it as though it's a dummy blue or red gun.

Never point your gun at anything that you are not willing to destroy! As we described in Chapter Two, our firearm needs to point somewhere, and when we dry fire, we ensure that it is ONLY pointed at something that can serve as a bullet stop and will not damage property or lives (pets included) if a round were fired.

Keep your finger OFF the trigger and outside the trigger guard until you are on target and have made the decision to shoot! Dry firing is one of the most effective drills that can be run to instinctively drill this rule into our brain. We never, never, never put our finger in the trigger guard until we have aligned the barrel on our dry fire backstop, and have made the decision to press the trigger. Performing this exercise thousands of times while dry firing will make it instinctive on the range or during a defensive use of force.

Always be sure of your target and beyond! On the range we're usually aware that there is an earthen or concrete backstop that can serve as an effective bullet stop. At home we need to be confident that our dry fire target can also stop a live bullet, otherwise we CANNOT perform dry firing at home. Effective backstops include cinderblock or concrete walls, but those run the risk of a ricochet if they were struck by a bullet. A better choice – and safer choice – would be to invest in an "Aim-Safe" dry practice bullet block from Gander Mtn. This floor standing bullet block absorbs most handgun, rifle and shotgun rounds without the risk of ricochet or splatter. Homemade options include a full box of paper reams or a bucket of dirt or sand.

Too often a dry firing exercise begins without planning. Dry firing requires MORE planning than going to the range because it involves the removal of ALL ammunition from our dry firing area and it involves TRIPLE checking that our firearm has been cleared. We find it best if we perform our dry firing exercise with three distinct stages – prior to, during, and after the exercise.

BEFORE DRY FIRING BEGINS

1 Remove ALL live ammunition and magazines (empty or loaded!) from your dry firing room. Better yet, pick a room which never has ammunition or magazines in it in the first place.

2 Establish a "bench rest" in front of your dry fire shooting position, just like you'd have on the shooting range. This can be as simple as a TV tray, but it should be at waist level.

3 Prepare your backstop and attach an actual target to the backstop. Never perform dry firing by just picking a spot on the wall, even if the wall itself can serve as an effective backstop!

DRY FIRING PROCEDURES

1 Clear your firearm in a room OTHER than the one you're using for your dry firing exercises. Take the round that was ejected from the chamber, plus the magazine, and lock it in your gun safe. Case the firearm with the slide / cylinder open and carry it into your dry firing room. Just as you'd do on the range, uncase your firearm and place it on the benchrest, muzzle down range.

2 Pick up the firearm and perform THREE clearance checks as described in Chapter Two.

3 Only now can you perform dry firing. If firing a true

double action, you can remain on target and dry fire as many "rounds" as you'd like. When dry firing a single action or striker fired semi-auto (which requires a racking of the slide between dry fire "shots") maintain good muzzle control when you bring the firearm off target to rack the slide, and take your finger OUT of the trigger guard.

AFTER DRY FIRING ENDS

1 As on the range, perform a clearance procedure and case your firearm. Return it to its proper place. Do NOT reload the firearm at this point.

2 Remove the target from your backstop.

3 After a reasonable amount of time has passed, you can reload your firearm in preparation to reholster it.

THE "DIME" TEST

When dry firing a semi-automatic, we occasionally add an extra factor to our exercises which helps to eliminate any "flinch" and works to ensure a proper grip and smooth trigger press. The "dime" test performs the dry firing exercise as described but has the shooter place a dime on the top of the semi-auto's slide. During dry firing, the shooter should focus on a solid grip and smooth trigger press so that the dime doesn't "dance" or fall off the slide. When you can consistently do this test without losing the dime, you're ready for the range.

Range exercise

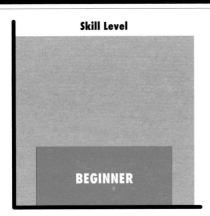

Skill Level

BEGINNER

Self-Led

Target: Official USPSA / IPSC Target

Description:

Starting from the low or high ready position, the shooter will fire a series of 2 to 5-round strings at the target's center of mass (the "A" or "C" areas of the target). If targets other than the USPSA / IPSC targets are used, the shooter should approximate an area consistent with the "cardiovascular triangle" described in Chapter Five.

Goal:

This exercise will "warm up" the skills being written to the neural pathways of the cerebellum (the "muscle memory"). The shooter's goal should be to vary the number of rounds in the string and integrate reloads into the exercise. The shooter should slowly increase speed, as long as he is maintaining "defensively accurate" hits. Any shots outside the "A" or "C" should cause the shooter to slow down until accuracy is maintained.

Distance:

7 – 14 Feet

Things That a Coach Can Watch For:

Watch for the shooter attempting to immediately progress to his fastest speed and accuracy combination.

THE "SHOOT SMALL/MISS SMALL" DRILL

Skill Level

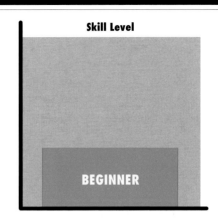

BEGINNER

Description:

Starting from the low or high ready position, the shooter will fire a single round at the back of a USPSA / IPSC target (or any piece of cardboard) then fire strings of 2 to 5 rounds at the hole she just made.

Goal:

This exercise is designed to force an intense concentration on accuracy by making the "target" no larger than a bullet hole. Many shooters will allow their degree of "slop" to be dictated by how large their target is, so the "Shoot Small/ Miss Small" drill is designed to force extra attention on precision.

Self-Led

Distance:

7 – 14 Feet

Things That a Coach Can Watch For:

Watch for the shooter attempting to use the same speed she uses for much larger target areas or for relying only on sight shooting to be extra precise. With plenty of practice (and these distances), the average shooter can become very accurate using point/instinctive shooting, even with a target as small as 22/100ths of an inch.

Target: Back of an Official USPSA / IPSC Target

DRAWING FROM THE HOLSTER

1 A safe draw from the holster uses a four step draw (performed smoothly) combined with the lessons learned from the four Universal Safety Rules. Step number one is to gain a solid grip on the firearm with the web of the hand high on the backstrap, as it would be once all fundamentals are established. (You should not need to adjust your grip once you've completed your draw.) The trigger finger should be straight and extended along the side of the holster. The support hand should be brought into the body to ensure that it does NOT cross the muzzle during the draw.

2 The firearm should be lifted straight up to ensure that it properly clears the holster, and immediately rotated forward smoothly in the direction of the target or attacker. The support hand should remain in close to the body until the firearm begins its forward motion so that the muzzle cannot cross the support hand. At that point, the support hand can move away from the body to meet the strong hand.

3 The support hand locks in with a proper grip with the fingers butted up against the bottom of the trigger guard. The now complete two-handed grip should *not* require adjustment once on target. Since we've already rotated the firearm toward the target once the firearm cleared the holster, we should now be transitioning through a high ready position.

4 The arms are punched out from the high ready, with the firearm elevated into the shooter's line of sight.

THE "FROM THE HOLSTER" DRILL

Range exercise

Skill Level

INTERMEDIATE

Self-Led

Target: Official USPSA / IPSC Target

Description:
The "From the Holster" drill is designed to add additional steps to the pathways being written to the cerebellum and is a repeat of the warm-up drill with the additional task of drawing from the holster.

Goal:
The shooter should conduct his draw from the holster as distinct steps until he has mastered the skills and can ensure that his support hand does not cross over the muzzle of the firearm.

Distance:
7 – 14 Feet

Things That a Coach Can Watch For:
Watch the shooter to ensure that he does not cross his support hand with the muzzle on the draw; watch for him to take his finger outside the trigger guard when he has moved off the target; and watch for him attempting to force greater speed and accuracy than is practical.

Alternatives:
1. Any of the other drills can be combined with the "From the Holster" drill.

THE "SEB" DRILL

Description:

Starting from the low or high ready position, the shooter will fire on command of an assistant. The assistant will vary the commands between calls of "Up!" and one of the numbers (such as "Two!") On a call of "Up" the shooter will fire at the large square in the high center of the silhouette and on the command of a number, the shooter will fire at the appropriately-numbered shape surrounding the large silhouette. The assistant can choose to call more commands of "Up" or more commands of the numbered shapes, in order to vary the shooter's need to balance speed with accuracy.

Goal:

This exercise will force the shooter to vary her balance of speed and accuracy on the same target and within the same exercise.

Distance:

7 – 14 Feet

Things That a Coach Can Watch For:

Watch for the shooter attempting to shoot the smaller, numbered targets with the same speed that she uses to shoot the larger square in the silhouette. If she is consistently missing the smaller targets, she'll need to slow those shots down. On the other hand, if she's shooting with a consistent speed for the large and small targets and consistently hitting each target, she can afford to speed up her shots on the larger square.

Skill Level

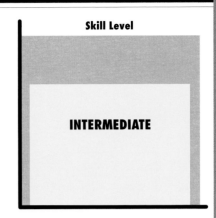

INTERMEDIATE

Instructor-Led

Target: SEB Training Target

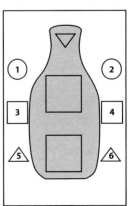

Range exercise

Skill Level

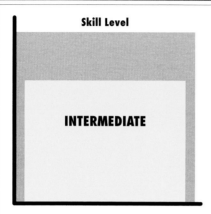

INTERMEDIATE

Instructor-Led

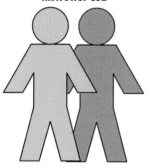

Target: Law Enforcement Target Co.'s DT-2C Target

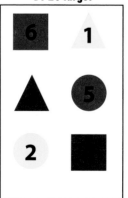

Description:

Starting from the low or high ready position, the shooter will fire on the command of an assistant. At stage one, the assistant will call four of the six colored numbers, an equal number of times. The distance to the target will then be doubled and stage two will be fired with the assistant calling the two remaining colored targets.

Goal:

This exercise allows the shooter to understand how distance affects his "personal balance of speed and precision." The shooter's goal should be to maintain 100% defensive accuracy (what Rob Pincus of the I.C.E. Training Company calls "Combat Accuracy") with no shots off the colored numbers.

Distance:

Stage One: 6 – 8 Feet

Stage Two: 12 – 16 Feet

Things That a Coach Can Watch For:

As with all exercises, watch for "fast misses," indicating that the shooter needs to slow down; or overly tight groups, indicating that the shooter can speed up.

THE "PUSH YOUR LIMIT" DRILL

Description:
The "Push Your Limit" drill was introduced to Rob Pincus by Brad Schuppan and is used to force students to shoot at a progressively faster pace until they eventually move beyond their own personal balance of speed and accuracy.

Stage One:
The shooter will fire five rounds at target #1 (the circle in the upper left hand corner) on a count of "one-one-thousand, two-one-thousand," etc., up to "five-one-thousand." This will require a shot fired approximately every second.

Stage Two:
Same exercise as above, into target #2 (the circle in the upper right hand corner) on a count of "one and two and three and four and five." This will require a shot fired approximately every half-second.

Stage Three:
Same exercise as above, into target #3 (the square in the middle left) on a count of "1, 2, 3, 4, 5" as fast as the shooter can count. This will require all five shots to be fired in approximately one second.

Goal:
The first string of fire allows the shooter to concentrate on trigger press and reset separately. The second string of fire will force the shooter to bring the two parts of the process together. The third string of fire forces the shooter to push herself to the limits of her ability. It's important to maintain the appropriate pace throughout the drill's strings, instead of relying on your perception of how long it should take to get defensively accurate hits.

Distance:
5 – 7 Feet
If the shooter was able to keep all 15 shots on the targets, the distance can be increased 3 – 4 feet and repeated.

Things That a Coach Can Watch For:
Watch for misses, especially on the slower paced rounds, which indicate that the shooter should return to the "SEB" or "Colored Numbers" drill which do not have the forced time limits.

Skill Level

INTERMEDIATE

Self-Led

Target: SEB Training Target

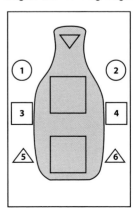

THE "SLAP, RACK, AND ROLL" DRILL

Skill Level

BEGINNER

Instructor-Led

Target: Official USPSA / IPSC Target

Description: The "Slap, Rack, and Roll" drill is designed to give the shooter opportunities to clear malfunctions while engaged in the exercise and to determine if he is prone to flinching in anticipation of the recoil. To conduct the exercise, an assistant will load the shooter's magazine with a mixture of live rounds and dummy rounds. When ready, the shooter will fire a full magazine.

Goal: This exercise allows the shooter to build appropriate neural pathways ("muscle memory") to quickly clear malfunctions. The shooter's goal should be to safely clear the dummy round while maintaining his eyes and muzzle on the target.

Distance: 21 Feet

Things That a Coach Can Watch For: Watch for the shooter to maintain his muzzle downrange when clearing the dummy round (which will require him to turn his body slightly, not the muzzle of the gun) and watch to see if he maintains his eyes on the target. Also watch for any flinch when the shooter pressed the trigger on the dummy round.

Alternatives:
1. The assistant can actually load the magazine in the firearm, which would allow him to have the top round be a dummy round.
2. Place two or more dummy rounds in sequence.
3. To simulate the effects of adrenaline on the hands, run this drill after holding your hands in icy water. In the northern states, an alternative is to leave your steel firearm in your car overnight on a freezing winter night, and shoot the next day on an outdoor range with no gloves. It's not fun.
4. To simulate the effects of auditory exclusion, run this drill with live stereo ear pieces inserted under your normal hearing protection. Turn up the volume loud enough so that the combination of music and hearing protection drowns out all other sounds. This will teach you to recognize your firearm's proper operation and failures by feel alone – you'll learn to trust that your firearm actually fired even though you didn't hear the "bang" and you'll learn to identify failures through a lack of recoil, rather than a lack of sound. During this version of the drill, the assistant will also be responsible for hearing any range commands and communicating them to the shooter.
5. An advanced version of this drill combines the dummy round exercise with either the "SEB" drill or the "Colored Number" drill.

FLASHLIGHT HOLDS

The flashlight holds described in this section offer a variety of methods for using a tactical flashlight to first illuminate a room or area to search for a threat, and then rapidly bring the muzzle in alignment with the light to engage the threat. All three holds have pros and cons, but it's fair to say that any handheld flashlight hold causes the fundamentals to suffer, and that these holds should be practiced frequently. Note that you can practice these holds on the range in full light to become comfortable with them, but we suggest that you invest in at least one session under true low light conditions.

FBI HOLD

The FBI flashlight hold allows the light to be positioned in a variety of locations and momentarily flashed to check out our surroundings. Positions might include placing the light high and outside our body, above our head or under our firearm. The theory with this hold is that if the light acts as a "bullet magnet," the changing light locations would confuse the bad guy about where we actually were. Drawbacks of this hold include the difficulty of lining up the light beam with exactly where you need to shoot. It also forces you to shoot one-handed, which is rarely as accurate as a two-handed hold (just ask Jack Weaver).

HARRIES

Like the FBI hold, the Harries still requires shooting one-handed, but the back-of-hand to back-of-hand pressure can steady your shooting hand. Ensure that you feel solid pressure between the backs of your hands, and are not simply resting the strong hand on the wrist of the support hand (picture holding a piece of paper firmly in place between your two backs-of-hands). Also, when setting up this hold ensure that you do NOT pass the muzzle of your firearm over your support hand.

SUREFIRE/ROGERS

Also described as a "cigar" hold, because it holds the flashlight between your index and middle finger. Best used with a light that has rubber rings around it to allow you to pull the flashlight tightly into your palm, which will activate a light with an end-cap activation switch. This hold keeps the light beam fairly aligned with the muzzle of the pistol, but with small motions of your palm allows you to move the light around. This flashlight grip comes the closest to allowing you to maintain all basic fundamentals, although it doesn't allow as solid a grip as you'd get with a mounted light and it still throws in the extra variable of activating the light, etc.

THE "LIGHTS OUT" DRILL

Skill Level

ADVANCED

Instructor-Led

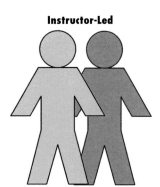

Target: Official USPSA / IPSC Target

Description: The "Lights Out" drill is designed to give the shooter opportunities to gain experience with the different flashlight holds and/or a mounted light. We recommend that these drills be learned first in a full light environment before transitioning to a low light environment.

Goal: The goal of this drill is to safely gain experience with the different flashlight holds. There is no time limit specified which will allow the shooter to ensure she is performing each hold properly.

Distance: With two targets one yard apart at seven yards, start with the firearm and flashlight on the benchrest. On command, fire two rounds at each target. Shooter MUST NOT fire until the flashlight beam has lit-up the target. Repeat three times.

Stage #1, FBI Flashlight Hold – Lighted Conditions
Stage #2, Harries Flashlight Hold – Lighted Conditions
Stage #3, Surefire/Rogers Flashlight Hold – Lighted Conditions
Stage #4, Mounted Light – Lighted Conditions
(Note that firearm MUST be cleared prior to attaching mounted light)
Stages #5 - #8, Repeat the exercises above in low-light conditions. This portion of the exercise MUST be instructor-led until the student has proven proficiency in low light shooting situations.

Things That a Coach Can Watch For: Watch to ensure that the shooter doesn't cross her hand in front of the muzzle when setting up the Harries hold, and watch for her ability to place the light beam on target with all three flashlight holds. The FBI hold and Surefire/Rogers hold in particular can take time to master properly aligning the muzzle and beam of light.

Alternatives:

1. An advanced version of this drill combines the "Lights Out" drill with either the "SEB" drill or the "Colored Number" drill.
2. Another advanced version of this drill combines the "Lights Out" drill with the "Slap, Rack, and Roll" drill. Ensure that the shooter has the flashlight's lanyard looped around her wrist so that the light can be "dropped" while performing the clearance procedure.

THE "LASER" DRILL

Description: The "Laser" drill is a scored exercise designed to allow the shooter to compare and contrast point/sight shooting to shooting with a laser.

Goal: The goal of this drill is to push the balance of speed and accuracy on all three stages. The "Comstock" scoring (which creates a composite score between time and accuracy) should give the shooter a good indication of how a laser might fit into his overall training and self–defense program.

Skill Level

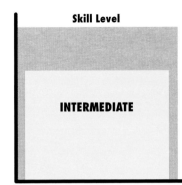

INTERMEDIATE

Distance:
Stage #1, Dry Firing
One target at seven yards, start with firearm on benchrest, dry fire five "rounds." Repeat three times. Focus on a solid grip and good trigger control. Instructor should watch for a "dancing" laser just prior to or after the trigger press.

No score

Stage #2, Left Target, with Laser OFF, From the Holster
Two targets one yard apart at seven yards, start with firearm holstered, on command fire five rounds at LEFT target. Repeat three times.

Scored Comstock (Score/Time)

Instructor-Led

Stage #3, Right Target, with Laser ON, From the Holster
Two targets one yard apart at seven yards, start with firearm holstered, on command fire five rounds at RIGHT target. Repeat three times.

Scored Comstock (Score/Time)

Things That a Coach Can Watch For: In stage one, watch for the laser "dancing" just prior to or just after the trigger press, which can indicate a grip or trigger control problem. On stage three, watch for the shooter falling back on either point/instinctive or sight shooting. It may take several runs through stage three before the shooter learns to trust the laser and begins picking up his speed.

Target: Official USPSA / IPSC Target

Alternatives:
1. An advanced version of this drill combines the "Laser" drill with either the "SEB" drill or the "Colored Number" drill.
2. If possible, the second target can be painted red or be covered in a red cloth. The laser will then be nearly invisible on this target, forcing the shooter to transition quickly between laser shooting and point/sight shooting. If he's trained consistently to elevate his firearm up into his three degree line of sight, this transition will be relatively smooth.

SUGGESTED READING

BOOKS

Combat Focus Shooting: Evolution 2010, by Rob Pincus

Deadly Force Encounters, by Dr. Alexis Artwohl and Loren Christensen

Lessons from Armed America, by Mark Walters and Kathy Jackson

On Combat, by Dave Grossman

Training at the Speed of Life, by Ken Murray

PAPERS / ARTICLES

If I Remember Correctly, by Dr. Alexis Artwohl

No Recall of Weapon Discharge, by Dr. Alexis Artwohl

Perceptual and Memory Distortion, by Dr. Alexis Artwohl

We Look But We Do Not See, by Dr. Alexis Artwohl

Why Didn't I Hear That?, by Dr. Alexis Artwohl

Reaction Times In Lethal Force Encounters – The Tempe Study, by Dr. William Lewinski & Dr. Bill Hudson

Combat Human Factors: Triggering the Survival Response, by Bruce and Kevin Siddle